POSTAL BLUES

A Murder Detective Mystery

Postal Blues

Published by We Must X-L Publishing
Kansas City, Missouri

First Printing, June 15, 2000

Copyright © Vincent R. Alexandria, 2000

Re-edited, April, 2004

Printed in the United States of America
Cover by Lydell Jackson/Ulisa Lathon
Photography by Gerald Grimes

ISBN 0-9749564-1-4
Library of Congress Catalog Card No. TXU958203
Original ISBN: 0-9666503-3-6
First Printing: March 2001

PUBLISHER'S NOTE
This is a work of fiction. Names, characters, places, and incidents are either the product of the author's imagination or are used fictitiously, and any resemblance to actual persons, living or dead, business establishments, events, or locales is entirely coincidental.

POSTALBLUES

A Murder Detective Mystery

VINCENT R. ALEXANDRIA

special thanks

I have to give thanks to God Almighty for his works and blessings He has bestowed upon and within me. To my children; Randi, Preston, Royce, Azia, and Nia, you are the poetry and creativity within me and without your joy and laughter my life would not mean anything. I love you with all that I am.

To my parents and family, for all the love, support, laughter, and prayers that you all have shared for me, thank you. You have made my life rich and full of love.

For my best friend's in the world, Derrick, Gino, and John, you guys have had my back from the beginning and keep me spiritually grounded. Thanks for the 25 years of love and brotherhood.

I can't say enough to my ace-in-the-hole, Victor McGlothin, your friendship in undeniable and I would die for you my brother. Keep practicing on them bones and I'll let you win one day. (Smile) To my editor, Susan Malone, you bring out the best in me.

Thanks to all the great authors that have supported the Brother 2 Brother Literary Symposium. We are making a difference promoting reading and literacy in America, thanks for believing in the vision.

acknowledgements

They say a person is as good as the people that supports him and I want to thank all those who have supported me in my writing endeavors; Jeanette Lewis, Patricia Oliver, The Rev. & Mrs. Gary Jones, Mother Jones, Jimmy "Jet" Alexander, Bernice McFadden, M.C. Richardson, Women of Wisdom Book Club - San Antonio, St. Louis Church Family,& Fr. John, Marie Young, Frederick & Venetta Williams, Linda Martin, Candice, Travis Hunter, Jackson Mississippi Book Club, Zane, Women of Word Book Club, Lorrie Goings, Eric Pete, Linda Alexandria, Katie Wine, Aaron Johnson, Jr. II, Perry Alexandria, Donald Johnson, Frederick Williams, Lorrie Goings, William Cooper, Tracey Grant, Regina & Beverly, Emma Rodgers, Mosaic Books, Cynthia Guidry, Cheryl Shelvin, Kimberla Lawson Roby, John and Karen Ashford, Sr., C. Kelly Robinson, Parry Brown, Sara Freeman Smith, Nina Foxx, Jacquese Silvas, Brenda Thomas, Evelyn Palfrey, Blair Walker, Dionne Driver, Sean Tyler, 103.3 FM-KPRS and the Carter Broadcast family, Greg Love, Lady T, Tre' Michaels and 107.3 FM Radio Station, The KC Negro Baseball Museum-Bob Kendrick and Johnnie Lee, Arzelia Gates and the Gates family, Victoria Christopher Murray, Donald, Lillian, & Albert Dean (Cuz), Mom & Dad Ashford, Alvin Brooks, Mom & Granny Young, Uncle Pete, Bob O'Brian, Damon Smith, Elaine Dibartilo, Frances Latimer, Gerald Grimes-the greatest photographer in the world, Ulisa Latham, Sheila Goss, Sheila Shelvin, Ilyasah Shabazz, Delores Thornton, Michelle Chester, Nichole Poignord, Jamila

Jagours, Katie Gibson, Kwame Alexander, Steve Perry, Lisa Cross, Lydell Jackson-the best artist in the world, Rosemary Kelly, Monica Miller, Dino Anderson, Omar Tyree, Patricia Haley, Peggy Hicks - the most spectacular friend and publicist in the world, Philena Wesley, PJ Jones, Quiana Williams, Renetta Davis, Cousins Verneal, Marilyn, Thelma, and Denita, Mary Jones, Pam & Rufus Williams, Steven Barnes, and to any others I forgot, I'm sorry! (Smile)

prologue

HE HEARS THE RING AT THE DOOR AND GETS UP TO ANSWER IT. She looks so lovely standing there in the hot-red, tight fitting, mini skirt. Her breasts almost spill out of her two sizes, too small, top, that reveals her nipples like cherries atop grapefruits as her jacket hangs from her shoulders. He has seen her on Independence Avenue plenty of times and they have been intimate on several occasions. He ushers her into the small station and strolls to his postal jacket to get her payment.

She licks her lips and smiles, "That's what I like about you, baby. Business before pleasure, " she compliments as she takes off her sweater, rubs her hands through his hair, grabs him in the crotch and sits in his chair with her legs propped open.

She knows he likes to peek and she obliges as she rocks her vivacious legs that once supported her cheerleading days in high school, back and forth. With excited anticipation he hands her the fifty dollars and falls to his knees to get a whiff of the joy he's paid for.

He sees her Tweety Bird panties and smiles as he reaches up to her blouse and pulls it to the side, revealing her colorful tattoo of the same cartoon character above her right breast. He smiles with pleasure and she giggles.

"Say it for me, baby, " she directs.

He takes another long peek between her legs as she reaches down and pulls her panties to the side to help his view. He looks up at her like a shy little boy. "I thought I saw a putty cat."

They both laugh as she stands to greet him. They kiss with a slezzy passion as she impatiently reaches for his belt buckle, unzips his pants and undoes his button. His pants drop to the floor around his ankles. They kiss some more as his nature rises.

He pulls off her blouse in their dimly lit space and reaches under her top and pulls it up over her head as she flings her shoulder length hair back and forth, to help it fall back into place. He traces the tattoo of the cartoon bird with his tongue as they both breathe heavy. She moans as she grips his manhood. Their movements get more aggressive as their body temperatures rise.

He grabs her breasts in his small hands and sucks her nipples. He quickly tires of this and begins kissing her neck and throat. She laughs as he reaches under her mini dress and pulls her panties off, one leg at a time. They almost fall losing their balance, but manage to stay upright in the heat of the moment.

He turns his paid-for-date around, kiss the Tweety bird tatoo on her rear, drops his boxers to the floor, and has sex with her from the back. Pushing, pumping, grinding, and banging his manhood between her legs as she moans with each forward movement. She sucks his fingers as he places them close to her face and he grabs her breast with one hand.

He comes once, then twice as his other hand searches the desk for the stun gun he has hidden under a postal mail bag. He pumps her harder, not wanting her to suspect what he's doing.

"Do me, baby! Do me!" She screams with pleasure as she climaxes and jerks with tender satisfaction.

"Is it good to you baby, cause I ain't through with your ass, yet, " he says as he hits her two times with the stun gun.

She screams and quickly falls to the floor with quick convulsions. He stands over her, pulling up his boxers and pants as she lay paralyzed and exposed on the floor.

"Thanks bitch, " he says as he pulls his leg far back and kicks her in the head, knocking her out cold. The postal employee reaches in her purse and pulls out his fifty dollars, walks to the phone, and slowly dials a telephone number.

After the conversation he goes to the back door to make sure no one is around. He looks up and down the dark back alley. When he gets back inside, the postal worker places a mail sack over her head, picks her up and manages her on his shoulder.

He carefully carries her to his truck and places her in the back seat, gets in, and drives into the night with his lady of the evening.

one

Clear and sunny! That is the weatherman's forecast this morning for
Kansas City, Missouri, the heart of America. Kansas City sits right in the
middle of the Nation. Our culture is as diverse as the economic condition
of the people. With a low jobless rate and high friendliness and morale,
we get the best of both worlds. We have the livability and pace of a country town, but the economy and urban core of the big city.

We have two major-league franchises with the Chiefs football and
Royals baseball teams. Known for its steaks, jazz, and stock yards, Kansas
City's second only to Paris with the number of fountains that adorn the
city parks and public locations.

Kansas City is my kind of town; it fits me like a well-tailored Armani
suit. I'm Joe Johnson, one of K.C.'s home-grown finest. Seems like I've
dreamed of being a cop for as long as I can remember, and probably a long
time before then. True to the blue is my motto. True to the blue. There's
something to be said for living your dreams; even the small ones.

I head out the door to meet the wife of my partner and best friend,
Detective Vernon Brown. Gertrude is planning a surprise party to celebrate their twenty-five years of marriage and my job is to get Vernon to
the celebration on time. I am not sure of what's expected of me and I

need to finalize some details on the party, so I'll drop by her job at the United States Postal Service building, near downtown Kansas City.

I maneuver my late-model black Nissan 300 ZX into one of the empty parking spaces at the front of the gothic building. The huge, white concrete structure has carved inscriptions. Two proud eagle gargoyles adorn the top of the east and west corners.

I'm reminded of a previous news story from a few months ago in Phoenix, where a postal employee was charged with attempting to kill some of his fellow colleagues. "Going Postal, " headlined the newspaper article, about a troubled postal worker who had reached a breaking point.

He blamed his reaction on stress and unfair practices on his job, which finally exploded into violence. Sounded more like "Postal Blues" to me. For the average person to suddenly, without warning turn into a mass killer would mean that he had suffered a great deal of pain, depression, and had not only lost all hope in himself but in everyone around him. Then again, my police experience taught me that signs always exist. But, most people tend to ignore things they don't want to see.

According to Gertrude, who has spent twenty-four years working for the Postal Service and has shared many stories in the ten years I've known her, the "Good Ol' Boy Network" is alive and well. She recently began contemplating retirement due to the current management's worsening human-relations problems. Some of her stories seemed far-fetched, but I've yet to hear Gertrude Brown tell me anything that didn't pan out.

I step behind two young ladies who look like they're dressed more for Sunday service than business. We seem to be going in the same direction. As they sashay down the sidewalk, I wonder what job lets one wear sun dresses and hats.

The taller of the two ladies asks, "Girl, did you hear the latest? They found another woman in the Missouri river. That makes fifteen."

"Was she black?" asks the one with the Carmen Miranda hat.

"Yeah, girl! They say she was a prostitute on Independence Avenue, like those others they found dead."

"The article I read in the paper said the bodies they found were white and Hispanic women. That's why I wasn't worried as much about it. I figured that meant the killer wasn't killing Black women."

"Ugh Um! You've got it wrong, girl. Three black prostitutes are still missing. Ain't no woman safe from this fool."

Peculiar that they would bring this up. Rumore has it that the services of some of the missing prostitutes have been used by postal employees working in the Independence Avenue area.

When we reach a glass door with the marking "employees only" one of the women lets her friend pass, and then holds the door open for me. She could be an Ebony Fashion Fair model, and her navy sun dress accents every voluptuous curve. Blessed with a perfect cocoa-brown complexion, her jazzy deep-set hazel eyes sweep over me, making me feel as if I am the special-of-the-day at the local supermarket.

I smile. "Thank you. How are you ladies doing today?"

Flashing a Colgate smile, the other woman, dressed in a similar brown outfit, turns to me. Tho smaller than her friend, and not as stunning, she clearly also knows how to work with what God gave her. "We're just fine, better than those missing prostitutes out there. I don't remember seeing you around here?"

I blush and answer, "No, I don't work here. Actually, I'm looking for a friend. She's a supervisor and works in the first-class manual unit."

The woman in the navy dress responds, "Lucky her, I wish I were the friend you're looking for! A six-foot, dark skinned brother with a football player's build would just complete my dream."

The smaller sister says, "Most of the men who work here ain't worth the energy it takes to look at them. Seems like we spend every waking moment of my day in this place."

"Thank you for the comment and I'm sure they have some good men in here, " I respond, backing away from the ladies who seem to get closer to me with each statement.

The taller one with those eyes says, "These people don't let you have a life, so it's hard to meet a nice man and God forbid have a family. We were just interviewing for another job, so we can leave this one, but until we do, here we are back again looking at another twelve-hour shift."

The woman in the brown dress reaches and gently touches her elbow.

"Oh! I'm sorry; I don't know why I'm dumping on you. You must think I'm crazy." She dazzles me with that smile and the way she licks her lips before she speaks makes my body warm. She pushes a long lock of hair from her eyes and smiles again. "The manual unit is on the second floor, we'll take you to the elevators."

She is fine, but I have to admit, "crazy" did cross my mind. Should I pull her close sympathetically and let her cry on my shoulder, or say thank you? I pick the latter.

I follow them as they accentuate their hip-throwing walk. How easy it is to get to the restricted side of a United States Postal Building. In this Federal building, no security is in sight. And that after the government's past experience with terrorism and disgruntled employees. It should be secure.

How easy planting a bomb would be. And what about metal detectors? Strapped to the calf of my leg is a holstered, ten shot, automatic 9mm pistol. How many employees are carrying concealed weapons in the building? Is a postal employee the serial killer hiding within these confines?

The elevator bell rings for the second floor. I turn to thank the ladies as I exit the elevator and catch both of them eyeing my behind. They blush as we all laugh with embarrassment.

After regaining my composure, I ask, "Can you ladies direct me to the letter manual unit?"

Smiling and barely able to look me in the eyes, the lady in the blue dress answers, "Just follow the yellow arrows that mark the floor."

"Thank you and good luck on your job search. You sistahs stay positive and safe." Still smiling, I turn and head for the manual unit, humming "Follow the Yellow Brick Road."

The yellow arrows lead me through the crowded aisles. Loud machines make beeping sounds while sorting mail all around. Above, the fire-alarm lights flash. Hesitant and ready to follow if any of the employees start to head in any certain direction, I keep moving. No one pays attention to the flashing lights. I stroll past mail-sorting cases as the employees begin to check me out. But, no one approaches me about my presence.

Finally, I spot Gertrude at her supervisor's desk in an area labeled "030 Manual Unit." She lifts her head and smiles warmly dropping her pen. She rises to greet me. Gertrude at forty-six years old looks to be about thirty-seven. Petite, she stands about five feet, four inches. I always tease her, because Vernon is at my height of six feet.

Her embrace is warm and she kisses me on the cheek. "Joe, how did you get all the way up here?"

"I just walked in with two women who were on their way to work and they told me how to find your area. All the way up here I was thinking about how easily I had access to this building. I see the fire-alarms lights flashing but no one is concerned."

Many employees have stopped casing mail and now eavesdrop on our conversation.

"Tell me about it, that's sensory adaptation. Those alarms go off so often that we've learned to ignore them. If there's trouble, they announce it on the loud speaker."

Confused, I ask, "Where are the security personnel?"

She heavily sighs, lengthening her round, pretty face. "They got rid of security about nine years ago. People get robbed all the time. Postal employee's cars are stolen so often on Preston Road and our parking lots, it's like a blue-light special at K-Mart. Women walk to their cars in pairs to protect themselves from being attacked at night." Gertrude places her well manicured hands upon her shapely hips in frustration.

"Bummer. You would think the post office would be more concerned."

"Isn't there someone you could report this to?"

I shrug. "Maybe I can speak to some people I know downtown about this security situation. I can talk to the captain about running some patrol cars by." My detective nature to fix everything has kicked in.

Gertrude looks at me. Sadness gently embraces her beautiful eyes. She looks like a child that missed recess. "We've expressed our concerns about security regularly, but the employees are not the primary concern of the Postal Service. It's scary if you think about it. This is one of the reasons I'm considering retirement. The safety factor alone is stressful."

"A Federal facility should take extra precautions, especially since the Oklahoma bombing attack and 9/11. You people are sitting ducks."

A frown creases her smooth, chocolate kissed forehead. "Joe, whatever you can do, we'd appreciate it. Come on, let's make you official and get you a visitor's badge."

After I get my visitor badge, we go to the employee break room. The room is painted a boring, light blue with tables and chairs and assorted vending machines.

The walls contain several information boards that are set up for union business, job announcements, and personal ads. The well lit place has several large windows. I get two cups of hot coffee from the vending machine and we sit at a table away from the few other employees in the break area.

"I like your pin-striped suit, Gertrude. You're looking awfully fine, Ms. Lady. Vernon better watch out for these dudes in here, " I tease.

She smiles that embarrassed, but 'I know you right' smile. Gertrude has shoulder-length black hair. She wears a size eleven and still has an hour-glass shape. I know her size because I've accompanied Vernon several times on the weekend, while he picked out an outfit for her in celebration of some event or for no reason at all.

Gertrude's nails are always kept in exquisite shape and I've yet to see her with a bad hair day. Made from a model's mold, she wears very little make-up. She and my wife, Sierra, ride their bikes every morning for an hour, unless it rains. Only Lena Horne could give her a run for her money in the beauty department.

"Joe, tell Sierra I really missed our ride this morning. I had an early meeting. How's she and that precious little daughter of yours?"

"Just fine. Nia's putting those puzzles you and Vernon gave her for her birthday together with her eyes closed. She's learning so fast and does something that makes us laugh everyday. She looks so much like Raymond, it's scary, " I respond.

Nia is actually Sierra's little sister. We adopted her after we were married two years ago, after Sierra's mother, Ebony and her sister, Diamond both become pregnant at the same time by my high school best friend, Raymond Tyler. Diamond has since moved to Denver with her son, Raymond Jr., and Ebony is serving her last two years of a five-year sentence for the murder of Raymond Tyler; Nia's father. Ebony felt that Sierra and I should raise the child as our own and she have the Grandmothers' role. She was wise enough to understand the bond Nia would form with Sierra and me, the five years she would be incarcerated. She wanted her daughter to have a normal life.

She was lucky that the prosecutor took into consideration her self-defense motion and worked out a plea bargain. When Nia gets old enough to understand the complexity of the situation, we'll sit down and explain it to her. Right now, we all just want her to be loved and raised in a two-parent home.

"It's really great how you guys have worked everything out. You two have really made us proud. Not too many people would have taken the responsibility you two have. I know Ebony Dupree must thank God every day to have such a wonderful daughter and son-in-law."

"Well, we've gotten a lot of support from friends like Vernon and you. We really appreciate you two being there for us and for being Nia's Godparents."

Gertrude blushes and gently touches me on the shoulder, "You know

Vernon and I wouldn't have had it any other way. You ought to see the rocking horse he's making for Nia. He's been working on it for two month and wants it just right. It looks great and Nia will be so surprised. He loves her so much. You ought to see the way he smiles when she calls him Uncle Vernie. She's so cute. How does Ebony handle being called Grandma, instead of Mother?"

I sighed, "It was an adjustment for all of us. My being called Daddy and Sierra being called Mama by her Mother's baby. I admire Ebony for being so unselfish and thinking of her daughter. It has to be hard for her to hear Nia call Sierra, Mommy and see all the love she's missing. But, enough about us. What about the anniversary party for you and my favorite detective?"

Gertrude's elegant brown eyes light up. "I can't believe it's been twenty-five years. It seems like a lifetime has passed in a blink of an eye. Vernon and I have had our rough patches, but we've had a blessed life together."

"Oh, so you trying to get brownie points for giving Vernon a hard time all these years?" I tease, smiling.

"See Joe, you trippin', I want to show Vernon and everybody just how much he means to me. And I know it will mean so much to him."

After taking a sip from her coffee Gertrude adds, "I'll just be happy when he retires from the Police Department. I know Sierra worries about you too."

"C'mon Gertrude, you and Sierra both knew what kind of men we were before y'all said, 'I do!' Believe me, we know it's hard on you and that makes us careful."

I've had this same conversation with Sierra and always end up feeling guilty afterward.

Three young women approach our table.

A very sexy young lady with a sprinters body, gold tooth shining it's reflection from her smile and a gold neck chain that reads "Adrian" places her hand on the table. "Ms. Gertrude, who is your friend? We didn't know you had it going on like this. We gonna tell your husband, girl."

The nosey women all giggle.

"Well, Ms. Adrian. This is Mr. Happily Married and Not At All Interested, Detective Joe Johnson. He's my husband's partner and my dear friend. Joe this is Adrian, Camicka, and Phyllis. Now where are you young ladies supposed to be, cause you just came off break twenty minutes ago?" Gertrude smiles that, "mind your business" smile.

Camicka crosses her skinny arms. "Dang, Ms. Gertrude. You ain't got to front us in front of your friend. We just tryin' to be hospitable."

"Yeah, Mrs. G, we were just making sure you were all right and stuff. You sittin' here with all this man, lookin' all handsome and fine, " Phyllis adds, making it a point for me to see her licking her red lips slowly.

Gertrude rolls her eyes as she shakes her head in disappointment. "Phyllis, you just need to slow down with your fast self and you ladies need to find yourself some work. Let's keep the mail moving, okay? I'll see you back in the unit, when I'm finished visiting with Mr. Johnson." The ladies reluctantly leave to return to their assigned unit, waving goodbye.

I return the farewell wave. "Are these sistahs always so aggressive?"

"Not all of them, but you have to realize that a lot of these sisters get very materialistic and start to live above their means when they get to the postal service. Most are only high school graduates and would not make nearly this much money in other work arenas."

"Yeah, but what does that have to do with anything? They're independent at that point and should be happy, shouldn't they?"

Gertrude shakes her head. "Joe, unfortunately, it's a soap opera in here. Many of these women have good men at home, but they lose sight of that, thinking the grass is greener. When they get income and benefits that they've only dreamed of, it brings a new sense of independence. They get caught up with the men in here, and they figure with another postal employee they can bring home sixty-five to eighty thousand dollars a year, easy."

Gertrude glances across the room at an older man making a selection from the vending machine. A Snickers bar drops to the open slot. Picking up his candy, he exits the break room.

In a lowered voice, Gertrude continues, "Now, they have access to the finer things in life, middle-class status and middle-class problems. Couples start buying stuff they can't afford, debt, gossip, back stabbing, and affairs are what they have to face around here!"

I hadn't told Gertrude about my conversation earlier with the two women who helped me find her. It was innocent flirtation, but for someone else it could have led to more. "Damn, that's deep. I see how it would be possible to get into relationships and have a man or woman at home, but it sounds like you're making excuses for bad behavior."

She shakes her head, "No Joe, I wouldn't condone this, but I'm trying to get you to understand how this could happen. Think about it. In their first five or six years of employment, they're working ten to twelve hours a day, six days a week. They're on the job more than they're home. A person on the job can relate to the frustrations and the stressful conditions they work under, and there's a language in the post office that only postal employees understand."

"Postal language? What do you mean by that?"

"We have so many acronyms for equipment and positions, that anybody at home would think we're talking French if we tried to explain our day. But, another postal employee can relate.

"Damn, Gertrude that could get ugly and dangerous, especially if they have to work together."

Gertrude swivels in her chair and crosses her shapely legs. Her shoulders seem to sag. "The worst part is the rumors, gossip, and slander that follows. People smile in your face while talking about you behind your back and heavy drama begins. Another stress-filled romance, destined to be destroyed, before it can even begin. There's bad blood and feelings flare, because someone always feels more used than the other. Then, the threats, jealousy, and before you know it, verbal or physical fighting. The saga continues."

"Sounds like a soap opera to me."

Sighing, Gertrude continues, "The new hires come in and the next fools fall into the same trap of greed and lust. Another chapter in the book of love and hate."

Gertrude adjusts in her seat and I can sense the pain in her voice as her eyes narrow with concern.

"So Gertrude, have you ever fallen into that trap?"

"Please, let a good man like Vernon get away? I don't think so. My mama always told me that if you get a man that loves, respects you, helps with the housework, and doesn't mind cooking, never let him get away. That's the same thing I told Sierra and you see how fast she grabbed you, huh?" Gertrude says, laughing.

I grin. "Oh, so that's why she married me so fast. Well, I guess I'll have to be careful from now on, seeing how you women are ganging up on me."

Gertrude and Sierra have become as close as Vernon and I. Which is good for us, because they have a support group within each other.

"Joe please, we just started doing what you and Vernie have been doing for years."

Relaxed again, I smile. "Well, I guess we should start talking about the party. How long do I need to keep Vernon out of the house?"

"Pick him up about 1 in the afternoon and meet us at the Marriott on the Plaza about 6 o'clock. That should be enough time. Everyone is to arrive around 5. That'll give people a little time to have a drink. Joe, don't go running your mouth and slip. Sierra told me to remind you of that." Playfully, pointing her finger at me, Gertrude threatens, "I don't want to have to beat you up, Joe. So get this right, okay?"

"See, you and my wife be trippin'. I know how to keep a secret. I'm hurt that y'all would even suggest such a thing. Like I always let the cat out the bag or something? I think you two just get paranoid because Vernon and I know what each other are thinking sometimes. Y'all got a lot of nerve." I poke out my bottom lip.

Clapping her hands and laughing, Gertrude can barely speak. "And the winner for the Academy Award for best actor goes to Joe Johnson."

I throw my hands in the air. "Oh, so you didn't buy that, huh?"

"Sierra told me you'd pull the innocent angel routine. She knows you pretty well, " Gertrude says with a big grin.

"You ought to see what Sierra and I got for the two of you. You guys will be very... What the Hell! That sounds like gunfire! Get Down!-Get Down!"

Three more blast above the screaming. People stampede every way. Gertrude and I remain. She crouches behind me, under the table.

Vernon and I have gotten out of tons of difficult situations. I will not be able to face him if I let something happen to his wife.

The gunman enters the break room. The profuse stench from his armpits fills my nostrils. His eyes are darting around the room and his nostrils are flared. Perspiration wets his collar and the top part of his tie. Sweat on his brow and his wide pupils alert me that he is on a mission. His brown eyes are affixed to mine and his lips twitch. This will not be a good time to go for my pistol.

The shooter stumbles a bit and looks confused getting his bearings. He has a .38 revolver in his right hand and a .45 automatic in his left. He has several bullet clips attached to his belt and I'm sure he has another pistol behind his back, cloaked by his grey suit jacket.

About thirty-five, light-brown complexion, with a medium muscular build, the man is smaller than my two hundred-twenty pound body. I have seen crazy men before, but this one makes me shudder. My senses tell me that he's reached the edge and is ready to jump off. He won't jump alone.

"Don't move and keep your hands where I can see them. I need you and Mrs. Brown to come with me now, " the gunman demands.

Gertrude, gasps holding her hand to her chest, "Victor? Victor McGregor, is that you, son? Why are you doing this? You're such a nice young man don't let them do this to you, Victor." Gertrude desperately looks at the gunman for some sign of rational behavior.

Desperate eyes dart back and forth between me and Gertrude. "Sorry Mrs. Brown, but I don't have a choice. I need you to come with me, now!" He looks over his shoulder as if expecting something to happen. He pushes us forward and directs us with his guns to leave the break room.

"Look brother, take me, you don't need her, " I say.

"Brother, I don't know you, but I know that when this is over, Mrs. Brown will get my story straight. My life is safe as long as I have hostages and since you two are the only ones available at the moment, it's your lucky day. So if y'all don't mind? Move your asses right now!" the gunman screams as his hands shake.

"All right, just stay calm. Everything will be fine, " I reason.

I keep Gertrude in front of me and the gunman. The noise of building alarms wrap themselves around us with chaotic assurance that this one's real.

We walk down the same walkway I had ventured through earlier. But this time, I have the barrel of a .38 caliber pushed into the small of my back. The 030 Manual Units where Gertrude works in is now abandoned by the fortunate postal workers who were able to escape this mad scene. I squeeze Gertrude's hand and give her a smile, prompting her to keep moving.

The wood floors are freshly waxed but the dust from the paper that the mail produces leaves a coating on the floors. So much sorting equipment occupies this floor of the building! One big mechanized machine after another.

A door swings open on the north wall. I push Gertrude down and lay over her. Two shots blast. Gertrude screams and hides her face in my chest. I think of pulling my gun, but decide to let the scenario play out and wait for my best opportunity.

The gunman is a crack shot. He shoots the Postal Inspector in the chest twice before the crew-cut blond man gets off one shot. He is killed instantly.

"Shit, after all these years, I finally see a Postal Inspector. The lazy bastard, " the gunman says.

The Postal Inspector lies sprawled across the floor. Gertrude vomits. Crimson-colored blood forms a big puddle under his right arm pit. I help Gertrude up.

"Mrs. Brown, go into the Tour Superintendent's office, " the gunman demands.

We step over the dead inspector. Gertrude opens the door to the office. We walk in, and the killer closes it behind us.

The gunman smirks like he enjoys this search as he walks us into each of the four offices and checks the closets.   "If I was a coward, where would I hide?   Hmm, let me see. I know, a closet."

We enter a medium-sized meeting room. A muffled thump comes from inside the closet. He motions for me to open the door as he aims his gun.

"Don't shoot, don't shoot, please!" The older white man with brown hair and a pot belly snivels as he and three women employees and one other supervisor spill from the closet.

"Well, I hit the jack pot. You are so predictable and pathetic, Mr. Hampton. I guess you do have skeletons in your closet, huh? I see you have your ass-kissing boy Fields with you. All y'all get over to the corner and sit down."

We all do. The angry gunman locks the door and forcefully wedges a chair underneath the knob. He then walks to the window, looks out, and throws a table up to block the view of the helicopter circling the building.

He says to himself, as he paces the floor, "Damn, the cops have made it here, already."

"We've been here all along." I watch his every move inconspicuously.

"So, why are you doing this, Victor? Do you understand the consequences of your actions?" Mr. Hampton asks with shaken authority.

"Like you don't know? I don't care about consequences right now. I'm doing this because of you and this fucking bureaucratic place, you trifling snake bastard. I ought to shoot you in your mouth for all the slander that has crossed your lying lips." He backhands Hampton across the face with his .38 pistol.

Mr. Hampton grabs his mouth. Blood spills between his fingers. I hand him my handkerchief. He puts it to his mouth, trying to stop the blood that slowly turns the handkerchief crimson red.

Mr. Fields starts hyperventilating and can't control his trembling. The three women, one black, and two white, huddle together, crying.

"Okay, Mr. Fields, I know most of the time you have your head so far up Mr. Hampton's ass you barely realize what time of day it is. I'm going to give you a crash course in diversity. You have three chances, but there is a consequence with each wrong answer. Now that you know the rules, let's begin. What do you see when you look at me?" Victor asks as he puts the forty-five automatic in his waist holster and grabs Mr. Fields by the collar.

Sweat engulfs Mr. Fields wrinkled forehead and trickles down his pink cheeks. "Uh-uh-uh, a black man."

"Wrong answer, " Victor snaps and slaps Mr. Fields across his cheek, leaving a faint hand print on his flushed face. "Two more guesses."

"Uh, an African-American man, " Mr. Fields responds, tears in his eyes.

"Wrong answer, " Victor snarls as he slaps Mr. Fields again with enough force to knock him off balance. When he regains his balance, he finds Victor's gun pointed in the middle of his forehead. Fields is perspiring profusely and his tan shirt is half soaked with perspiration, yet he tries to concentrate on the riddle, while wiping the sweat from his pointy chin.

"Mr. Victor, Sir, this has gone far enough, " I say. "You made your point. Look at him; you see the man is scared shitless. Let him be."

Victor walks up to me and puts his gun in my face. "Sit the fuck down! You see, this is the trouble with management. We should be impressed with the talent and not with the color of one's skin. Mr. Fields, this is your last shot and excuse the pun, Sir. What do you see, when you look at me?"

Victor yells.

Everyone holds their breath. Tension engulfs the room. I slowly reach for my leg holster, trying to be inconspicuous. If he shoots Mr. Fields, I'll have no choice but to take him out. I pray he gets the obvious answer.

"A man, " Mr. Fields sobs. "A man!"

Victor pulls the gun from Mr. Fields head and pats him on his pudgy shoulder. "I knew you could do it, Fields. That's all I wanted around this place was to be treated as a man. A man!" Victor says softly with tears in his eyes.

Gertrude moves closer to me and is calm; trusting that I will take control of the situation.

"Brother, Victor. Can I call you Victor?" I ask.

Victor rolls his eyes and takes a heavy breath as he moves closer to me. "Yes. Who are you anyway?" He stares into my eyes.

I can see the twitch that divides sanity from insanity. A subtle blackness deep in his lost soul. He stands before me, his gun aimed at my chest. I sit erect and avoid sudden movement. I raise my eyebrows and expose the palms of my hands with a slight smile.

"My name is Joe Johnson. I'm a friend of Mrs. Brown. Her husband and I are best friends. Whatever it is bothering you; this is not the way to resolve it. I have problems at my job as well, but I don't let the problems dictate my actions.

Victor responds, "Oh, is that right?"

"Yes Sir, and if you care for Gertrude as you say, then you would not be putting her through this."

"Am I supposed to be moved by that shit? You don't know me or anything about me. I shot the people who have made my life a living hell. I killed four people today. Mr. Frost, Mr. Ray, Mr. Nunally, and Maxine Mitchell."

Victor pulls up a chair and sits in front of me. "Since you want to go down memory lane, let me tell you about my memories. Mr. Frost was killed for raping a female friend of mine and getting away with it by threatening to fire her if she told anyone. She told me and that was that. I killed Mr. Nunally for always calling me a son of a bitch behind my back. I heard him one time too many."

"Victor, it's only words, man."

Victor leans forward and responds, "My mother is not a bitch. Mr. Ray was killed for blocking me from getting transferred to Dallas. He was my supervisor and because he didn't like me, he wrote a nasty review on my job performance. Even though I received a superior review, Dallas turned down my transfer which I really needed. Later he smiled and told me that if I got on his good side, he could pull some strings to get the transfer approved. That pissed me off, so I pulled his strings instead. I'm not counting the Postal Inspector. Just consider him a casualty of war."

"What is it that you want?" I ask trying to keep him talking, maybe the police outside will find some resolution.

"I wanted to be treated as an intelligent man, to be left alone to do my job, to not have to play politics and I wanted to be recognized for my hard work. I wanted people to stay out of my business and I want to be able to attain a position I am qualified for, not having to cater to the white man's ego.

Hampton says, "Victor, there are other ways of expressing your anger other than killing people."

Victor snaps, "Yeah, but killing people sends a message that the atrocities that go on within these postal walls can't continue. I've seen Manager Frost's daughter come in as a temporary employee and get promoted so fast, that even the white people couldn't believe it. And to top that, they created a position for her. Ain't nepotism against the law?"

Hampton explains, "He was reprimanded, Victor. We treat all our employees the same, " Hampton says, his fat face and neck turning red with anger.

"Is that right? Then why is it when a black supervisor was accused of sexually harassing a white supervisor, he was demoted to clerk. To pour salt in the wound, they put him in the same unit under the supervision of the supervisor whom he supposedly harassed. Now, this just proves how separate and unequal this place is." Victor gets up and kicks yet another chair away from him. Foam is forming on the corners of his now dry mouth.

Hampton puts his head down. Helicopters continue to circle the building. I know by now the SWAT Team is getting into position and a negotiator will soon be calling to get the demands and try to circumvent the situation with as few casualties as possible. Yet, the truth is that they will take Victor out as soon as they have the slightest chance. A black man with hostages doesn't have half the chance a white man has. It's not right, but it's true. And I know it.

How can I rationalize with this disgruntled postal employee and possibly save his life as well?

"I need to pee, " one of the receptionists complains.

Victor narrows his eyes and tilts his head with displeasure. "Well, you better get one of those plastic-lined trash cans. You can go in that closet that you love so much, cause this ain't no joke, Ma'am. You won't be leaving this room."

We all look at each other. She reluctantly gets up, takes the trash can, and enters the dark closet, closing the door behind her. We try not to hear the tin clinging rhythmically. The woman is scarlet red with embarrassment as she emerges from the makeshift commode and returns to her place on the floor. She never looks up and folds her arms across her knees, burying her face.

"I'm truly sorry for the embarrassment, Ma'am, " Victor sincerely apologizes. "But just magnify that ten times and you can start to imagine how a black man feels everyday when he is deprived of respect or talked down to just because of the color of his skin."

The phone rings. Decision time. Our fates will be decided in minutes. It is now 3:30. If I can't talk Victor out of this hostile situation, I will have to kill him.

Victor answers the phone.

He pauses, then, "I want to talk to the press and tell them what brought me to this point. I want to talk to my Pastor, Reverend Royce of Holy Rock, CME Church, and I want to talk to my wife. I will release one hostage when each request is met."

Another pause. "If the police try to enter this room, I will kill everyone!"

He nods, "Yes, I will show my good faith and send out one hostage."

Victor moves the chair from under the door knob, points his gun at the secretary who urinated and motions her to get up and leave.

She gets up looking at no one and says thank you to Victor. Victor winks at her. She disappears out the door. Victor re-secures it and the other ladies start to sob. Gertrude pushes closer to me. I position myself so my hand is on top of my leg where my gun is located.

"Victor, man we can end all this here. If you let us all go and walk out with us, they won't harm you. You have the press and all the postal people outside as witnesses. Your story will be told, " I pledge.

"Those postal people out there are part of the problem." Victor paces, scratching his temple with the barrel of his gun. He slams his fist down on the table angrily, "God, I can't believe I'm in this mess. I shouldn't have killed those people. Jesus, my head is hurting and I'm so tired."

He slumps down the wall to a squatting position with his gun still pointed in our direction. I have a shot, but choose not to take it. To kill this man, would only traumatize the hostages and besides, I feel sorry for the brother. He is a killer, yet he is a killer by circumstance.

Some people react differently when they feel forced into a corner with no options. How could postal management let one of their own get to this crisis point?

This whole scenario could have been avoided. To be fair and equitable is not so hard to do. A bullet started this grizzly situation. I hope it doesn't end it.

two

GERTRUDE SEEMS DEEP IN THOUGHT. SHE GAZES AT THE yellow-spotted, water-damaged ceiling. I have always respected her strength. I can tell she feels partly responsible for Victor's actions. Maybe something was not said. Maybe not enough was done. She is always maternalistic.

Gertrude looks at me and I smile. Does she see this young man throwing his life away with so much potential, as I do? People take different paths to get what they strive for. No matter what one has done positive in an entire lifetime, one bad choice can spin life out of control. Everything comes crashing down. Victor is a man engulfed in hopelessness. He can't see a way out and is determined to do something drastic if choices aren't put in front of him.

The phone rings again. We listen to Victor's conversation, hanging on every word and earnestly waiting for some resolve.

"Yes, I'm here."

"This is the FBI?"

"Yes, I realize this is a federal offense."

"Agent Royal James, did you locate my wife and Pastor?"

"I will release a hostage, but only after I talk to them."

"Yes, two hostages. I am a man of my word. Please, put my wife on, Sir."

He pauses and his bottom lip begins to tremble. His eyes water and his shoulders slope down. "Hey, baby. I didn't want it to come to this. I'm very sorry. I can't get out of this one. It's gone too far now. I've made bad choices and I accept responsibility for my actions. Forgive me for putting you through this."

Victor rubs the phone with his thumb as a single tear rolls down his saddened face. "I love you, too. Remember that no matter what. Everything will be all right, sweetheart. Just be strong. Let me speak to the pastor."

Again he pauses and takes a deep swallow, "Reverend Royce? Please pray for me."

"Yes, Sir. I've considered my wife and what I have done."

"Yes, I'm trying to do the right thing. I pray that God will forgive me. Let my parents know that I'm okay and I love them. They are probably going crazy. Tell them I'm sorry."

"Yes, Sir. If you could put the FBI agent back on the phone, Sir. Yes, I will."

His eye brows raise and his young face hardens as he clenches his fist. "I'm sending out all, but three hostages."

"No, I do not plan on hurting anyone, Sir."

"Yes, Sir. I want this over too."

Victor hangs up the phone with tears in his eyes. He wipes them away with his jacket sleeve and slowly looks at everyone. His head hangs lower and he is not as cocky. His lean face has a softer look to it. He even seems remorseful as tears stream down his face. He slowly moves the chair from under the door knob.

Victor announces, "Everyone except Mrs. Brown, her friend, and Mr. Hampton can leave!"

These people get up and leave without saying goodbye. Not one of them looks at us with regret. They are so caught up in getting out, that they don't even realize that three of us are left.

Victor puts the chair back under the door knob. Now that the FBI is in charge, Victor's chances of survival are minimal. I've worked with Agent James before. He's a no-nonsense guy who goes strictly by the book.

The first thing SWAT will do with hostages is interrogate them, to get the names of the people detained and get a description of the room, the hostage taker, and the weapons that he has. I know most everyone on the force and they run background checks on hostages to see if any medical attention is needed and to make sure the criminal doesn't have another accomplice on the inside. They'll know I'm a hostage when my name is given. Law enforcement will realize that one of their own is a hostage. It will probably buy Victor some time. This is more than likely the reason the FBI, SWAT, and Police Department haven't kicked in here and blown his head off. They would not put an officer in harm's way, if they could avoid it. They are waiting on me to hopefully make my move.

Victor's eyes start to dart back and forth anxiously and that puts me on alert. I can reach for my gun within seconds. Victor jumps up and grabs Gertrude. I pull out my 9mm(millimeter) pistol at the same time.

"All right Victor, the ship stops here, buddy. Stay cool. I'm a detective with the Kansas City Police Department, " I announce with the gun pointed at his chest as he walks toward me.

Victor has his gun aimed at the side of Gertrude's head. Gertrude looks at him with a small smile and reassuring expression. She looks as if she's made peace with God and her fate is in His hands.

"Victor don't do this. It doesn't have to end this way, man. Is this what all this was for? So you could give up, and quit in the end? You said yourself you're not a quitter. Don't go out like this, Victor. Please!"

I stand a foot away facing them with my gun aimed at Victor's head.

"You mean to tell me, you're a cop and let this situation get this far?" Mr. Hampton asks as he backs away from the path of our aim.

"Shut up, Hampton! You've done enough today." I turn my attention back to the gunman. "Victor, let her go, brother. She ain't in this. Take me instead."

"I'm not taking anybody. What do I have to look forward to after today? I have shamed myself and my family. I'm a killer now and I can't spend my life in Leavenworth. You have a choice to make, detective. I'm going to count to three and if you don't kill me, I'm going to kill Gertrude."

"We really don't have to do this. We can put down these guns and walk out of here together, Victor."

Victor stares blankly, determined to see this lethal situation to its deadly end.

Gertrude prays, "Our Father, which art in heaven..."

"One!" Victor says calmly."

"Victor, we can work this out, " Hampton pleads as sweat engulfs his face and his eyes widen with fear. "I'm sorry for what I did to you. I was wrong, but this will not solve anything. For Christ's sake man, don't do this." He grasps his jacket lapels.

She continues, "Thy will be done, on earth as it is in heaven..."

"Victor, think about your wife, please!" I state, yet take steady aim for a kill shot. I have to take him out and not give him time to pull the trigger and harm Gertrude.

Victor yells with his index finger on the trigger, "Two!"
Tears are rolling down his face and his body begins to shake. He has made up his mind. I pray for all of us.

"As we forgive those, who trespass against us. Amen." Gertrude prays.
"Blam! Blam!"

The gun barrel smokes. I grab Gertrude. Blood spills from Victor's head and splatters onto Mr. Hampton's face and clothing. Victor's body collapses. Something inside me falls when Victor hits the floor. His open eyes seem to fade as life escapes his body, hopefully to a better and peaceful place.

The SWAT Team bursts through the door with the FBI in their steps.

I raise my hands, not to be mistaken for Victor and killed on the spot by anxious agents. I show my badge and identify myself.

"Stand Down!" FBI, Special-Agent-In-Charge, Royal James commands. "You okay, Johnson?"

I respond, "I've had better days, Royal. Glad you could make it."

"We'll need a statement."

"Sure thing. I'll take care of it."

"Uh, thank you, Detective Johnson. We owe you our lives, " Mr. Hampton states.

"Mr. Hampton, people died here today. I don't know what part you or your people played in this, but this is not a time for thank yous. Good day, Sir."

I pick up Gertrude who has fainted and am met by Vernon, who is frantic just outside the office doors.

"Oh God! Is she hurt Joe? How in the hell did you get here before me?" He looks puzzled as he gazes deep in my eyes for an explanation. His lip twitches and he wipes the tears from his eyes.

"I would not let any harm come to your wife, Vernon. You know that. I've been with her the whole time. We were planning your anniversary party, when the gunman took us hostage, " I respond.

Vernon accepts his wife from me as she starts to come to. He embraces and kisses Gertrude. "Honey, I'm here. You're fine."

"Thank you, Joe, " Vernon says with his hand on my shoulder. Gertrude smiles, and then breaks down crying in Vernon's arms.

"No problemo, partner, " I say as I step away and give them a moment to themselves.

"Gertrude, today I felt like I died, when I thought I had lost you. I would not be able to live without you, sweetheart. Your twenty-five years of love have been the most fulfilling times of my life. God has truly blessed me twice: once by bringing you into my life and again by delivering you to me unharmed. You are my beauty, my color, my weather, my life, my breath, my desire, my romance, my best friend, my strength, my motivation, my inspiration, and my happiness, Gertrude Brown. I love you so much, sweetheart." Tears run down his dark brown face as he kisses his wife, smiles and softly sings Phil Collin's song:

"...Wouldn't you agree, baby you and me,

got a groovy kind of love..."

Vernon told me awhile back that "Groovy Kind of Love" was their song of devotion to each other. I have to admit, I've never seen this side of Vernon. I am truly touched. This is the first time I've seen Vernon cry. He is always so tough.

I think of Sierra and Nia and how blessed Vernon and I really are to have such good women in our lives. I want to rush home and be in my woman's arms and tell her how much she means to me. I want to play with Nia and give her a loving kiss and tell her she's her daddy's everything. I love them both so very much.

Emergency personnel and crime-scene investigators, as well as Postal Inspectors pass me by. I take the elevator down to the ground floor. What secrets are kept in this place? What could drive a person with so much potential to self-destruct?

Please let this tragedy be a learning tool for the postal service. A small dog pushed in a corner will defend itself against an aggressor. I don't condone what took place today, but I understand.

The scene outside is chaotic. Media trucks are all over the place, two television helicopters flying above, fire trucks, the SWAT van, Red Cross Emergency Care vans, assorted police vehicles, and several ambulances hover.

I go over to my car, blocked in by the crime-scene tape, and sit on the trunk. Curious bystanders and postal people stand behind the blockade to get a glimpse of the victims to this tragedy. I pull out my cell phone and call my wife.

"Hi baby, I just wanted to let you know that I love you."

"Yes, I'm okay. I'm sorry you had to find out on the television. Is Nia doing okay?"

"Kiss my baby girl for me and let my parents know that I'm fine. Gertrude is fine, too. She's with Vernon now. As soon as I wrap up here, I'll be rushing home to you, baby."

"I'll be there soon, don't worry. Bye for now, sweetheart. I love you!"

Captain Wayne stands talking and comforting a petite woman. This must be Victor's wife. I approach them.

Captain Wayne asks, "You all right, Johnson? Did Brown find you?"

"Yes, Captain, I'm as well as can be expected, and Vernon found me. He's with his wife, " I respond. "Excuse me. Are you Mrs. McGregor?" I ask compelled to reach out to someone Victor loved. I feel I owe it to him.

She responds with teary, swollen eyes, "Yes, I am."

She has reddish-brown hair, very light skin with freckles and a small oval face. She searches my faces for understanding. My gut swells with anxiety.

"Mrs. McGregor, I'm Detective Johnson. I'm very sorry for what happened, but Victor left me no choice. I did everything I could to defuse the situation. I tried to reason with him, but his determination to die or kill a hostage put me in a precarious situation. I had to do my job."

The distraught woman lunges, slaps me, and starts beating me in my chest. Captain Wayne takes a step to intercede, but I shake my head. Some things have to be played out.

She screams as she buries her head in my chest and breaks down in a tearful moan. "Why did you have to kill him? Why did he have to die?"

I put my arms around her and share her pain. I only did my job and this man was a killer, yet I took a man's life. I stroke her reddish-brown hair and ask that God show her the way.

I look at Captain Wayne and he assists Mrs. McGregor to the squad car. The media will soon pounce upon her, like a hungry lion on its injured prey.

Dusk has fallen upon the Kansas City skies as death has fallen upon this postal facility, suddenly and without hesitation. Souls have been cast out of bodies, like shadows on a cloudy day. I trust that the essence of all the fallen will be looked upon favorably by the Almighty and the hearts of their loved ones be cloaked in the grace and love of the Lord.

"Joe, are you all right?" A familiar voice asks. "I heard you were inside. I was so worried about you. Do you think you can tell me anything about what happened?" Tracy Jackson inquires as she pushes a KC-TV 7 NEWS microphone in my face and her news beat, camera man aims his video camera at Tracy and me.

I hate the media. They're blood suckers just waiting for bad things to happen to get a story. The more grim the scene, the better the ratings.

"Tracy, you know how I feel about reporters. What made you come out in front of the cameras, anyway? I thought you loved editing?" I ask as I motion the camera man to get out of my face. Tracy is an ex-girlfriend who tried to shoot my "Willy" off. We didn't end on the best of terms. She's as beautiful as ever with her almond-brown eyes, long black hair, caramel-kissed lips, and ebony-hued skin.

I understand why the network decided to put her in front of the camera. She is well versed, very intelligent, and has always been on top of the political and social government issues in Kansas City. She has a gift of intuition and an excellent fashion sense. We had problems with trust in our relationship and when we broke up, I met Sierra.

"It was an executive decision and a promotion. I like it and it pays the bills. So, I hear you are the one that took out the shooter. Is that true?" Tracy asks as she orders the camera man to start shooting with a quick snap of her fingers.

"No comment!" I answer as I motion for the camera man to stop shooting. "Please Tracy, I've been through enough today, give me a break. I don't have time for this."

Tracy moves closer to me, just out of earshot of the cameraman. "Like you gave me a break, Joe, when you broke my heart and put me on probation for two years?"

As an agreement not to give her jail time, Tracy received two years probation and violence counseling.

"Tracy, you tried to run me over with your car and then tried to shoot me. If it wasn't for Sierra, you might have succeeded. I cared enough to keep you out of jail."

"So how is the bitch who stole my man?"

"She's Mrs. Sierra Johnson now and she's doing fine."

"Congratulations. That was supposed to be my name, but you made sure that didn't happen. I can't believe how much I loved you, Joe. I hope you are happy and I'm sorry I bothered you. Thanks for everything, Mr. Joe Johnson."

I look at her incredulously. "So you had no part in my decision, right? You know as well as I do that I tried like hell to make it work. You wouldn't communicate with me and you didn't trust me. Look, that's all in the past and we both have moved on. I have never done interviews and don't plan on starting now. You know the department will have a press briefing any minute. Go bug them."

"What time?" Tracy asks tilting her head suspiciously as she raises an eye brow.

"I don't know, but FBI Agent Royal James likes to talk to the press and he'll be out in a few minutes."

"Joe, you know I'm not the one to be played with. He better be out here. Come on, Antoine, we need to get some live feeds and interviews for tonight's spot. Look, they're bringing out bodies, get some shots of that. Thanks for the tip, Joe. I hear that you and Vernon's names have been thrown around for that prostitute murder case. Is that true?"

"I haven't heard anything and the FBI is all over that case. Why would they need us?"

"I suspect they feel like you two can get more information than they can from the ladies of the night. I also heard they've questioned a postal employee. There could be more than one killer lurking behind those postal walls. Oh, your pimp friend, Pretty Kevin's name came up, too. They say birds of a feather, flock together, huh, Joe?" Tracy cut her eyes away from me.

"Yeah, there could be more than one killer, but I doubt it and for your information, Pretty Kevin is a friend I grew up with in my old neighborhood and was my roommate in my junior year of college. He's just an associate now. I haven't seen him in years and what's that bird stuff supposed to mean?"

Tracy's camera man whistles her over as people start appearing from the postal building. I shake my head and watch her rush up to one of the hostages. She shoves her mike in his face, asking questions with her camera man capturing the personal invasion.

That's why I left her butt!

three

I ENTER THE HOUSE AND HEAR THE RAPID PATTER OF MY little girl racing to the doorway. I love the big kisses and hugs from the two women in my life when I get home from work. My daughter meets me at the door. Nia always takes a running jump and I catch her in the air and swing her from side to side like a rag doll. Her two big pigtails flap freely as tho she's about to take flight. She gives me a large toothy grin and giggles.

My heart is at ease as she hugs me tight around my neck, kisses me on the cheek and says, "Daddy's home."

I return the love, put her down, reach into my pocket and get the package of soft-chew, Life Savers I picked up in the postal break room. I put my hands behind my back and we play her favorite game. I pull my big closed hands from behind my back and one conceals the sweet treasure.

"Which hand is it in?" I ask.

She cracks me up - she puts her finger to her chin as if she's in deep thought analyzing the task at hand. "This one, " she says as she grabs my right hand to reveal her prize. It's amazing how bright she is, because ninety-percent of the time, she chooses the correct hand. "Thank you, Daddy. You the man, " she says as she runs toward the dining room.

I say as Sierra approaches me and jumps in my arms, "Something sure smells good."

"Daddy's home, " she yells as we both fall to the floor.

She kisses me deep and holds me tighter than usual. "I was so scared for you, Joe. Vernon called and I saw things on the news. Don't you ever scare me like that again. I love you so much."

Nia yells as she jumps on top of us on the floor. "Unnhh! Mommy and Daddy kissin'!"

I yell, "Group hug!"

As we embrace each other, I thank God in a silent prayer. Heaven must feel like this.

We finish a dinner of short ribs, macaroni, green beans, cornbread, and peach cobbler. We talk a little of the day's events and I answer Nia's questions of how daddy got on television. We give her a bath and tell her a bedtime story. I kiss Nia goodnight and leave Sierra to tuck her in.

I run the bath water for Sierra and me. The lights are out and one purple, jasmine-scented candle is burning. The smooth sounds of the Temptation's "I'm On Fire" plays in the bathroom tape player, from one of Sierra's home-made, slow jam tapes. The water is soothing, but the sight of Sierra as she enters the bathroom with two glasses of Chardonnay takes my mind off the water and places it on the burning passion I feel for my wife.

She sits the wine on the table by the tub, disrobes, slowly gets in, and lays her back against my hairy chest. I kiss the top of her short-cut curly hair. I watch her shapely size seven frame and know by the stern expression on her small caramel colored face, reflected by the mirrored wall that she has something serious to talk to me about.

"Joe, I don't know if I can take another day like this. I don't want to lose you, baby. I was so scared. Gertrude must have been a wreck. Is being a detective and putting your life on the line day in and day out worth it?"

I kiss the back of Sierra's neck, rub the Oil of Olay soap in my hands and massage her shoulders.

"Baby, protecting and serving people is what I get paid for. What if I wasn't there today? Would Vernon still have Gertrude? I understand your concern, believe me."

"I was so nervous I couldn't stop trembling. I thought I was going to lose you, baby."

"I know you must have been going crazy today. I realize it's a high-stress life I put you through, but God is with me, baby. I'm sorry for the situations I put you through and what they do to you, sweetheart."

I move my hands down Sierra's back, rubbing her tense spots and hoping my passion will alleviate her concerns. "Sierra, I hate when I leave you and love when I return to your caramel kisses and loving touch."

"Every time you leave home, I wonder if this is the day I become a widow and Nia a fatherless child. I try to put the bad thoughts out of my mind, but when I hear a siren, I wonder if it's for you. It would kill me to lose you, Joe."

Sierra turns, faces me, soaps a towel, and washes my chest. Her dark almond eyes are soft, like she's trying to understand the daily crisis I put her through, yet they're filled with love and desire.

"Baby, I love my work, but I love you more. I will give up this job, if that's what you truly want. I care for you that much, darling."

Sierra hands me the towel to wash her shoulders and breasts.

"I'm sorry for all the stress and all the days you worry about me, but I stay safe, so I can fill your nights with love. You and Nia are my reason for living. Not only have I married my friend, but my comforter as well."

I wash Sierra's small feet. The fear and concern in her face starts to melt as I kiss her softly around the face. I kiss her toes delicately, rub her ankles, and move up her legs with the soapy towel.

"Joe, you know I won't ask you to give up your job. I'm just very concerned for your safety. There are crazy people out there and they don't care who they kill. Look at the person killing those prostitutes on Independence. I worry about my man out there, facing all that evil and ugliness." She moans as I rub her favorite spot.

"Sierra, I'm not out there alone. Vernon has my back and I have his. We keep things in perspective, baby, and we don't take unnecessary risks."

My wife kisses me as she washes my stomach.

"You stir things inside me, I never knew were there. I promise to do everything to keep you happy. Woman, I love you so much."

Sierra drops her wash towel and kisses me with such depth, the sparks inside me bursts into flames.

"Joe, I'm sorry I worry so much and I try not to panic. You are my man and I know I never have to worry about your devotion or how you feel about me, cause you show me each moment we're together."

"Thank you baby, for having faith in me."

"You stood by me when I was a suspect in Raymond's murder. You put your career on the line for me, Joe, and you didn't have to do that. You stayed by my side when it wasn't easy and you had everything to lose, even your friendship with Vernon. I will never forget that."

"You meant that much to me, sweetheart."

"The love you have for Nia and my family makes me proud to be your wife. You respect me and treat me with chivalry. You fulfill all my desires and your imagination drives me wild. You are spontaneous, understanding, charming, romantic, humorous, strong, intelligent, family oriented, and you spoil me."

"Damn, I do all that?"

"Stop playing, silly. Just be careful, baby, " Sierra says as she rubs the hair on my chest, while nibbling on my bottom lip the way I like it.

We step from the cooling water of the bathtub and towel dry each other. Once in the bedroom we massage each other's body with cucumber-melon lotion and light several candles. Sierra's naked body is firm and lustful as she wears a small blushing smile.

I know I'm forgiven for the drama that I put her through today. I apologize until she tells me to quit. Then I kiss her until she moans provoca-tively in my ear. The moon blushes like a shy child as we make love well into the night to the tunes of, "So Amazing, " by Luther Vandross and "Turn off the Lights, " by Teddy Pendergrass.

The sounds and scents are harmonious, as the candles reflect shadows rhythmically dancing on the bedroom walls and ceiling, imitating our love ballet. The stars in the black night form a constellation in honor of our intense passion.

Sierra has her head deep in my loving chest and pulls my arm around her tighter, as I pull the covers around us. I kiss her once more, say a thankful prayer, and surrender to fatigue.

WE SPEND THE DAY AT THE ZOO WITH NIA. SHE LOVES ANI-MALS, but her favorite is the sea lion. She likes the way they swim around care free and get a kick at how their bark is similar to a dog's. She rides the pony and the camel, as well as the train. We eat hot dogs, nachos, cotton candy, and peanuts. When we finally make it home, she goes straight to sleep.

Sierra and I are busy getting dressed for a well-deserved evening at Three Black Cats Jazz Club and Restaurant downtown on 18th and Vine. KC has always been known for its jazz in that area.

Such greats as Duke Ellington, "Cannonball" Aderlly, Charlie Parker, Sarah Vaughan, Ella Fitzgerald, Lester Young, Count Basie, and Miles Davis have played here at the Reno and Hey-Hey Club. During the 30's, you were not a recognized jazz musician until you've played in this music Mecca.

The internationally recognized song, "Going to Kansas City, " was spawned about the importance of this Black area. It was the hot spot for Negro league players such as Josh Gibson, Buck O'Neil, Satchel Paige, Jackie Robinson, and even boxing greats such as Sonny Liston and "Sugar" Ray Robinson.

Kansas City was wild and wide open. The Eighteenth & Vine area was black owned and operated, from the soda shop, newspaper, juke joints, barber, beauty, and shoe shine shops, to the grocery store, restaurants, Gem Theater, hotels, clothing stores, and cab company. Everyday was Sunday on Eighteenth and Vine, because people always dressed their best.

Everyone congregated together too, from teachers and hustlers, to deacons, pimps, lawyers, and train conductors. It was a place to let your hair down and let the good times roll.

Sierra has on her tight-fitting olive leather dress with matching purse and pumps. My blue suit shows off my dark skin and muscular physique. It is accented by a blue-olive mix tie, an Italian, crushed silk, olive shirt. I sit on the bed admiring my wife as she applies her make up.

Sierra looks at my reflection in her mirror and asks, "What time did you ask Hilda to be here?"

I walk up behind her and kiss her neck, whispering in her ear softly, "Seven-thirty, so that means we have a half hour before she gets here, " I say raising my eyebrows.

"Baby, we don't have time for that, you know Hilda always gets here early, but am I good for a rain check later tonight?" she asks with a devilish grin while powdering her face.

Hilda is a six feet-five, two hundred and twenty-five pound transvestite. We met at the Pink Oyster on a case Vernon and I were working on, investigating suspects for Raymond Tyler's murder.

Hilda was a bouncer at the gay club and beat Vernon and me up. We later became good friends and he loves children. So, we let him watch Nia for us when we need a night out and he gladly obliges. Nia enjoys his company as well and we know Hilda will protect her with his life.

"Girl, I ain't even thinking about no quickie when we get home. We gonna take our time and do it right, " I answer, kissing her softly on the lips.

Sierra says laughing, "Joe, I just put this lipstick on, boy..."

The door bell rings.

"See I told you he always gets here early. You need to wipe that lipstick off before you go downstairs. I don't want Hilda getting the wrong impression."

"Oh, so now you got jokes, right?" I reply as I leave the room and run downstairs to open the door.

Hilda steps inside the foyer and gives me a hug as he sets down his bag, takes off his hat and coat, and adjusts his blond wig.

"Hey, Joe. Where's my little pumpkin' at?"

"She's upstairs and you'll probably want to wake her, she's been waiting for you, " I say with a smile.

He snaps his finger two times and with the other hand fans himself. "Don't you just look like the man? You're wearing that suit, boy."

"Don't play, dude, " I warn as I lead him up the stairs.

Sierra stands at the top of the stairs, arms outstretched, waiting to give Hilda a hug. "Hi girl, it's been so long. You have to come by more and we really appreciate you sitting for us tonight."

"It's my pleasure. I picked up a couple of videos on my way over, " Hilda explains. "I got Iron Giant and Mrs. Doubtfire. I just love those movies. I brought some chocolate chip cookie dough, so we can bake some cookies, too. I hope you guys got milk."

"Yes, down in the refrigerator. Sounds like you two are going to have a ball, " Sierra says as she goes into Nia's room with Hilda.

I get our coats from the hallway closet and enter my daughter's room as she awakens with a big smile and hug for Hilda. Hilda catches Nia as she jumps from her twin-size bed into his massive, loving arms.

Nia asks, wiping the sleep from her eyes, "Aunt Hildy, when'd you get here?"

"I just got here, cutie. I got us some movies and we're going to bake some cookies and just have a great time, girlfriend." Both their eyes light up with excitement.

He swings Nia around his shoulders and she rides his back as they head downstairs.

WE ARRIVE AT OUR FAVORITE JAZZ CLUB, THREE BLACK CATS. Eddie Penrice, Eddie and Earl Baker opened the place about two years ago. It quickly became the favorite spot for musicians to hang out. Eddie and Earl have a long history of jazz music. Eddie plays jazz piano professionally and has even played for President Clinton with his Trio.

I walk into the club with a sense of pride, my lady on my arm and with a peace of mind. It's like my second home. The place is pretty full for 9 o'clock. Eddie and Earl walk up and greet us.

"Hey, Catdaddy! Earl says as he walks up to us with rusty brown skin, gray hair, and a full set of pearl white teeth shining from ear to ear. "Good to see you, detective, and I see you have your lovely wife with you. How you doing, Sierra?" Earl shakes my hand and kisses Sierra's. His brother does the same.

Eddie is of the same skin color but is four years younger and has salt and pepper hair and a noticeable bulge over his belt. "Joe, you didn't bring your bass, what's wrong with you coming up in here without your ax, dude? You know we gone be mixin' it up in here. I sent you a letter saying that we were jammin' on Friday's. You know you gone want to get part of this, man?" One of Eddie's bushy eyebrows is raised farther than the other.

"Don't worry, he can use Marlon's bass, he ain't getting away that easy. Sierra, you heard Joe play?" Earl asks as he puts his arm around her and lead us to a table up front by the stage.

"Just at home, Earl. He usually comes up here with Vernon on Sundays, " Sierra answers holding her hands up to her face to hide her excited grin.

"Okay, I'll sit in on a few, " I answer, not wanting to disappoint anybody.

"Well, if you play you got to sing one with me too, " Earl insists.

"Dang, next y'all want me to start waiting tables, Earl."

"I don't think you got the legs for that, " Eddie rebuts as we all start laughing.

Earl calls the waitress over. "Let me see, Jennifer, let's get two Miller beers and a couple shots of tequila for the lovely couple, " Earl orders and instructs her to put us on the house tab. I thank Earl and Eddie as they stroll around the club taking care of other guests.

Sierra raises her beer for us to toast the night out. "Joe, here's to you, baby. This is so exiting and I can't wait to hear you play."

"Sierra, remember the last time we drank tequila we ended up in a hotel room, " I remind her as I throw my hand around her shoulders and we drink our toast. I lean over and kiss her as Eddie Penrice comes from the stage after finishing his sound check.

Eddie shakes my hand, kisses Sierra on the cheek, and teases, "Joe and Sierra, I see y'all still acting like college kids, kissing in public."

"Eddie, don't be hating, before I go over there and tell your wife you meddling in grown folks' business, " Sierra threatens as she waves to Viola, who's looking our way.

Eddie, motions to Viola that he'll be right over after she looks at her watch as tho he's leaving her alone too long. "It's good to see you guys. When are we going to get together again and play spades? Me and wifey want our revenge. We got whipped up on pretty good last time."

I start laughing and give Sierra a high five. "Just let us know when your wounds heal."

Eddie shakes my hand again and heads over to his wife, who immediately cuts into him for having her wait so long.

"Baby, you wouldn't front me in public would you, " I ask, feeling sorry for Eddie.

Sierra says, laughing, as she punches me in the side, "Naw baby, I'd ask you to step outside."

"Thanks boo." I say as I rub my side. She kisses me and apologizes.

The musicians take the stage. Eddie Baker on piano, Lisa Henry, Geneva Price, Earl Baker, and Sharon Thompson on vocals, Benny Jet on drums, the legendary Sonny Kinner on guitar, Ronnie and Lonnie McFadden on sax and trumpet, Leroy Butler on trombone, Jerry Cartwright on keyboards, fabulous Charles Williams on piano, and Marlon Bankston on bass. Musicians on stage wave hello to us before they start their set.

People stand three deep, crowding the outer edges of the stage. The band starts out with "Birdland" by Quincy Jones and they are rocking the joint off its foundation.

Everybody in the place is moving to the music and even the smoke from the cigarettes seems to rise to the beat. They flow from one song to the next, grabbing the crowd and shaking it up with horn and vocal solos. People dance in their chairs and take to the dance floor adjacent to the stage.

Sierra and I get up and dance to the jazz and blues. Drinks are flowing, the music is blowing, the joint is jumping as the bass is thumping, feet are tapping, and fingers are snapping. Everyone's worries take flight, if only for tonight, fun is the medication, mixed with intoxication as the singers scat and everyone jams at Three Black Cats.

Eddie calls musicians up for the next set and calls my name as the bass player and vocalist, along with eight other musicians and vocalists. We start off warming up and jamming to the key of "G". The next tune we play is "One of a Kind" by Fattburger.

"This song is going out to my wife, lover, best friend and source of all my joy, Sierra Johnson." I blow her a kiss and her eyes mist up as the crowd applauds.

"You're magic, you're one of a kind and I love you every time I'm near you...

You're one of a kind and I love you every time I kiss you, you're magic, you're one of a kind."

Sierra comes up to the stage and kisses me and returns to her seat blushing, mouthing the words, "I love you" as she sits at the table with the crowd applauding and women in the club wiping their eyes. We play a couple more grooves and finish the set for the night with a grand finale of "Going to Kansas City."

Sierra is fast asleep on my shoulder, embracing my arm as we drive home. I thank God for a wonderful family, friends, and the beautiful city I live in. There is nothing like the twinkle of the city lights on a dark night with the moon shining down on you and the stars sparkling like effervescent champagne bubbles.

four

TWO WEEKS HAVE PASSED SINCE THE HOSTAGE SITUATION AND Things are back to normal. Vernon and Gertrude are on their way over to our house in South Kansas City. It is much bigger than the loft Sierra and I used to share. Our corner red-brick ranch house. Our home is much larger inside than it looks from outside.

Sierra did a magnificent job decorating it with an African cultural flare. I feel proud each time I walk in the door. The art work and intrinsic artifacts we collected are accented by aesthetic black and cream furniture.

The live plants and potpourri bowls adorning small tables around the house give off pleasing fragrances. Yet nothing beats the smells rushing from the kitchen, where Nia is helping Sierra put the finishing touches on lunch.

"Joe, I know what they mean by the terrible twos, " Sierra says with a smile and heavy sigh.

"Daddy, I helped Mommy cook, " Nia says smiling from ear to ear in her yellow daisy apron and yellow and pink Sesame Street, Big Bird outfit.

I embrace and give each of them a kiss. "Baby, you have really out-done yourself. You lookin' all good and the food smells delicious. I can't wait for Vernon and Gertrude to get here so we can eat."

"Joe, while you were downstairs working out, Dad called and asked that you not forget to come over this evening, " Sierra says while taking the garlic bread from the oven.

My stomach growls as the scent tempts my pallet.

"Mr. Man, while you're over there staring at that garlic bread, you could be in there setting the dining room table. Let Ms. Nia help you so I can finish this pound cake, " Sierra says as she places the cooled cake onto a plate and turns it over, in preparation to spread a lemon glaze on top of it. I go to the chair my little girl is standing on, let her get on my back, and we gallop into the dining room.

"Daddy, are monsters under my bed?"

I reply smiling, "No Nia, there is no such things as monsters. Besides if there were monsters they wouldn't want to mess with a pretty little girl who has a police detective for a daddy."

"Well, Mommy an' me were watchin' T.V. They said some ladies in the night are killed and put in the river by somebody and Mommy said who's doing it's a monster, " Nia explains, wide eyed.

I pick Nia up after we finish setting the table and sit her down on my knee. "Baby girl, you know the difference between nice people and bad people, right?"

"Un-huh. Nice people like Grandma and Grandpa and Uncle Vernie and Aunt Diamond and stuff like that. Bad people, shoot people and stuff, " she says puffing her little chest out with confidence and pride of a lesson well learned.

"Very good, sweetheart. Well, there is a bad man out there doing bad things to people like those ladies. Sometimes we call bad people, monsters. They are hardly ever under the bed though, and me and Mommy check under your bed each night when we tuck you in."

"Nobody better not mess wit' me, cause my daddy's da' man and he kick butt, " Nia says as she jumps off my lap, punches me in the stomach, and runs giggling into the kitchen.

I sit back down. Who would frequent the Independence Boulevard prostitute district? Who could have easy access to this area and go unnoticed? The person would have to know the area. Tracy's words from the post office pop into my mind, 'There's probably more than one killer in there.' I shake my head. This is the FBI's case and not my problem.

I go to answer the knock at the door. "Vernon, how you doin', man? Our doorbell does work. Hi, Gertrude, come on in. Nia and Sierra are in the kitchen. If y'all were a minute later, you guys would have been eating left-overs, " I tease, greeting my friends with hugs and kisses.

"Joe, come help me with Nia's surprise, " Vernon says as we walk back out to the car, so not to be heard by Gertrude. "We need to have a serious talk. I'll pick you up Monday for work and we can have breakfast at Niecie's Restaurant."

"Everything okay?"

Vernon puts a cigar in his mouth, his eyes glaze over and I can feel he is somewhere else lost in thought. He has never been one to put anything off, especially conversation. "Trust me on this one, partner, we'll talk Monday. I got some more thinkin' to do."

We have always understood not to push one another. So I respect my partner's request, but I'm concerned. He opens the back door of his Jeep Cherokee and pulls the canvas tarp off the most beautiful wooden rocking horse I've ever seen.

"Vernon, buddy, you got mad skills. This is excellent. Look at the craftsmanship. Nia will love you for this, " I state as Vernon inspects the black-painted rocking horse with black cloth twisted braids for the mane and tail. It also has brown leather reins and a saddle, with gold trim fringes. Nia's name is printed on each side of the pony. Rubber covers the curved bottom of the rocker.

"Yeah, I know, Joe. That's why I made it. She's my God daughter, what you expect? Help me bring it in."

Before we can get it all the way into the house, Nia runs out screaming with joy, "Uncle Vernie!" Nia yells with excitement.

She jumps into his arms and gives him a big hug that makes me a little jealous.

"You made this for me, Uncle Vernie?" Nia asks, hugging the big eyed, black pony. She climbs on and Vernon adjusts the leather straps, placing her feet in the brass stirrups.

Nia commands the pony as she rocks back and forth on her precious gift. "Gitty yup!"

"Ride em', cowgirl!" Vernon yells.

"Weeeee, this is cool, Uncle Vernie. Thank You!"

"You done good, old man, " I say.

"Watch your mouth, boy. I ain't too old to knock you out, okay?" Vernon says as we shadow box in the front room.

Sierra says as she enters the room with Gertrude, "I don't know which one is the kid in here. Oh, Vernon, you shouldn't have. That is so sweet. You did this all by yourself?" She admires the beautiful rocking horse.

"Look, Mommy. Looky at what I got from my Uncle Vernie? Ain't it cool?"

"Way cool, Nia, " Sierra answers.

"That man tinkered with that thing so much, I thought he'd never get through with it. It had to be just right, but that is the kind of man he is. Ain't that right, sugar?" Gertrude says as she snuggles into Vernon's arms.

Vernon teases, "You know it baby and it's all right to call me 'Big Poppa,' Joe and Sierra are family."

"All right now, Big Poppa, don't hurt nobody. You got 'Big Daddy' over here too, " Sierra says, giving a high five to Gertrude.

Smiling, Vernon brags, "I taught him everything I know."

"Yeah, but I don't take Viagra, " I joke as I grab Nia off the pony and head for the dining room to a roar of laughter.

"That ain't funny, Joe, not one bit funny, " Vernon responds.

We all sit at the table, hold hands, say grace, and eat. After dessert, we all retire to the family room. Nia rides her horse, while we watch the video movie, Down in the Delta. The movie hits close to home, because my parents are elderly and my dad is fighting cancer and the middle stages of Alzheimer's disease.

Vernon says as he starts to put on his shoes, "That was one hell of a movie. Alfre Woodard and Wesley Snipes know they can act."

"I really liked the ending, " Sierra states.

"So, what are you guys going to do about the party? I ask, just like Gertrude had instructed me to.

Gertrude looks at Vernon and touches his shoulder, while addressing my question. "Joe, after what we been through, I really don't want a party. Having Vernon here in my life is party enough for me."   V e r n o n hugs his wife and gives her a kiss, while Sierra and I sigh. Vernon agrees with Gertrude, not knowing that the party is already planned.

"Well, Joe, I want to thank you and Sierra again for having us over and we'll see y'all next week at our house. C'mon sugar, let's get you home, so you can show Big Poppa just how thankful you really are, " Vernon says.

"Yeah, Gertrude, get him on outta here, before I have to throw some cold water on his old butt."

We all laugh, hug, and kiss goodbye as Vernon and Gertrude leave for the evening.

"Joe, it's 6 and remember we still have to go to your parents. Dad said he wants to talk to you."

"Thanks, baby. Get Nia together and I'll straighten up down here. Give me five minutes."

MOM'S AND DAD'S HOUSE IS A BIG THREE-STORY BRICK STRUCTURE with a full basement and seven bedrooms. The place is huge, it had to be to house fifteen kids. Joyful memories erupt every time I step through the doorway. My parents are from Louisiana, so the kitchen is the focal point for our family. Times got rough with a big family, but Mom knew how to make magic in the kitchen, so food could go around.

No one was ever late for dinner. The food was always "seasoned to the bone, " as Mom would say.

"There is love in the food and the food feeds the soul, " as Daddy always said.

Nia and Sierra go upstairs and I go straight to the refrigerator, grab a couple pieces of fried chicken, cut a large piece of chocolate cake, and grab a Pepsi to wash it all down.

When I get upstairs to my parents' room, I am quickly relieved of my edible treasure.

Sierra pulls the chicken thigh and half my cake from my plate. "Ain't you nothin', just getting food for yourself."

"Yeah, Daddy, " Nia says and grabs the plate with the remaining drumstick and the rest of the cake.

I state, "...and this little piggy had none!"

"C'mon Nia, let's go get Daddy something to eat, since he was so nice to think about us, " Sierra says, licking her fingers. Nia puts down her plate and tags along as Mom and Dad laugh at me.

"Joe, I need about forty dollars to go to the boat, " Mom asks as I give her a hug and a kiss.

I lecture, "Mom, you know how I feel about that boat. You can give your money away, but not mine. If I want to give away forty bucks, I can go and lose it myself. When Daddy drank fifteen years ago, I never bought him a drink. I don't supply people's habits. You need to stay off that boat anyway. That's probably why you don't have forty dollars."

"See, you don't know what you're talking about. I won four hundred dollars last week on the boat and I'm old. What other entertainment I got?"

"Mom, you can join a church group, do volunteer work, tutor children, help out at a homeless shelter, be a teacher's assistant, open a restaurant, anything but give your money away at the boat. And if you won that much, why you asking me for money now?"

Mom looks exasperated as she starts fidgeting with her fingers. "I paid off some bills. You know we on a fixed income and you know how I hate bills."

"Well Mom, if you stop making bills, you'll stop having to pay them. Do you see where I'm going here?"

Daddy wears a frustrated smile as he rubs the back of his neck, "Boy, you fighting a losing battle. Your Momma gets with her friends and they be gone most of the night gambling. It don't make no sense, " Dad complains, as Nia and Sierra return with chicken and cake for me.

"Thank you for the drink, sweetheart. So Mom, how's all the family doing?" I ask as Nia grabs my Pepsi, drinks, and passes it to Sierra.

Mom sits back in her chair and her full figured smile lights up the room. "They all doing fine. Everyone will be here for Thanksgiving. You and Sierra are supposed to bring the ham and a couple of Sierra's sweet-potato pies. Girl, you know you can make a good pie, " Mom says as Sierra blushes.

Sierra hands Nia--who is now sitting in the chair with Dad-- my Pepsi.

"Thanks, but my pies are not nearly as good as yours, Mom."

"You heard from your brothers, Joe?" Dad asks.

"Yes, Sir. Perry and I do lunch once a week and I talked with the rest on the phone after the postal incident. We'll get together in a week to play dominoes."

Dad grabs Nia and playfully pulls her to him as he tickles her. "Nia told us about her new pony Vernon made for her. How is he and Gertrude doing?"

They're doing all right. Things are getting back to normal. They said to tell you hi and Vernon said he has some popcorn for you two."

Mom putting her hands over her heart, "He's so thoughtful, but y'all scared us to death, with that post-office incident. We had people calling and asking for your address and phone number. I assume they were from the press, but I don't give out phone numbers. You never know who is calling you. Don't it make you nervous, Sierra, to have him in situations like that? It really scares me sometimes."

Sierra frowns at me. "Yes, Ma'am, it bothers me. We just had this discussion last week."

"Uh-oh, Daddy's in trouble again, " Nia says as Grandpa rocks her on his knee.

"Thanks, Mother, but we definitely don't need that conversation again. Nia, mind your business, " I say, playfully sticking my tongue out at her. Dad laughs.

Dad comes to my rescue. "Leave the boy alone, honey. You just starting stuff cause he wouldn't give you that forty dollars."

"Mom, we had our discussion about his job and he knows how I feel. I love him anyway, " Sierra says, rolling her eyes at me playfully.

"I love him too, with his cheap self. That reminds me. I was out at the store and bought you two matching pajama sets. Come on downstairs with me to get them. They're the cutest things you've ever seen, " Mom says clapping her hands as she leads Nia and Sierra down the oak wood steps.

Dad grabs me by the hand and whispers, "Son, I need you to help me take a bath. I'm not as strong as I used to be and have a hard time getting out of that high antique tub."

"No problem, Dad. I'm glad to help. You ought to let me buy you all a lower bathtub you can get in and out of."

"Your mother loves that tub and it's been in our family for over eighty-five years. It's priceless to us."

He is right. The pearl white tub has a brass outer shell with feet of lizards grasping balls. It is a valuable antique.

I run the water as Dad gets undressed. This is only the second time I have witnessed my father in a weak state his entire life. My father has lost more than 30 pounds due to cancer.

He has shown so much humility in his request. I know how hard it has to be for him to ask for help. Yet, I admire his humbleness and courage in reaching out to me, and am honored, being the youngest child of the fifteen.

I help Dad step into the tub of warm water and notice the grimace on his face, from the pain of his arthritis and the difficulty of getting into the tub. His physique still has the remembrance of being strong and masculine, but his muscles have softened and his skin is loose. He is still a handsome man. The hairs on his chest are grey and his chocolate-brown complexion has become a shade darker, probably from the chemotherapy. Yet, the man within is still strong willed, wise and proud.

Dad smiles admiringly at me. "I remember when you were thirteen years old and got in trouble for fighting. I believe one of your friends had lied and said they slept with your sister, Leslie. Boy, you got madder than a tick at a flea-collar convention." Dad chuckles. "You didn't hesitate to stand up for your sister's honor and you whipped that young man's ass pretty good, as I recall. Your sister told me that the guy later apologized to her."

"I wasn't going to have those bad rumors going on about my sister, " I respond, blushing.

"That's what I'm talking about. Family has always been important to you and that has filled me with pride. That's why I asked you to help me. I could have asked one of the other kids for help today, but this is a passage of wisdom, youngest and oldest sharing a bond. I had to care for my father and his father cared for him. One day, your son will care for you." Dad wipes a tear from his eye and I fight back the one that begins to swell in mine.

Dad gathers his emotions and continues, "Family is important. When I pass on, it's up to you to keep this family together and pass on the heritage and love that flows down from generation to generation. Keep our children on a positive path and be an example. One generation should always leave it better for the next. You understand what I'm saying, son?"

"Yes, Dad."

"Remember that I only had a fifth-grade education, but I made sure that each one of you received a college degree, " Dad explains placing his hand atop of mine, passing down the responsibility to me.

We are silent as he soaps a towel and starts to wash his face, chest, and arms. He hands me the towel to wash his back, then I help him up and wash his legs and feet. He washes his mid section himself. I put shampoo in his hair and begin washing his scalp.

"I remember when I used to give you baths as a child. I really appreciate the help. I wonder if God makes you weak in body and mind as you get older, to make life easier? What you think, son?"

I bite my bottom lip, "That could be so. We go through so much turmoil in our life, that it would be good to be stress free when we get older. I know I see you as the strongest man I've ever known, and I'm proud to be your son, Dad. You've always worked hard and been fair. You taught me to love God, family, and be an asset to my community, but you were also an example. You made it with limited resources and education. I really respect that."

"Joe, you make me proud. You have never been a problem for me and your mother. You have been a spoiled brat at times, but besides that, you have been the ideal son. I just want you to know how much I love you. You are my baby boy and I know I treated you a little different than the rest of your brothers and sisters and they tease you about it, but you always take responsibility for your actions. I respect that. You also have been able to admit when you're wrong. You're all right, son."

"Thanks, Dad, and I love you too, " I reply, getting teary eyed along with my father.

"Damn, boy, get me out of this tub. My nuts are beginning to look like prunes." We both laugh.

I help my father out of the water, dry him off, and help him lotion his body. We get him into his pajamas and meet Mom, Sierra, and Nia downstairs in the kitchen drinking hot chocolate.

Nia inquires with a smiling, chocolate-marshmallow mustache, "Grandpa, we got hot chocolate. You and Daddy want some?"

"I think I will, baby girl, but only if I can get some of those marshmallows you have there, " Dad answers, smiling as Nia runs to the counter where Sierra hands her the bag of marshmallows and cups for Dad and me.

We finish our cocoa and help wash the cups, then ready to leave.

"It was good seeing you all again and I'm making gumbo next week, " Mom says.

I lick my lips at the thought of mom's homemade Louisiana gumbo. "We'll be here, next week too."

"Just make sure you bring that forty dollars when you come, boy." Mom winks.

"Yes, Ma'am. For gumbo, I'll bring you fifty."

five

I STAND IN THE DOORWAY OBSERVING THE NEIGHBOR-HOOD kids playing as they wait to board their school buses on this sunny morning. The laughing and screaming of the children reminds of my fourteen brothers and sisters and how we played in and out of the house for hours on end.

Mom and Dad made it with fifteen children and two bathrooms. Ten boys and five girls. Our parents had a system and we didn't even realize it. Mom made us bathe at night, that way in the morning all we had to do was wash up and brush our teeth. We always made it to school on time. What a wonderful job they did, sacrificing and organizing constantly to make ends meet.

Memories of my father bringing his paycheck home and only putting five dollars in his pocket, makes me warm inside. Mom made oatmeal with butter and brown sugar, no one can make it like that.

Our parents gave us birthday parties on our sixth, thirteenth, sixteenth, eighteenth, and twenty-first birthdays. Each and every one of us. So parties were going on all the time. The family would push the living room furniture to the side and take some upstairs to make this huge dance hall out of our downstairs. We would put in black light bulbs and Dad would walk around patrolling for kids necking in the dark corners. It was so much fun.

We would barbecue at Swope Park on all the major spring and summer holidays. People probably considered us poor, but we never knew it. We were treated as well as any rich kid; and probably better, because our parents spent time with us and didn't send us off somewhere. I smile.

VERNON PULLS UP IN ONE OF THE UNMARKED, SQUAD CARS. A dark blue Crown Victoria. Vernon resembles Danny Glover a little bit. In good shape for a man of fifty, he keeps his weight at one hundred and ninety pounds. He has a rich brown skin tone, salt and pepper hair, and a graying mustache. What does Vernon want to talk to me about? He hasn't said much since the hostage situation. I run upstairs where my wife and daughter are sleeping. Nia has crawled in our bed and is resting happily in Sierra's arms. I can't help taking a few moments to admire the two most beautiful things in my life. I lean over the bed and kiss them both.

I go to my gun safe, unlock it, and retrieve my 9mm and Smith and Wesson .45 automatic. Then I insert my bullet clips into the guns and grab a couple of extra clips. I place the guns in my shoulder and ankle holsters. After locking the safe, I return downstairs closing the front door behind me and get in the squad car.

"Good morning, Vernon. How you doing, brotha?" I ask with a big smile.

Vernon groans. "Fine. What the hell you smiling about?"

"I'm just happy to see my partner, and get back to work after that two week administrative leave, " I explain.

"It's good to have you back. I was just as tired doing all that desk work by myself. Man, I'm hungry as a bear and since you been sitting at home getting paid for nothing, you buying breakfast."

"Vernon, you just don't want Myra to talk about your cheap butt, that's all."

"Joe, that shit ain't funny. It ain't funny, one bit."

"Just drive, Ms. Daisy, " I tease.

"What would be funny is me putting your ass out on the street."

Something is bothering him, even tho he tries to laugh at his own dismal joke. The restaurant is about half full. The smell of black eyed peas, candied yams, bacon, sausage, grits, pork chops, greens, and macaroni and cheese fill the air.

Niecie waves at us from the counter, looking lovely as ever. A voluptuous woman with full lips, hips, bright eyes, and Hershey chocolate-brown skin, Niecie is always pleasant and committed to her community. She rarely says no to someone in need.

She and her husband, Perry, have been in the restaurant business for fifteen years in the heart of the city and people travel from all parts of Kansas City to get the best soul food in town. The rich, poor, professional, blue-collar worker, clergy, pimps, drug dealers, teachers, criminals, lawyers, law enforcement personnel, drug addicts, high school graduates, and people with Doctorate degrees all congregate together at Niecie's. All God's children need a little soul and they get it through the food that is cooked with love and seasoning at Niecie's.

"Hey, Joe and Vernon. How you gentleman doing today?" Niecie asks with a gracious smile and her face lights up in a way that you can't help but feel welcome.

"We doing fine, Niecie, now that we about to get our grub on, " Vernon responds.

"Well, I'm happy you boys came to my place. Make yourself at home, and Myra will be over in a minute. Joe, why you acting all shy and stuff with your fine self?"

"Hi, Niecie. I'm sorry, I'm just concentrating on those pork chops on that dude's plate over there. They're lookin' and smellin' great. I'm 'bout to ask him for some, if Myra don't get over here, " I joke, as we sit at our table.

"Myra will be there quick. As soon as she see you guys're here, you know you'll get the royal treatment. Now Vernon, be nice, " Niecie scolds shaking her finger at Vernon, playfully.

Vernon says with his fingers crossed across his heart like a boy scout, "Yes, Ma'am, I'll be on my best behavior."

Niecie shakes her head and attends to the next customers. Myra waves as she heads our way from the other side of the room wearing the hospitable smile of a dear friend. Myra is a caramel smooth, Indian-skinned woman. Shapely, with medium-length hair, full hips, and a small waistline, she is attractive, with the facial features similar to my favorite female rap star, M.C. Lyte, and she has a gold crown on her front tooth that radiates her charming smile.

"What's up, Joe, how you doing? You know I miss you when you don't come in, " Myra says, flashing that gold tooth as I rise and give her a warm embrace.

Vernon asks, "What about me, Myra?"

Myra places her hands on her hips and throws her head to the side as her eyes roll in his direction. "What about you?"

"You don't miss, me?"

"Vernon, I miss you about as much as I miss cramps each month, " Myra says and people around our table bursts into laughter. "Vernon, you know I miss you too, baby, with your old hateful self. I'm glad your wife is okay, " Myra says as she kisses Vernon on the cheek.

"Thank you, sweetheart, you ain't so bad. You could use a breath mint, but that's all right. You cool as you are, girl, " Vernon states as the place fills with laughter once again.

"See, I can't be nice to your old butt. You guys want the sunrise special with pancakes, smothered potatoes, eggs, and bacon?"

"Yes, Myra, that will be great with two cups of coffee and small orange juice, " I answer.

"Vernon, I'll try not to drop your eggs on the floor, okay sugar?"

Vernon returns Myra's evil grin. "Yeah, you try real hard."

When Myra walks away, I turn to my friend. "So Vernon, what's going on with you, man? We've been friends for too long for you not to tell me what's been eating at you. I respect how you keep to yourself, but whatever this is, it's starting to scare me. You haven't been your usual sarcastic self. You do trust me, don't you?"

Myra places two cups of coffee and glasses of water in front of us and leaves. Vernon stares into his coffee, takes a sip, and looks at me with troubled brown eyes.

"Joe, you are one of the few people I do trust, and I consider you my closest friend. I guess you do have a right to know, since it will affect you in the end."

I sit back in my chair and try to get ready.

"As long as we've known each other, I've avoided talking about this and I thank you for not prying. I've been with the department for twenty-five years. I'm forty-nine years old and headed for fifty awfully fast. My mother used to say, 'a loose shoe or a shoe too tight can both do damage to your feet. Always get a comfortable fit in whatever you do.' I seen a lot of shit go down. I've been through the racism, race riots, and been passed over for promotions more times than I'd like to think about. I didn't care because I love the work. You know, making a difference. Doing some good."

"That's why we do this job, Vernon."

"I gotta tell you, Gertrude is the best thing that ever happened in my life."

Vernon rubs his chin slowly. His shoulders sag. Looking around the room he grabs his forehead and rubs it with his fingers. He takes a drink of water and stares me deep in my eyes.

"Joe, what I'm about to tell you, only my wife has knowledge of. My Dad abandoned me and my mom when I was nine years old. You know the routine. He went out for cigarettes and never came back."

"I'm sorry, Vernon. That's jacked up, dude."

"He was never heard from again, Joe. So I became the man of the house. Helping out with whatever I could. Mom was always depressed, but did the best she could. She held down two jobs. She was so heart-broken by my dad that she never dated again. She hardly ever smiled. I hated that, because she was such a beautiful woman."

Vernon takes another drink.

"Vernon, I'm sorry dude. If you don't want to finish, I understand. I didn't mean to stir up bad memories."

"That's all right, Joe. You need to know this about me. I was drafted by the Army to go to Vietnam. I'd write my mom every week and called as often as I could. I would never tell her about how my life was in dan-ger each day or how I lost twenty-eight of my high school friends within three months. I never shared the ugliness of war with her. About the peo-ple I had killed for my country. I knew she'd worry and I loved her too much to put that stuff on her mind. Shit, my mind was full enough for five or six people."

I shook my head. "Nothing can prepare a man for the ugliness of war, but you made it through."

"Yes, I did. I was released from the Army after my obligated two years. When I returned home, I was greeted by our neighbor, Mrs. Collins, who walked from her porch to meet me when she saw me coming down the street. She was so proud of me in my uniform."

"I bet you were looking good, too."

"Joe, I was lookin' sharp, but there was something wrong, because she held me too long when she hugged me. I asked her had she seen my moth-er. I could tell by the look on her face and the tears that formed in her elderly eyes, that something terrible had happened. She sat me down and explained as best she could that someone had broken into our house and my mom had been raped and beaten with a baseball bat the night before I arrived home." Vernon's eyes are misty.

"Vernon, I'm so sorry. You don't have to go down this road, bro."

Vernon takes a handkerchief, wipes his eyes, and continues, "I immediately went to St. Luke's and the condition my mother was in was devastating. I barely recognized her. Her head and arms were bandaged. Her head was swollen as well as her eyes and face. They really did a number on her, Joe." Vernon's face tenses up and he stutters.

I reach over and touch his hand, but he shakes his head, determined to finish.

"I was mad as hell and full of hate. I wanted to kill that day. My mama was in a coma and never regained consciousness. I stayed at her bedside for seven days, before she died. She never saw me in my uniform, Joe. I was never able to tell her that I loved her. I felt like I had failed her."

"There was nothing you could do. Only God knows the time and the hour, Vernon."

Vernon clenches his fist and his jaw tightens. "I should have been home to protect her. I was devastated, guilty, angry, and felt cheated out of the only person I loved in life. I couldn't believe God would let something like that happen. I stopped going to church. I didn't have any more faith in anything." Vernon pauses as Myra brings our food and places it on the table with orange juice and hot sauce.

Myra approaches slowly looking at us and seeing us for the first time without smiling. "Excuse me. You two need anything else?"

"Thanks, Myra, that's all for now, " I respond with a smile and a reassuring wink. We say grace and begin eating.

I say with a mouth full of hot-sauce-sprinkled, smothered potatoes, "Go on, Vernon, I'm listening."

"I met Gertrude about five months after I buried my mother. She had just graduated from Lincoln University and taken a job at the post office. We met at a car wash. I was in the stall next to hers and Marvin Gaye's song, 'What's Going On', was on the radio. It's kind of funny, me there, minding my own business, about to turn the wax on the automatic wash, when Gertrude asked me if I had change for a ten."

I grinned. "I bet you would have went to the store and back to give her change."

"You know it. She was so pretty and she had this little country slang in her voice. I later found that she was from Little Rock. When I first laid eyes on her, my mind was made up that I could not live without her. I just stood there with my mouth open and fumbled in my pockets, until the water shut off from the car wash sprayer. She smiled and laughed with me about my being smitten with her. My car or the wash didn't matter anymore. Eventually, I found the change and even helped her wash her car." A little smile dances on his face.

"We went to eat after that, dated for six months, and have been married ever since. Her parents and I hit it off from day one and they treat me like their own son."

"Yeah, they are really nice people."

"Her dad worked construction and her mom was a grade school teacher. No other woman has ever turned my head. She is my soul mate. I got my religion back, and I thank God everyday that she loves me, just as hard as I love her, " Vernon says, while sprinkling hot sauce on his eggs.

"You are a lucky man to have a woman like that, Vernon."

Vernon smiles, "Joe, I'm not just lucky, I'm truly blessed. She has stuck with me through thick and thin. I believe God sent her to me to replace all the pain I endured."

"The Lord is good and never leaves us alone. I really believe that."

"You never asked about my former partner, Walter Williams. He was a good cop. The top of his class in the police academy. What I remember most about him is his hair was kind of funny, it kind of did what it wanted to do. He could never style it right, but he was sharp as a razor blade with his instincts and he was smart."

"Sounds like the perfect partner."

"He was the best, Joe. The guy was the only person I knew who had a photographic memory. He could tell what was in the paper last week, line for line and could tell what you ate for lunch a month ago. He was a little bit smaller than you and a few years older. He was a great partner and friend."

I pause and bite my lick lip. "What ever happened to him, Vernon?"

"We had this serial killer case back in July, 1982. Children were coming up missing in The Wayne Minor projects. The papers called him, 'the Boogey Man,' because this is how the kids referred to him. He would strike in the early evening, just when it was getting dark. There was a big playground area in Wayne Minor with a sandbox. This is where most of the kids spent their time. You could always find children swinging, playing on the monkey bars, teeter-totters, and stuff that kids do. A total of eight little Black girls were snatched from the play area."

I nodded. "I remember that. The people in the community were up in arms about that and ready to riot if the killer wasn't caught."

"The Mayor and the press were hard on the department to find this killer and fast. The Black church and community leaders demanded that black detectives have a direct role in the investigation. They demanded that their best interest be represented. They accused the department of putting little value on the life of an African-American."

"So you two were the detectives that got the case?"

He looked up and rubs the cup in front of him. "Yes, Walter and I were assigned to the case. With the help of the children in the area, we quickly got a composite of the man. We also got very lucky when we started interviewing the older adults who had windows facing the play yard. They were and still are a great resource. They sit around and notice what's going on in the neighborhood. They love company and like to talk."

Vernon wipes his mouth, belches, then continues, "The composite matched the description of the ice cream man. The older residents said he came around Wayne Minor, right before dark and the children would come running at the sound of the ice cream bell. It was so obvious that it was overlooked by the White detectives who had the case before us. Walter came up with the plan for us to go under cover as winos."

"The brother had skills like that? That was a smart move."

Vernon smiled and nodded. "We staked out the play ground for three days, before our ice cream man showed. The guy would lace popsicles with Ipecac. It's a syrup that induces vomiting. It's a common over-the-counter drug that most people keep around the house in case their child drinks poison."

Vernon takes a drink from his juice. "Where was I?" Vernon asks.

"The ice cream man was about to show up, " I remind him.

"Yeah, when we spotted the ice cream truck, we approached and identified ourselves. The guy was a very dark Jamaican dude. We later found out his name is Felix Oyeleye. The guy looked normal, like he could have been one of your next-door neighbors. A good-looking fellow in his mid-thirties. He had nice dreads, clean shaven, had an honest face, but the guy's eyes were blood-shot, yellowish in color, and his pupils were blueish-grey."

"Damn, that's a weird mix."

Vernon rubs his shoulder and arm. "It was the strangest shit I ever saw in my life. We pulled out our badges, told him we'd like to question him, and asked him to step out of the truck." Vernon pauses and takes another drink of his juice. His hands tremble and his face is solemn.

"We didn't see the double-barreled, sawed-off shotgun he was hiding behind the red, clown-faced, ice cream truck door. He took Walter out with both barrels, shooting him in the neck. He almost took the man's head off his shoulders. The only thing holding Walter's head to his body was skin and vertebra. He was killed on the spot. I can still see my partner's body, damn near headless. Blood gushing everywhere. Children dropped their bomb pops, fudge bars, and popsicles, running in fear from the sound of shotgun blast and the sight of William's body, kicking like a chicken with his head cut off on the ground.

"I called in for back up with my walkie talkie and let them know an officer was down. I jumped in my car and followed Boogey Man, who had taken off, to a warehouse in the stockyard area, by the river, around fifth and Gennesse." Vernon fidgets with his watch. His long face stretches tight and his eyes seem to wander as he continues, "The place was dark and damp, with a foul odor, like nothing else I've ever smelled. I followed the stench with gun and flashlight in hand. I came upon a room in the basement. It was a refrigerated room, petitioned with thick strips of plastic lit by a red light. It had to be about forty degrees in there. The further in I ventured, the stronger the vile odor became.

"The source of the odor?"

"There they were. The eight missing, innocent, baby girls. Their ages were between seven and twelve. Their faces were made up with red lipstick and rouge. Their hair combed with red ribbons tied to their pony tails and their bodies were discolored, bruised, naked, and dead cold. They were lined up against the walls like mannequins and all the little girls' eyes were wide open. The freak was saving them. Using them as sex toys to feed his perverted sexual appetite. He used the cold room to preserve their bodies."

Bile rose from my belly as the scene captures my mind, "Did you ever find him?"

"Felix sprang from behind some boxes and fired his shotgun at me. I quickly jumped out of the aim of the blast. The shot struck and riddled the dead children's bodies. Before I could fire on him, he struck me in the ribs with the butt of his now-empty shotgun. I could hear one of my ribs break and the pain called out to me. I never released my special Police-issued eight round, .38 revolver and before he could hit me again, I emptied the eight bullets in his chest. I quickly reloaded and shot him two more times to make sure he was dead. I don't take chances with crazy people."

Vernon has never talked much about his partner and I feel even closer to him, knowing that he trusts me with his past.

"I remember those blue-grey, dead eyes staring at me when he died. When my backup arrived, I was still staring in this guy's eyes. It was the strangest shit I had ever seen. It was like dormant evil. I went to a psychiatrist for three months to get my head right."

I nod. "That was a traumatic experience. I can see why you would need to talk to someone to get you through that."

"Joe, I'm telling you all of this because the word is you and I are going to be helping the FBI with the prostitute murders. This is not the work of some pissed-off pimp. This is the work of a serial killer. From what I hear, this guy is not just raping and killing the women, this freak is cutting them up. I don't know if I can go that route again."

"Man, we don't even know if we'll get that case."

Vernon rubs his forehead and frowns. "Gertrude is real supportive of me. I don't know if I can ask her to do that again. I'm trying to be honest with you, because you are my best friend and my partner." Vernon pauses and looks me steadily in the eyes.

"Gertrude understands the kind of work you do."

"I've never regretted being a cop. I love what I do, but I adore my wife. If I have to choose between Gertrude and this job...well, the choice is easy for me. My wife comes first, Joe. There are two things I live by: live each day like it's your last, and don't love anything that you're not willing to die for. I realize that I've seemed mean and rough sometimes, but life has not been easy for me or to me, Joe. I take shit very serious. All I got is my wife, her parents, you, and your family. That's all that matters to me. God, family, and you."

I think of Nia. I would hunt a person to the end of the earth if they harmed my child in any way. Pushing the thought of rage and retribution out of my mind, I refocus on my partner.

"Vernon, I'd expect nothing less. I'm sorry about what happened to your mom. I'd give this shit up myself in a Kansas City minute, if it was the only way to keep Sierra."

I think back to the near tragedy in my life. "My road has not been much easier than yours. I have almost been killed three times."

"Damn, I never knew it'd been that many, " Vernon responds, as his mouth hangs open.

"The first was when I was seven years old. My brothers John, Ronald, and I were in our upstairs bedroom playing with Dad's twelve-gauge shotgun. John decided to point it at Ronald and myself and was ready to pull the trigger when we pushed the barrel of the gun away and warned him that the shotgun could be loaded. John, being the oldest, assured us that it wasn't and to prove it, aimed the gun at the wall across from us and pulled the trigger. The gun fired with a force that knocked all three of us off the bunk bed."

"Was anyone hurt."

"No, we just looked at each other in a daze, but not for long. Dad came running up the stairs. As soon as he realized what had happened and checked to see if we were all okay, he gave us each a whipping that we'd never forget."

"Joe, you know you had an angel with you that day."

I take a drink of water and continue, "The second time I was driving from St. Louis after having a big argument with my girlfriend. I hit a patch of ice that had formed from the falling sleet and skidded. I fought to control the car, but it wasn't working. I quickly pumped the brakes and was on my third spin, when I got calm and took my hands off the steering wheel and put my life in God's hands. My 1985 Toyota Corolla flipped onto the snow-covered embankment and rolled twice, landing on the driver's side. I looked out the car windows and all I saw was white. I checked myself for blood, but I was not hurt. Dude, it was the strangest thing, when I returned to work to find that a co-worker had been killed in a similar accident." I knock on the wood table.

"God has truly smiled on you. You've escaped death twice, but don't forget about Dr. Death, " Vernon reminds me.

I nod. "The third incident when the hit-man, Donald Dean, better known as 'Dr. Death,' shot me in the Research Medical Center Morgue. The bullet went straight through my shoulder and I survived. Every time I see the wound in the mirror, it reminds me of Officer Rico, the rookie who was shot in the head and killed as we searched for Dean in the hospital boiler room and morgue. Dean paid for that murder with his life. I can't help the thought, that I've been truly blessed." I bite my lower lip. "I realize what you mean when you say that you found your religion. My faith was at the crossroads when I found the children who were killed by their mother, but it has been solidified with each divine encounter. The closer I was to death, the more I thought that God had a plan for me and He is watching over me. My life has been spared three times. I will unequivocally submit to whatever He asks."

"Amen to that, Brother!" Vernon says.

"My life philosophy is simple, Vernon. Believe in God with all my existence. Love, nurture, and protect my family and extended family. And last, treat others as I would like to be treated, with dignity, compassion, and respect."

"I hear ya, man."

"You are like a brother to me, Vernon. I would never ask you to do anything that is counter to your beliefs, my friend." I grasp my partner's hand and shake it.

"Well, Kansas City's finest. How you two fellas doing this morning?" M.C. Richardson jokes as he and brother Bill Grace stop at our table. "The last time I saw you two was at Smoke Me Baby Bar-Be-Cue. It seems that the only place we run into each other is at eating establishments. That probably explains why my stomach is hanging over my belt."

Brother Richardson has a talk show, "Guess Who's Coming To Kansas City, " on KKFI, a local independent community radio station. The brother does a great job, keeping up on topics that affect the black community in greater Kansas City. The disappearances of the women on Independence Avenue has been one of the issues on his show, along with the massacre that occurred at the post office.

Brother Bill Grace is one of the Founders of W.E.B. DuBois Learning Center, which helps troubled students with math, reading, and science. They also build self-esteem and character through teaching African History. They too, have professional mentors who go into the classrooms and help the students with homework and understanding the importance of learning. I've worked with Bill at the center as a volunteer and I've also appeared on Mr. Richardson's show.

"We're doing fine, Mr. Richardson, and Mr. Grace. Good to see you, " I respond.

Vernon just smiles and nods with his mouth full of pancakes, as brothers Grace and Richardson excuse themselves and are seated at their table. We sit a few more minutes saying nothing.

Missouri State Legislator Lloyd Daniels comes in and sits at our table. "Joe, Vernon. How are you gentleman?"

Vernon answers, "Brotha Lloyd, if I had your hand, I'd throw mine in."

"Yeah, Brotha Lloyd, you've been on the case, man. We've been following you in the papers. You're doing a great job addressing issues for the community, especially the elderly. I really appreciate you dropping in on Mom and Dad. They were happy to have the company."

Brother Lloyd is a peanut-brown complected, thin man with a handsome presence. "Joe, we're from the same hood. Believe me, the pleasure was all mine, especially when your mom fills me with peach cobbler and coffee. Man, you can't beat that." We all agree and laugh.

"Vernon, I heard about the incident with Gertrude and I'm glad she came out of it all right, " Lloyd says. "Joe, great job, buddy."

Vernon nods.

"We have to watch each others' back, Lloyd, and do the best we can."

"Well, great. I've been hearing great things about you gentleman. Now, you did not hear this from me, but I heard you two made Sergeant. You really deserve it. Well, I don't want to hold you good brothers up. Take care and be careful, gentlemen, " Lloyd Daniels says as he shakes both our hands, then sits with M.C. Richardson and Bill Grace.

Vernon asks rubbing his chin, "Are you beginning to think that we're the only two people who don't know what's going on in our lives?"

"This is getting a little ridiculous, but congratulations, Detective-

Sergeant Brown.

"Look Joe, don't be drinking milk if you don't own a cow. All this shit is hearsay. We can celebrate when we have the gold shields in our hands, okay?"

I nod.

"You guys ready to cash out?" Myra asks.

"Yes, Myra, and thanks for the great service, " Vernon says, handing Myra a fifty dollar bill. "Keep the change."

Myra puts the fifty up to the light, then dips her finger in the water glass on the table and rubs the bill. "Joe, this ain't counterfeit, is it?"

"No, " I answer.

Myra puts her hand to Vernon's forehead to check for a temperature. "Vernon, you okay? You never leave a big tip. Better yet, you never leave a tip. Thanks, brotha, " Myra, says smiling.

Vernon says smiling, "I know what's important in life and you've always been an excellent waitress, even with your bad attitude."

"Joe, nobody hit Vernon in the head or nothin', huh?"

I shake my head.

"Thanks Vernon, thanks a lot, " Myra says, giving him a kiss on the cheek. "You guys take care and come back soon, " she says as she takes our dirty dishes into the back.

"That was pretty good, Vernon. Do I get a fifty too?"

"Joe, don't try your luck, Mr. Funny Man. Myra's a good young lady. I should show her more appreciation. But, I ain't gettin' soft. So don't even say it, " Vernon tilts his head, smirks and says with an, 'I dare you' look in his eyes.

I explain, smiling confidently, "I didn't have to say it. It doesn't mean you're soft by being nice, Vernon. You can be masculine and a nice guy at the same time. Look at me."

"Yeah, pull your pink panties up, nice guy, " Vernon says with a hearty laugh.

We walk outside and to our surprise, Pretty Kevin Wine, my neighborhood friend, pulls up in a 1998 blue Cadillac Seville. He stops the car, honks, and waves us over.

Vernon cocks his head at me and nods. "A friend of yours, I presume?"

"Yeah."

We approach the car, which is blaring the song "Roxanne" by the rock group, Police, from the stereo. Pretty Kevin is smiling a wide-toothed grin. He has perfect teeth and one gold tooth. He is wearing a blue FUBU sweat suit, with matching blue cap and gold Rolex diamond watch with matching bracelet. A two-carat diamond stud shines from his left ear. His necklace is gold as well, with a gold Greek coin, trimmed in diamonds.

He has not lost his good looks. Kevin has never been one to work a normal job. He never had to. Women threw themselves at him and most were happy to play second fiddle as long as they had part of Kevin in their lives. He could charm an old lady out of her heart medicine or swoon a section-eight lady out of her welfare check. When we were in high school, he picked me up in one of his teachers' cars to go roller skating. We stopped by her house on the way home, so he could show off and introduce me to her. She had to be about twenty-seven or twenty-eight and was fine. I had much respect for the brother.

"Joe, good to see you, brotha. I've been trying to get in touch with you. Who's the old guy?" Kevin asks peering over the rim of his Ray Ban sunglasses.

Vernon says with a threatening smirk, "I'm the old guy who can whip your ass up and down Prospect."

"He's my partner, Kevin, and he doesn't like to be referred to as 'old guy'."

"I'm sorry, Pops, I didn't mean no harm."

Vernon takes a step toward the car and Kevin leans away from his approach. I put my arm out to stop Vernon from teaching Kevin some much-needed manners.

"What's your problem, dude? Look, I didn't come here to start no trouble. I was coming to eat and ran into you cats. I meant no offense. Tell him, Joe, " Kevin says.

"Vernon, he's cool, man."

Vernon glares at Pretty Kevin. "Well, he better learn to watch his mouth and he better learn pretty damn quick."

"No problem, I got the message. Just cool out, dude. It ain't that serious, " Kevin states with his hands in the air. "Joe, we need to talk, but not around here. People see me with you and might think I turned snitch or something. You know what I mean? I got this serious problem, I need your help on. Can you guys follow me to Swope Park? You know where we used to party with the college girls?" Kevin brushes lent off his clothes as he smiles at Vernon.

"Yeah, I know the place. We only got about an hour, Kevin, so don't be wasting my time, all right?"

Kevin sucks his gold tooth and winks. "Joe, time is money and I don't have either to waste. This is some serious shit I need to talk to you about, man."

I look at Vernon, who nods. "Lead the way, " I order.

We follow Kevin to Myer Boulevard, turn right, and head into Swope Park. One of the largest parks in the country, it sits in the middle of the city. It has a zoo, bandstand, over 15 shelter houses and an outdoor concert hall. At one time it was closed to African Americans. Once integrated, we frequented "Watermelon Hill, " named for obvious reasons, a large area around the water lagoon and public swimming pool.

We triumphed and embraced our newfound freedom on the spot of land in Swope Park we carved out for our own. We shared our weekends with family and friends drinking, having barbeque's, dancing, playing dominoes, cards, softball, and having fun. It was a communal place.

We stand outside our cars on "Watermelon Hill, " waiting for Pretty Kevin to reveal the secret of his distress. Vernon takes out a Cuban cigar and places it in his mouth. He never lights it. He says he just likes the taste and feel of it hanging from his lips, but he really only does this when curious or nervous.

Pretty Kevin approaches, looking around and over his shoulder. With each car that passes on the road, Kevin looks in its direction for a recognizable face behind the wheel.

Vernon snarls impatiently, now holding the cigar between his two fingers, "Come on, boy, you move like a sixty-eight-year-old sissy. Shit, you making me nervous with all that fidgeting. You got us out here, what you want?"

"You need to ease up off me, old man. I ain't no sissy. A brotha can't be too careful these days, " Kevin explains.

"What's up, Kevin? We're on a time schedule here. Start talkin' or we walkin', " I say.

"Okay. I hear you two are supposed to be on the Independence prostitute case."

I shake my head. "We haven't been assigned to the case, regardless of what you heard. The FBI has it."

Vernon asks with a frown, "What the case have to do with you, anyway?" He bites his cigar as he stares at Kevin, waiting for an answer.

Kevin reluctantly answers as Vernon's clenches his cigar tight between his teeth. "Four of my bitches are missing. I ain't heard from them in five months. They wouldn't just leave me like that. They didn't even say anything to none of the other hoes. I can't understand it. I been good to them bitches. They had to have gotten snatched."

Kevin's total disregard for the women makes my blood boil. I feel the hairs on my neck stand on end. I reflect on my daughter and her being mesmerized by a smooth-talking man like Kevin and falling prey to his manipulating ways. Damn him and his manipulating attitude.

I'm surprised when I knock Kevin to the ground with a right cross to his jaw. Vernon picks him up and starts slapping him around, then turns him loose. We both start to head for our car, leaving Pretty Kevin bruised, but not hurt.

"What the hell was that for? You mother-fuckers crazy or something?" Kevin screams. He's pointing a .45 automatic pistol on us. We simultaneously draw our guns on Kevin.

Vernon spits his half-eaten cigar to the ground. "Bad career choice, Kevin."

"Drop the gun, Kevin. The only reason you're not dead is because you're an old friend of mine."

Kevin smiles and puts the gun back in his crouch holster. We put our guns away as well and approach Kevin.

"Look, guys, I wasn't going to use it on you, I just wanted your attention. Lisa 'Cherry' Chavez is my old lady and she's one of the missing women. She's four months pregnant with our baby, Joe. Something has happened to her Joe." Kevin wipes the tears from his eyes and his bottom lip is trembling. "Please help me, man. I love her."

Vernon says, "Yeah, enough to sell her body on the street and call her a bitch. That's some real love, my brother. You make me want to puke. All you're doing is exploiting those women for your own financial gain."

"Joe, look man, you owe me. I'm sorry about the pimp talk, but I'm scared for these girls, man. I take good care of my women. I don't be beating up on them and shit like that. They're all getting their associates degrees and Cherry has a Bachelors. It's just a business decision and agreement. There's a killer out there. Aren't you guys concerned?"

I bite my bottom lip. "Kevin, if you were so damned concerned you wouldn't have them on the street in the first place, now would you?"

"Look, I'll pay you guys whatever you want, just bring my girls back safe, " Kevin pleads.

Vernon has a mean frown on his face, "It don't work like that, Kevin. Besides, how do you know they just didn't get tired of you and the street walker life?"

"Cherry is pregnant and she loves me. None of the girls took any of their stuff and they each have over ten thousand dollars in their banking accounts. None of it has been touched. Does that make sense to you, Detective?" Kevin clenching his fists.

Vernon and I look at each other. Good grief, we're not even official-ly on the case!

"Kevin, we have a friend in the FBI who can get information into the case. We'll get back to you. Until then, make a report at the police station and give the names and description of the missing women. That's all we can do for now."

"Joe, anything that you can do, I'd appreciate. Thanks for looking out, " Kevin says wiping the tears form his face.

Vernon walks up to Kevin and sucker punches him. "Don't ever as long as you black, point a gun at me. Sissy!"

Pretty Kevin hits him in the gut, then in the jaw with a left upper cut. "I ain't gonna be too many more sissies, punk!" Kevin screams.

"That all you got?" Vernon yells as he pimp slaps Kevin with a pow-erful back hand. "Pull up your pink panties, girly man."

Kevin tackles Vernon and they wrestle on the ground. Cars pass by and I wave hello as I let the fellas blow off steam. After about two min-utes, I pull them apart.

"All right, you two, that's enough. Party's over. Time to go, " I order.

Pretty Kevin says as he straightens his wavy hair and snazzy clothes, "Yeah, Vernon, you lucky Joe pulled me off your old ass. I was bout' to have you screaming like a little bitch."

Vernon hits Kevin one final time. Kevin is dazed and off balance. I grab him and help him to his car.

"Who's the bitch now, you little punk?" Vernon asks with a grin as he tucks his shirt in his pants and knocks the loose grass from his clothes.

I shake my head and roll my eyes. "You both need to grow up and stop trippin'. Kevin, see what you can find out from your associates on the street. We'll do what we can on our end. If you hear from any of the ladies before then, call me at the downtown homicide unit."

"Nice meeting you, Pretty Kevin, " Vernon says as he gets in the car.

Kevin repeatedly gives Vernon the finger. "Like wise."

six

WHEN WE GET TO OUR DESKS, WE HEAR CAPTAIN WAYNE'S door open and his huge body fill the doorway. His ugly brown tie is almost as ugly as his mint green suit. His salt and pepper hair and mustache matches his bronze skinned complexion. He points his finger at us with an agitated look in his eye. "Johnson and Brown, get your asses in here."

We pass the other detectives on our way to the Captain's office. Jim, Clarence, Jessica, Daniel, Mike, Kimberly, Leo, Sergeant Lopez, and Janet tease us because we are in trouble, once again. Vernon ain't seeing no humor in the situation.

We enter the office and close the door behind us. We know the routine, we've been in this predicament on more than one occasion.

Captain Wayne asks rubbing his hand wearily over his face, "Would you guys like to tell me what the hell was going on in Swope Park?"

"Joe, do you know what he's talking about?"

"Vernon, I don't have a clue. Captain, what makes you think we were in Swope Park today?"

"Well, we had a citizen call in our office and report a fight around Watermelon Hill and said a blue unmarked police car was parked near the incident. What color vehicle are you guys driving?"

Vernon answers, "Blue."

"Dark blue Captain, there must be a mistake, " I say looking up at the ceiling, intentionally avoiding the Captain's glare.

"Blue is blue, Johnson. I don't have time for your smart-ass comments. I know you two were in the park. Look at Vernon's suit. He has grass stains on his pants leg and grass hanging off the back of his jacket."

I brush the grass off Vernon's jacket.

The Captain says, "Who were you guys fighting with?"

"Captain, we don't know what you're talking about. I don't know how Vernon got messy this morning. He was probably doing the wild thing with his wife in the back yard or something like that, huh, Vernon?" I wink at my partner.

"Yeah, something like that, Captain."

"Well, I happen to know you're both lying like carpets. That's all right, you're gonna be out of my hair for a while. I have some breaking news for you knuckleheads. The good news is that you both have been promoted to Detective-Sergeant. Give me your silver badges, " Captain Wayne orders as he stands.

Captain Wayne is a little taller than me with a robust build. A fair man with a no-nonsense attitude and a deep bronze complexion, he hands us our Gold shields and we place them in our pockets. We shake hands.

"Congratulations, you've been deserving this for a long time and I made sure you got what you deserved. You guys are the best detectives I've got. You're full of shit, but you know how to take care of business and get the job done. Thank you, not only for the professionalism that you bring to this department, but for the friendship we share as well. We've been through a lot together and you two have aged me more than Mother Nature herself. But, I've never met more committed men than the two of you."

I ask, "So Captain, this means a big pay raise, right?"

"Yes, Johnson. I don't know about 'big' though, " the Captain answers.

Vernon says, "Thank you, Captain. This really means a great deal to us and we'll continue to do our best for the department, sir."

The Captain walks over and puts his hand around Vernon's shoulder. "Vernon, you deserve this more than anybody in this department. I know the discrimination that you've endured over the years. I know it too well myself, but you've hung in there with your head held high and I respect you for it, brotha."

"Thank you, Captain."

"Now, for the bad news. You two have been assigned to a special assignment with the FBI. Report to Agent Royal James tomorrow. He will brief you on the Independence Prostitute case. You two were hand picked for this case. Someone is noticing the great job you've been doing. This is a great opportunity. This doesn't happen everyday. So, be careful and watch your backs. Come back in one piece and Joe, don't be a hotshot. Please go by the book and try to get along with the Feds, okay?" The Captain frowns hard.

"Why you pick me out like I'm the trouble maker? I know how to get along, don't I, Vernon?"

Vernon just looks at me and says nothing.

"Oh, so it's like that, huh brotha? Leave me hangin'? 'Ah yeah, I got your back, Joe. I'm your partner. I won't let you down, Joe.' That's cold, Vernon. Just cuff me and push me off a cliff, why don't you? You dudes be hatin' because I look good, that's all. No problem, I'm cool. Is that all, Captain, or do I need to stand here and get disrespected a little while longer, with Sergeant, 'I-got-your-back,' Brown?"

The Captain and Vernon laugh.

Vernon explains, "Joe, you cool and all, but you know you do things your way. I'm surprised you and me hit it off, but I know we play off each other. We ain't saying you bad, or trying to hurt your feelings or nothing, we just saying you can be hard to work with at times, that's all."

"Whatever, Judas!" I reply, rolling my eyes at Vernon.

Vernon laughs again. We shake the Captain's hand and receive our assignment briefing on the Prostitute Case.

When we walk out of the Captain's office, we're greeted by the applause of our fellow detectives who have a cake, chicken salad sandwiches, and punch waiting on our desks along with a gift for each of us. We open the gifts and find silver-plated, sixteen round, fully automatic 9mm Walther P99 pistols with black leather shoulder holster straps equipped with white tactical lamps, and laser aim.

Sergeant Lopez states, "Since you boys are going to be with the big boys, we thought you should have the big guns. You guys be careful and hurry back."

"Y'all are the greatest." Vernon responds. "We thank you and pray that you all will be careful and have all these cases closed by the time we get back, " The detectives burst into laughter.

"Seriously, you guys. We really appreciate the friendship and support you have shown to us. Vernon and I are working with the best precinct in the department and when we work with the FBI we'll show them what the Kansas City Homicide Unit is all about. Thank you, guys, for being here for us. This is really touching and as a newly appointed Sergeant, I wish to use the phrase of a group of prophets, A-W-B, 'Cut the Cake'!"

The Captain joins us, raises his cup, and we all toast. Vernon and I look at each other with school-kid grins and wink, Sergeant to Sergeant.

We leave the office around 6. It is just getting dark when my cell phone rings. Vernon and I look at each other.

Vernon asks, "You expecting a call, son?"

"No, but I'm getting one, ain't I?"

"Boy, one of these days, your smart-ass mouth is gonna try my patience and I'm gonna have to whip your ass, like that Pretty Kevin friend of yours, " Vernon says, squinting at me.

I answer the phone on the third ring.

Pretty Kevin screams, "Joe, get over here, man! I got some guy who broke into my place and tried to kill me, man. I have him tied up. I'm holding him for you. Man, you ain't gonna believe who he's working for."

"Where are you, Kevin?"

"7077 Manchester in Sheraton Estates. Man, get here as soon as you can, before I have to kill this fool!"

"Kevin, keep your cool and don't do nothing stupid. We're about five minutes away. Just hang tough. You got it?"

"Got it."

I explain the call to Vernon.

"Huh, I guess that Kevin ain't all punk after all, " Vernon says as he puts his unlit cigar in his mouth and picks up speed.

Kevin's house is a split-level ranch-style home with a two-car garage and a nice, well-kept, front yard. As we approach the front porch, Kevin greets us at the door.

He closes the door behind us as we enter his foyer. Kevin glimpses up and down the street through the door window.

"You guys weren't followed were you?"

"No, Kevin. Relax. Where is this guy?" Vernon asks.

"I got him hooked up downstairs, but you guys need to take your shoes off first, " Kevin says.

Vernon scrowls, "What the hell we need to take our shoes off for, fool?"

"Look at the carpet, you old fart. This is Persian White and very expensive. I don't want it all messed up with the dirt you bring in and I know on your salary, you can't afford to pay to have it cleaned, " Pretty Kevin explains.

Vernon says, "I don't give a shit about your Persian carpet."

"But I do, and if you want this guy and the information I found out, you need to come out of those cheap-ass ugly shoes you're wearing, brotha, " Kevin demands.

Vernon starts toward him as Kevin throws his fists up. I step in between them.

"All right Kevin, we'll do it your way. Leave the shoes, Vernon, " I order.

Vernon grumbles as he unties his brown leather shoes and sets them inside the shoe holder that Kevin has placed by the front door.

"See, that wasn't that hard was it? You better be glad Joe saved you from another ass whippin', " Kevin says, smiling as he leads us through his contemporary Oriental designed home, his furniture is bordered with jade and the room is accented with brass and red cherry oak tables. It is expensively furnished from the aesthetic art work to the Oriental throw rugs.

We proceed down the stairs, into his basement. Vernon is silent, but I can tell by the way he's mumbling to his-self, that he isn't going to let that last comment Kevin made slide.

I do a double-take of Dennis Forest, a known killer-for-hire dog-tied to a chair. We've been trying to catch this guy for years, but haven't been able to get enough evidence to make a case against him. Wanted in six states, he's good at his job. Linked to at least seventeen murders, Dennis is 6' 5" and has the build of the WWF wrestler, Hulk Hogan. His hair is blond, close shaven, and several tattoos adorn his arms. His thin-trimmed mustached lip is swollen from an apparent blow at the hands of Kevin.

His only other visible injury is a bump on his head, which is now a black, reddish-blue color. Tied up with tennis shoe strings and extension cords, Dennis' arms are bound behind his back and his legs and ankles are bound to the legs of the big oak chair. He is gagged with what looks like a dirty tube sock. The chair is placed in front of an old paint tarp that has been suspended from the ceiling beam.

I ask laughing, "Damn Kevin, you can't be putting your dirty socks in people's mouths. Have you heard of cruel and unusual punishment?"

"It wasn't more cruel and unusual than him breaking into my house to kill me, was it? I only wore those socks a couple of times. Let's see. I played a couple of hours of basketball, and then I wore them around the house, while I cleaned up. They can't be that funky and that was the only thing I could find to shut him up. He was screaming like a little girl." Kevin winks.

He gets behind big Dennis and starts playing with his hair singing in high falsetto "Roxanne, " a song by the group, Police. We all began to laugh, except for Dennis, who looks as if he's about to throw up.

"Well, you should know about screaming like a little girl, " Vernon teases with a sinister grin.

"Look, Vernon, you ain't gonna be disrespectin' me in my own house. I kicked your old ass once. Don't let me have to take you out to the shed, " Pretty Kevin warns as he starts imitating he's spanking somebody.

Vernon frowns up and his jaw tightens. "Kevin, you can call me Detective Brown or Mr. Brown. You call me anything else and I'm going to have to whip your butt, again. You know what they say about a hard head?"

"Yeah, Vernon, I know, they say a hard head whips a soft butt. You better ask this fool Dennis what happens when you mess with a pimp like me." Kevin slaps him in the back of the head.

Dennis struggles to get at Kevin, while trying to spit out the dirty sock.

"So, Kevin, how'd Dennis get the bumps on his head?" Vernon asks with one graying eyebrow raised and his cigar hanging from his bottom lip.

Kevin answers, "A seven wood."

"A seven wood?" Vernon and I ask simultaneously.

"Yeah, I came into my house and noticed the door had been jimmied. So I grabbed my seven wood golf club and sneaked into the living room. As soon as I heard something move, I did my imitation Tiger Wood's swing. When I turned on the light, I found blondie here knocked out. I dragged him down here, put him in the chair in front of this canvas tarp I use to practice hitting golf balls, and tied him up with whatever I could find. I decided to get some information out of him, although he was a little reluctant. Here is the gun he had." Kevin hands me a forty-four Magnum equipped with a silencer.

Vernon says, "Kevin, you're lucky you weren't killed. You did a good job. I'm impressed."

"What you find out, Kevin?" I ask.

Kevin twirls the golf club in his hand. "He told me he was working for somebody important in Missouri Government and if he told me who it was, he would have to kill me. So that's when I called you guys."

"Good idea, Kevin, " Vernon states as he approaches Dennis and takes the sock out of his mouth.

Dennis screams, looking at Kevin, "I'm gonna' kill you sucker!"

"Shut up, Dennis." Vernon says. "You're in no position to be threatening anyone and talkin' all bad. You broke into this man's house and tried to kill him. Don't you know that's against the law, fool? You must be slipping. Now, either you tell us who sent you and why, or we let Pretty Kevin here play golf with your punk ass, like he's at Pebble Beach."

Kevin demonstrates with a swing of his golf club coming only a few inches short of the killer's head. "I've been trying to break in this nine iron. I'm always hitting the ball wide right."

"You guys can't do that! You're cops, for Christ's sake. I know my rights and that's against the law!"

"Haven't you heard, Mr. Forest?" Vernon asks. "We're working with the FBI? We can do anything we want. We'll say we stopped over at a friend's house and there wasn't anyone home. So we left. Right, Joe?"

"Right, Vernon. We didn't see nothing. And as they say, nothing from nothing leaves nothing." I smile devilishly.

"Vernon, how does my golf swing look, man? Am I turning on it too fast or what?" Kevin asks as he takes twelve steps back, places a golf ball on a tee facing Dennis's chair.

Kevin winds up and swings, hitting Dennis in the right shoulder with the ball. Dennis screams and Vernon shoves the dirty socks back in his mouth.

Vernon smells his fingers and winces from the funk. "Damn, that sock stinks. I don't know if it's Dennis's breath or your socks, Kevin? You ever wash your feet, boy? It smells like you got athlete's foot. You need to get that shit checked out." Vernon wipes his hands with his handkerchief.

Kevin rolls his eyes. "Vernon, the only thing that stinks is that cheapass cologne you're wearing. Ain't nothing wrong with my feet, they just sweat heavy, that's all."

The hit man's eyes are shut tight as he fights off the pain from the golf ball.

I ask, "Dennis, oooh man. That must have hurt, huh? You ready to talk yet?"

Dennis looks up as pain dances across his face. He realizes that we don't intend to stop Kevin from his game of golf torture.

Kevin shrugs and retrieves the golf ball. "I think I'll try the five iron this time. I got it from the Lee Trevino collection a couple of weeks ago. I just took it out the box last night. Vernon, I bet you five dollars I can hit him in the same spot." Kevin pats Dennis on the shoulder saying, "Don't worry I can do it."

Dennis' bushy eyebrows raise as he shakes his head at Vernon.

"The same spot. I can't pass that bet up and I know you don't have skills like that. Joe, you in?" Vernon asks as he lays his money on Kevin's Formica-topped bar table and sits on the leather bar stool for a better view.

I lay my money atop of Vernon's. "Yeah, count me in and don't be tryin' to cheat, Kevin."

Dennis' eyes widen as Kevin tees up again. Kevin sizes up his target and takes a masterful swing. The ball rips into the exact spot on Dennis' shoulder, but on the left side. Dennis moans loudly.

I cringe and exclaim, "Oooh damn. That looks like it stings!"

Kevin boasts, "Told you I could do it."

"Fool, give me my five bucks, " Vernon orders as Dennis doubles over in pain.

Kevin explains, "What you talking' bout? I said I would hit him in the same spot and that's what I did."

"The same spot is the same shoulder, you little cheat, " Vernon growls as he grabs Kevin by the collar.

"Pay up, Kevin. I told you about cheating. Man, you never learn, do you?" I scorn.

"Hold up, dude. Here's yours and Vernon's five bucks. Vernon, you got this thing about grabbing people's clothes, huh? That's the second time you wrinkled one of my shirts. Don't let that shit happen again, " Kevin says as he straightens his Italian crushed silk shirt.

"Boy, don't let me have to hurt you, okay?" Vernon warns.

Kevin puts up his index finger. "One more time, " he says to Vernon, then turns his anger and attention to Dennis. "Look, killer-man, I'm almost as tired of you as I am of Vernon with his old ass, Red Foxx actin' detective self. You ready to talk or shall I pull out my seven iron and have another swing at it." Kevin places another golf ball on the tee. "Make the bet double or nothing?"

"Um-hmmm, " Dennis grunts as he nods.

Vernon grabs the dirty sock out of Dennis's mouth.

"I was sent here by Tom Brush. He wants you dead for pimping his step-daughter. You stupid fuck. You're the only man I know crazy enough to pimp the Governor's daughter and think you'd get away with it!" Dennis says, laughing and grimacing from pain at the same time.

Vernon and I look at each other then to Kevin for an explanation. Kevin throws his hands up and backs away from us shaking his head in denial. "Hold up, man. I ain't never tricked no Governor's daughter, honest. This dude is full of crap. Put the sock back in his mouth, Vernon, while I get my seven iron."

I hold out my hand. "Wait, Kevin, what if he's telling the truth? What proof you got, Dennis?"

"Her name is Courtney Roberts. Her street name is Candy and she has a tattoo on her right butt cheek of a sucker with the word 'candy' in the middle of it. Yeah, shit ain't funny no more, huh? Look at his face. You been pimping the Governor of Missouri's daughter and didn't even know. Damn, you stupid. The Governor wants you dead and wants his daughter back, " Dennis says, laughing as the revelation registers on Kevin's face.

"Shut up!" Kevin screams as he shoves the soiled sock back into Dennis's mouth. He sits next to Vernon at the bar and pours himself a double shot of Hennessy.

Vernon says, laughing, "You done did it now, son. You done wrote a check your ass can't cash. You better send that girl home to patch things up with her pappy."

"Vernon, I liked you better when you were grumpy and quiet. This is some serious stuff. Can you give me a break?"

"He's right, Kevin. You need to send the governor's daughter home so she can get that guy off your back. He's not a person to mess with. He has a lot of influence."

Kevin rubs the back of his neck. "I can't send her home because she's been missing for two months. She was one of the women I was telling you guys about. Man, I've searched everywhere I can think of for my women and even offered ten thousand dollars for a reward and still got nothing. You have to help me, Joe."

"Look, Kevin, get some stuff together and find another place to stay. If Dennis can find you here, somebody else can too. I'm sure there's a contract out on you. You know how to get in contact with me. We'll take Dennis in and charge him with attempted murder. You can file a complaint in the morning. Then just lay low until we can figure something out, got it?"

"Yeah Joe, thanks man. I owe you and Vernon big time, " Kevin states as he finishes his second shot of Hennessy.

seven

THE DAMP EVENING AIR IS CRISP AND THE WIND OFF THE
Missouri river is rich with the mushy smell of earth and the surrounding
industrial plants. The night is aglow with a full moon and an ensemble of
stars. The gurgling of the slow-moving water has a meditating effect.

When he looks up the Milky Way and Pegasus are visibly noticeable in
the black sky. The light damp breeze blows across his flushed face and
cools the sweat that has formed on his brow. He confidently smiles and
adjusts the heavy load on his back.

He remembers the evenings he spent with his dad, fishing and throwing rocks into the mud brown river that Missourians lovingly call "The
Muddy Mo." The River is majestic, its awesome force, capturing. Yet, you
respect its silent rage that can consume you in death, just as fast as it can
bring you life from the water it provides to the bi-states of Missouri and
Kansas.

He worships the river and has a bond with it. An understanding, if
you will. He had lost his footing and fell into it at the young age of ten
and no one was around to help the drowning boy who was snatched by an
aggressive undertow. When he awoke from the trauma, soaking wet
and half choking, he was on shore three feet from the water's edge. There

was no explanation how or why it happened. It might have been a miracle. It could not have happened by chance, he rationalized. One thing he did know was the river spared his life that day. He was grateful.

He never told a soul, because he knew his strict father would have his hide. So they kept his secret, the river and him.

He moves more cautiously now, going into the woods, through the moss-covered trees to the secret stream that feeds into the river. The creatures of the night - crickets, tree beetles, frogs, toads, owls, and possums - sing songs of desecration and scream to no avail.

Just as she had when he amputated her limbs one by one. She excited him even in death. The way she fell to her knees so often when they did their business. The twenty-five dollar special she called it. He went along with the program for a while, but why have to pay for what should be free in the name of love?

She would say she loved him when he asked and would always get an extra ten dollars for her affectionate lies. Yet, he believed her. He was different from the other Johns, she would say. He was special.

She was special too, he thinks as he pulls her long, discolored legs from the black plastic sack and places them into the stream that flows into the Muddy Mo. He takes out her arms and kisses and holds them close. The way he did when she held him close and told him she loved him.

He can still smell traces of her Enchantment perfume. He kisses the palms of her hands, then places the arms in the water as well. The arms and legs are slowly caught by the current and buoyantly make their way into the mouth of the river. He reaches for the remaining bounty in the plastic sack and slowly unveils her torso.

"She is so beautiful, " he thinks, stroking her long blond hair out of her face. He stares at her lifeless blue eyes and is enchanted. He cups her breast and kisses her on the neck and shoulders only to find himself becoming aroused by his limbless corpse.

He kisses her on her red-painted lips and holds the cold, discolored body close. The gurgling water, the insects singing, the owl, possum, they all watch on curiously as he plays and fondles the clammy, naked torso.

To love you one more time, he thinks as his erection gives way to his morbid desire. He lays the cadaver on the ground and unzips his pants. The owl flies off and the insects, frogs, beetles, and nocturnal animals are attentively silent.

Only his love, sadistic panting, grunts, and broken breath could be heard. Moments later, a big splash breaks the silence of the night and once again the insect and amphibian symphony consume the evening.

The tree fell as she had into the night, as well as the water. No one had heard. No one; except for him.

WE ARRIVE DOWNTOWN AT THE FBI HEADQUARTERS AROUND 8 in the morning and Agent Royal James greets us. A medium, athletic-built man with honey-brown skin and a freshly trimmed, low-cut fade hair cut, he is clean shaven and is all about the business at hand. He approaches in his usual off-the-rack Sears dark blue suit, tie, heavy starched white shirt, and with his hand extended. He is always meticulously and conservatively dressed.

"Joe, Vernon, welcome to the Federal Bureau of Investigation, gentlemen. We're happy to have you aboard and I'm sure you'll be a valuable asset. I took the liberty of having your identification badges made for you. You are officially considered Federal Agents and work for the U. S. Justice Department from this point, until we solve this case. I hear congratulation is in order, Sergeants, " he says, shaking our hands with a firm grip and hospitable smile.

Vernon and I check out our new FBI badges and the well-kept professional Victorian-decorated downtown office.

I inquire and by the look Vernon gives me, he is thinking the same thing, "Royal, you look cool and all, but do we have to dress like that?"

"That won't be necessary, guys. We brought you here for your investigative skills, not your attire. However, you are representing the bureau and you are expected to act and report appropriately. I have no problem with the way you dress. You're in the field so just dress accordingly."

We all smile. Vernon and I normally wear suits, but I prefer to wear cotton or silk t-shirts with mine. Vernon wears loud ugly ties and rarely buttons his collar. He says he wears the ties to give him the edge. Most people focus on the tie and it allows him the opportunity to throw the first blow if needed. He has a point. They get my attention all the time.

"Let me introduce you to the team you'll be working with, " Agent James says.

We walk down a long hallway and enter a huge conference room with a brilliant fourteenth-floor view of downtown Kansas city Sky-line and Missouri river. It has a huge conference table and it is set up with a slide projector and crime chart.

We are handed confidential folders of the serial-killer case files. Three others sit at the table in the usual FBI attire, dark suits. They rise simultaneously as we enter.

I notice the black female agent at once. Our eyes make contact and she looks away. She is quite stunning, even in her FBI wear.

"Detectives, let's get started and get down to business. Joe and Vernon, you have the privilege of working with the best agents we have in the Central State Region. This is a dream team if you will. To my left is our agency's brightest computer engineer, Agent Pho Li. He will be running all our computer research, cross sectioning with other departments, and pulling and entering forensic data. He will also be handling our link with the FBI National Crime Information Center. Mr. Li can get into anything that has a microchip. He caught several computer hackers who made their way into large corporation data bases."

Pho Li shakes our hands and sits. He is a small man with glasses and a genuine smile. His hair covers his somewhat large ears, but he has the body of a kick boxer. I hope he can fight as good as he can work the computer.

Agent James turns his attention to a red-haired, burly guy. The way his shoes are shined and the crease in his shirt and pants speaks of the military.

"Next to Agent Li is Agent Purvis Smelly. He will be in charge of the reports, crime data, suspect chart, and case files. He will work closely with our communications unit. He will also cross check the backgrounds of the missing women, suspects, and the victims. He too, will also handle all media with me. I know how you guys hate the lime-light." Agent James smiles as Vernon and I breathe a sigh of relief.

"Last but not least is one of our exceptional agents. She was first in her class at the academy. Agent Cheryl Chase will work with you guys. Her field is criminal and abnormal psychology. She will serve as our profiler. She should be able to help us narrow our suspect pool, develop motives, and hopefully give us a lead on why and where our killer will strike next."

Agent Chase nods to us and continues to avoid eye contact as she sits. She is strikingly beautiful with shoulder-length hair, dark brown hair. Her eyes are captivatingly shaped like a Siamese cat's and she wears little make up and shows a natural beauty. Her golden-brown skin shines smooth as pearls. Her smile is warm and dangerous. She looks mysterious, yet charming.

"Agents, I would like to introduce you to Detective Sergeants Vernon Brown and Joe Johnson. The detectives are two of Kansas City's finest. They get into places we cannot, and they've solved some of the hardest cases their department has been assigned. I'm positive that you will give them the respect and cooperation that is expected in this department. You're now a team. I expect you to work as such. I will oversee the progress and you will report to me weekly for updates. This situation has made the national media, people. All eyes are watching on this one. Let's give it our best. You were all brought here because you are the best of the best. I have complete faith that we can stop this killer, before this turns into a media circus." Agent James opens his case file and instructs us to do the same.

"Okay this is what we have to this point. Let me remind you that everything we say here is confidential. That is to be understood." He looks at each one of us for confirmation that his instructions are clear.

"Let's proceed. The police department, the Wildlife Reserve, Missouri River Port Authority, North Kansas City, and Riverside Police Departments have compiled the information in front of you. This is two years of investigative work. They have narrowed the suspect list to four individuals. In no way does this limit additional suspects as we see fit. There are some additional postal employees that did not make our primary suspect list, but give them a once over."

Agent James opens his folder and continues, "As you see we have twelve female victims. All prostitutes who frequent the Independence Avenue district. To this point, we have an additional four females reported missing. One white and three black. Please note that the prior victims were White or Hispanic. It looks like our killer has acquired diversity in his sexual appetite."

Agent Li asks, "Is there a timeline on these ladies disappearances and missing person reports?"

"It's been hard to get an accurate history on the women and when they were first noticed missing. They're normally outcasts and on the move. Family ties are for the most part severed. We have a list of people who still need to be questioned."

Pretty Kevin's name is on the list and I bring it to Vernon's attention.

Agent James let's me know that he knows Pretty Kevin and I are friends. Is he aware of yesterday's events? All of the suspects on our list either live or work in the Northeast general area. We're questioning a couple of players from the football team, but we have to be careful not to step on anyone's civil rights. I hope this is not too close to home for some of you and I hope personal friendships won't get in the way of us doing our job.

"Let me make this clear--these women's occupations and way of life will not interfere with our investigation, people. These are somebody's mothers and children and we will proceed with that mentality. We have a sexual predator in our town. We also believe this person suffers from necrophilia. If you look at the coroner's report, you'll see it is believed that some of the corpses have been penetrated. This person is twisted. If you look at the photos provided by the coroner's office, you'll see what I mean."

There are assorted pictures of the victim's grotesque bodies with their limbs missing or placed next to where they should be attached. The water damage has a serious affect on the bodies. Eyes and hair are missing as well as skin and chunks of flesh from the dis-colored bodies. The bodies are also swollen from the water and internal gases.

"This person is believed to be quite intelligent and has some sort of medical training due to the amputation of body parts. He has stayed one step ahead of the investigation. Let's get this sick bastard before he strikes again and hopefully save the ladies who are missing."

We all look at each other, a sense of urgency at hand. Vernon gives me the thumbs up.

I finally make eye contact with Agent Chase and she wears a half smile. Agents Li and Smelly both continue to look at the photographs of the victims. We all feel the responsibility and grab the case with both hands with no plans of letting go until this serial killer is caught.

"We will be domiciled on the corner of Benton and Independence Boulevard on the second floor of the building. Use the back entrance to gain access. Everything we need is being set up as we speak. I took the liberty of having vehicles as well as cell phones and pagers assigned to you. Pick them up in the compound on your way out. Have your pagers with you at all times. We have our own two-way paging frequencies with the Nextel cell phones. There are subsequent numbers on the back of each phone in the order that you are seated, please make note which number you are. We will meet at our focal point at 2200 hours. I suggest you get some rest in the meantime. We're dealing with nocturnal people, so this is when we will get most of our information. You're dismissed."

Everyone on the team shake hands and exit for the compound area.

We have already broken into cliques. Vernon and I walk behind the

FBI agents. I decide to break the ice with small talk. "So Agent Smelly, where you from and how long have you been with the bureau?"

"Five years. I'm from Nebraska."

"Hold up! I remember now. Purvis Smelly, #52 linebacker for the '85 Champion Nebraska football team. Dude, you were the shit! You had four sacks in the championship game and your sack with twenty-eight seconds left put Oklahoma out of field goal range. Man, I won three hundred on that game. Let me shake your hand. I thought you looked familiar. Why didn't you go pro?"

"I got picked eighteenth in the first round by the Bills, but I got in a car wreck and tore the cartilage in my right knee. So, here I am, " Agent Smelly responds, smiling.

Vernon says, "Agent Li, that was nice work on the Matrix Link Software Company security breach. I remember the article in Time magazine. You could have made millions working in Silicone Valley, why the FBI?"

Agent Li and I both look at Vernon with amazement.

"I knew that I would get to use my skills for the good of the people and not for my own wealth by working for the bureau. This is more like a chess game. I can match my skills against the best minds out there and get paid for it. You can say I'm securing cyber world." Agent Li says proudly as he puffs out his chest.

We all laugh at his weird sense of humor and his superhero impersonation.

"Well, Agent Chase, where you from? What's your claim to fame?" I ask as we all stop and wait.

"I'm from Columbia, Missouri. I attended Missouri University. My parents wouldn't have it any other way. They're both alumni. I've had several articles published in Psychology Today magazine as well as Science Magazine and the Journal of Abnormal Psychology. I've worked on three prior serial-killer cases including the Indiana case of 'Chester the Child Molester'."

We all snicker, except for Vernon and Agent Chase. This is a common play name kids used when someone was acting weird in grade and high school.

We quickly straighten up after the looks we received from the both of them. We continue our journey to the compound in utter silence.

At the garage sits a fleet of cars. I am truly amazed at what the FBI has to offer in vehicles. Jaguars, Lexus, Cadillac, Mercedes, Porsche, BMW, Corvette, and even a couple of Ferraris are lined in the garage along with trucks and sport utility vehicles. Agent Chase notices my mouth drop open.

"We do a lot of undercover work and we have to dress the part, if you know what I mean? Our transportation is over here, " she directs as she smiles at my embarrassment.

Vernon nudges me. "Oh, that was real smooth. Can you roll over, too?"

"It ain't even like that. I was just admiring the automobiles."

Vernon says, "And the view of Chase as she walked away. I saw you staring at her behind."

"Whatever! She does make that suit look good though, " I admit.

We approach the vehicles and I am fitted with a burgundy Dodge Durango. Vernon has a blue Ford Explorer and Li and Smelly get black Ford Crown Victoria's. Cheryl gets a grey Range Rover.

We retrieve our pagers as they go off simultaneously. I pull my phone and dial the number that is preceded by 911. Agent James gives me instructions and directions to proceed immediately.

"It was Agent James. They've discovered another body in the river by Highway 69, just east of Burlington Avenue. He wants us there pronto." We jump in our vehicles and head for the discovery area.

Clouds that look like over-sized cotton balls, cloak the sun. Our drive is swift and the flow and tide of the current of the muddy river is breath taking. Small white-head water caps caress the swirling waves.

The barges that trudge up and down the long river are magnificent as they push cargo to their destinations along the riverbank. Cranes and other waterfowl take flight as our caravan pulls into the dirt and gravel drive area that leads to the crime scene in a dust-filled flurry. The local police, forensic team, and wildlife rangers are already at the river bank.

We walk up and display our federal badges. One of the local officers walks us to the narrow and wooded location of the body, while the other personnel walk the steep muddy banks looking for evidence.

"Hi, I'm Officer Susan Hart. We figured that the Fed's were involved with this case?"

"Yes, ma'am. We're heading up the investigation now, but we can use all the help we can get, " Agent Smelly diplomatically states.

Officer Hart is very cute and has a face that reminds me of Marie Osmond. "Well, I hope y'all don't mess up your nice shoes, and watch out for the snakes. Some are poisonous and they like the sunny banks on the river. They get pretty big too."

Everyone looks around.

We walk about twelve feet to a gully where the body has become lodged in tree branches that have fallen into the river and protrude upward out of the water like out-stretched hands. We make our way to where the discolored and bruised corpse lies nude and slightly submerged.

Her face is grey, yet her full lips are still the color of her red lipstick. Her long blond hair dances in the water's current as if she's still alive. Her once blue eyes now have grown opaque. Her arms have been removed at the shoulder and her legs from the upper thigh area. Her extremities have been food for the fish and insects that inhabit the river. She looks around twenty-seven or so.

"What a way to die, " Agent Chase states.

Agent James asks, "So, what do we have, people?"

"The body is yet to be identified, " Agent Li explains. "The Park Rangers are approaching in a boat from the river to dislodge the victim from the trees. Forensics is here and a search is in progress to find her missing limbs."

The rangers open a black body bag inside of the motorized flat boat and retrieve the water-damaged body from the river. Crawfish detach themselves from her submerged amputated flesh and fall back into the water. As her body is over-turned the tattoo that the hitman Dennis Forest told us about shows up. A lolly-pop on her right buttock with the word 'candy' in the middle of it.

"Courtney Roberts, " Vernon and I say aloud in unison as the rangers zip up the body bag and head downstream toward the waiting white coroner van.

"How do you guys know who she is?" Agent Chase asks as the others look on curiously.

I answer, "My friend, Pretty Kevin, reported her missing and gave us a description. She's also the Governor's step-daughter."

"What the hell, " James says. "Oh, this is great. You get that pimp in for questioning and I mean now. There's gonna be hell to pay. Keep this under your hats, people. The press has already arrived. Don't let this leak out. Johnson, your friend's in deep shit, you got a problem with that?" Agent James' bottom lip quivers with anger.

I answer knowing that I won't let Kevin be a scapegoat for a crime he didn't commit. I don't condone his way of life, but I know he's not a killer. "It's his shit, Sir."

"Okay, wrap it up here. Li and Smelly, you two help with the forensic team and see what information you can find out. Johnson, Brown, Chase, I want you guys to go ahead and rendezvous at the Benton location, then bring in pimp dude for questioning. We'll meet in three hours, " Agent James orders.

eight

HE METHODICALLY PULLS OUT HIS MAGAZINES ONE BY ONE, retrieves his razor blade and adjusts the light in the dark cool confines of his forbidden sanctuary. He cuts out letters from the magazine with surgical precision, just as he had the limbs of the lady of the evening, Tammy "Brown Sugar" Collins.

They get together two times a week. He loves her thick lips and the way she likes it from the back. She has dancer's legs and a voluptuous rear end. Her nipples are long and her breasts are round and firm. She can always make him laugh. He truly loves her. Each and every time they are together. He walks over and removes the tourniquets from his victim who is lying on his homemade operating table and places them in a sanitized bag.

The stitches are holding and the ice packs he placed on the severed ends have stopped the blood flow to the extremities. He kisses her softly, raises the sheet covering her sedated body, and reaches for the moisture between her hairy legs. As if smelling a rose, he brings his soiled fingers to his nostrils and breathes in deeply.

"Just lovely. Won't she be surprised." He takes her sugar brown, amputated arms and legs and places them in plastic bags in the refrigerator.

With a handy wipe he cleans his rubber gloves of the sensual vaginal scent. He returns to his desk and pastes the paper alphabets carefully to a sheet of typing paper to complete his twisted message, intended for the new black detectives.

Excitement fills his body from the intellectual challenge that maybe, he has found a worthy nemesis who can bring his tormented years to closure. He has made a mockery of law enforcement to this point.

"It has been too easy. I take what I want, " he says crying and laughing at the same time. It has been so simple and the previously assigned agents were clueless.

He takes his stethoscope and checks his victim's heartbeat. "The fools even picked up a John and tried to pin it on him. The only charge that would stick was check fraud. He was just a sex-deprived guy who wrote bad checks. How could the idiots think that he had the knowledge, intelligence, and skill to exercise such a disciplined plan?"

He kisses his patient and continues his conversation. "They know nothing about love, sacrifice, and the saving of souls. They don't appreciate the river and what she offers and provides. They could never match the lust, passion, and desire I hold in my soul. They see me as a mere killer, not the sanctified man that I am. They don't understand do they, sweetheart? But, they shall. They will realize that this passion lies within all of us." He seals the envelope that contains the message for the detectives.

He takes a stamp, licks it slowly, then places it on the letter. Turning the envelope around, he licks the glue on the fold and seals it, smacking his lips at the bitter sticky taste. He gets up from his desk and walks to the table where she lays, still unconscious. "Another successful procedure of love, my darling, " he says as he strokes her permed black hair and checks her pulse and temperature.

She slowly awakens from her chloroform tranquilized sleep. He removes her oxygen mask and gives her a warm caring smile.

She inquires with difficulty through her dry mouth and intense pain,

"What are you doing to me, you sick fuck?"

"Here, have a sip of water. You've been unconscious for about seven hours. I just saved your life and your soul. And to think, this is how you greet me. You need to show some gratitude, Tammy!"

"Why are you doing this? What have I done to you? Where are the others?" Tammy asks, not seeing the other women she had been held hostage with as tears roll down her face.

He dries the tears away with a soft cloth and strokes her face. "Don't worry about the others, my dear, they are safe. You're the one I care about. You're the one I need. Who else could sacrifice what I have and accept you the way you are? I see your transgressions and forgive you for them. I rebuke the sins Satan cast upon you. You've been sanctified, Tammy. You owe me your life and your soul."

"Please untie me. My arms and legs are itching very badly. I promise I won't run."

"Well, my dear that is something that you will never have to worry about doing, " he says with a sinister sneer.

She reads his face. Trembling she slowly turns her head right and left. She raises her head and thighs where her legs once were, only to notice two bloody bandaged stubs.

Through the tremendous pain she yells, "God, no! You sick son of a bitch! You cut off my arms and legs. How could you? You crazy motherfucker! I hate you...I hate you!" She screams hysterically, twisting her body until the bed topples over sending the surgical instruments next to the bed flying everywhere.

He jumps atop her in tears and in a rage puts his hands around her throat. "After all I've sacrificed? After all I've done for you? You're like all the rest, you ungrateful whore. Die then, die like all the rest. You never loved me! You never understood!" he yells through his grinding teeth while squeezing with all his might.

Tammy's mouth flies open and the bloody stubs of her bandaged arms fly loosely and aimlessly about.

He intently watches as she tries to find something to grasp hold of. Her eyes widen. Then, her body collapses as life escapes with one last gasp for air. For the last time, her lips form the word, "Mama."

"Why did you make me do this? Why couldn't you have just let me love you. Why? Why?"

He falls atop her warm torso as the last tear she will ever cry falls from the corner of her eye. He cradles her and sobs like a baby, rocking her ragged body back and forth as the phone rings, unanswered.

***

Pretty Kevin fidgets in the makeshift interrogation room as Agent Chase, Vernon, and I wait for Agent James to enter on the second floor of the Benton Boulevard corner Building.

"So, Joe, what's up, man? Why y'all bring me here and who's the chick?" Pretty Kevin asks.

"Chick! Oh, you're real smooth. I see why the women fall for you, " she says as she tilts her head and frowns. "My name is Federal Agent Cheryl Chase."

Kevin looks her body up and down as he sucks his gold tooth. "Slow your roll, sister, I meant no disrespect, although as fine as you are I could take you to Hollywood and make you a star with that money maker you got. Well, let's just say you would be the gem of my life. You'd probably bring in about a thousand a week, if we worked it right."

I put my hand on his shoulder. "Watch your mouth, Kevin. Aren't you in enough trouble already?"

Vernon just shakes his head.

"You talk a weak game, player. It would be the other way around. I'd have you out there tricking old ladies with your punk-ass. I'd say you'd probably bring about a hundred dollars a week and that's working it real hard. You know what I mean, brotha?" Cheryl stares Kevin down.

"Yeah, I like the roughneck type. You can spank me now if you like, " Kevin says.

Agent James enters the room before Cheryl can react.

Agent James interrogates Kevin as he sits on the desk in front of Pretty Kevin with a scornful expression that distorts his face, "Well, if whippings are what you like, we can just release you now. There's a twenty-five thousand dollar bounty on your head. I'm quite sure when the Governor finds out his daughter is dead, he will triple that. So, you want to keep being a smart mouth or are you ready to tell us what we need to know?"

Kevin folds his arms and smirks. "Is that supposed to scare me? I ain't got nothin' to tell. You can sit there like my daddy if you want to, but I ain't got shit to say. So kiss my ass!"

"Let's cut to the chase, shall we, smart man? You got a girl friend who is missing and pregnant. We're the only chance you got at seeing her alive or do you even care? Well that's a silly question, isn't it? You're pimping her, aren't you?"

"You don't know nothin' about me, agent man. So, like I said, kiss me where the sun don't shine, " Kevin says as his jaws get tight.

"Look, Kevin, we're here to help you and try to get the women you are responsible for out of harms' way." Vernon says as he slams his hand on the table. "The Governor's daughter is dead. He'll hold you responsible. We can connect you with that death and three other women working for you have disappeared. What's to say that you aren't the killer? You have access to them and could be playing some sick copy-cat game."

"What? Get outta here. For me to copy, there has to be someone else, right? Why would I kill my income? That shit don't make no sense. Tell them, Joe. I ain't no killer, am I?" Kevin asks, beginning to bite his fingernails.

"Not the Kevin I grew up with, but I don't know what you're into now, Kevin. I haven't seen you in over a year."

"Oh, so you gonna roll over on me, huh?"

"No Kevin, I'm just giving the facts. You work with us and we'll work with you and that is that."

"Man, you think I'm crazy? I talk and you bring me up on charges.

No thanks. I'll take my chances with the Governor. Y'all got nothing on me or I'd be locked up already, " Kevin announces as he folds his muscular arms in his chair and looks at all of us.

"You give us what we want and nothing you say will be held against you, " Agent James says. "That's the best I can do. You're starting to piss me off and that's a place you don't want to go, believe me. This is your last chance or I'll have your ass up in Leavenworth before lights out tonight."

Kevin looks at me and I nod.

"What you want to know?" Kevin asks with a heavy sigh. We all pull up to the table.

Agent James asks, "Who are your ladies' clients?"

Kevin answers, "Look, dude, they have some pretty important people who frequent the Independence Avenue area. You probably wouldn't believe me if I told you."

"Try me, " Agent James demands with a frown.

"We have politicians, professional football players, lawyers, business men, postal guys, officers, college students, convention people, husbands from the area, and regular Joe's looking for a good time. No pun intended Joe, " Kevin says smiling at me.

"None taken. We'll of course need a list of your clients, Kevin."

"No problem, I can do that."

Vernon questions, "Have your girls ever told you about any John who has been to medical school?"

"Not that I recall."

"Have they ever told you about anyone being overly possessive or longing for words of affection, like wanting them to say they loved him repeatedly?" Agent Cheryl questions.

"Shit, that could be all of them." He pauses and rubs the back of his neck, then snaps his fingers. "Wait, there is one guy they had regular schedules with. They said he would pay extra if they told him how special he was and that they loved him. The girls used to joke about him a lot. I just thought he was some lonely guy. I never got a complaint about him getting rough or nothing, so I blew him off."

Kevin snaps his fingers again as he tries to conjure memories. "There's a cab driver named Amir, a postman named Willie, and a clerk named, Frank, at the 'Gas It & Get It' store who are weekly clients."

We all look at each other with surprise. Kevin has named all the prime suspects we have listed in our investigation folder, except for the ten dollars, "say you love me" John. We know he's being straight with us.

Kevin's forehead wrinkles as he looks at me for help. I know and I'm sure he is aware that his life is still in danger as long as the Governor has the contract out on him.

I say, "Royal, we need to talk to the Governor and get this hit taken off Kevin. He needs to be informed about his daughter anyway. Let us talk to him.

"Joe, you and Chase drive to Jefferson City tonight. I want the Governor informed as soon as possible. We'll get his address for you. You guys have been up all day, so stay overnight and head back first thing in the morning. I don't want you killed on the highway. Handle this diplomatically, Johnson."

Agent James turns to Vernon and Pretty Kevin. "Brown, I want you to get Kevin into a safe house and sit on him until the smoke clears. I'll share this information with Agent Li and Smelly. They can take first watch and try to question some of the prostitutes."

Then Royal turns to Kevin and continues, "Kevin, I checked your background. You have so much going for you. You're educated, smart, and have common sense. Why do you need to pimp?"

Kevin folds his trembling hands in front of him and answers, "You guys might not think it, but I am saving these girls' lives. They were gonna trick with me or without me. I provide them with health plans, mutual funds, housing, education, and clothing. They are drug free and don't have to worry about getting beat. Each of the ladies has more than ten thousand dollars in their personal accounts."

Vernon spits, "Yeah, but you have control of the money, right?"

"Yeah, we have a three-year agreement. Shit, I have a waiting list of over fifteen females. The bottom line, it's about the money."

"So you think that's impressive, you exploiting women?" Agent Chase snaps.

"Each girl makes five hundred dollars a day. They are required to work five hours a day, five days a week. Multiply that times twenty-six weeks and that amounts to sixty-five thousand dollars a girl. I got seven girls working for me. That equals four hundred and fifty-five thousand dollars in tax free money per year. I get twenty-five percent netting me a profit of one hundred thirteen thousand and seven hundred fifty dollars per year. Now, if you can find a job for a college-educated brotha that pays that, I'll give it up in a Kansas City minute."

"Kevin, you come across like you're the savior of hoes or something, " Vernon says.

"Vernon, I don't push drugs and don't force the women into this and I don't give a shit about impressing you or Agent Chase. They make the choice and I provide the business. I have the finances. Don't judge me and I won't judge you, " Kevin answers as he stands up and straightens his shirt in his pants.

"Kevin, the women are still exploited, " I state.

"Yes, but willingly so. I just provide a service and like they say, 'don't kill the messenger'."

"The service is still illegal and it's only a matter of time before they pull your number, Kevin, " Vernon explains.

"Let me worry about that, Vernon. All right?"

Vernon replies as he takes Kevin by the arm, "Your funeral."

"Joe, we have corporate accounts with most major hotels. All you have to do is show your badge. You guys better get going, it's getting late, " Agent James orders.

We exit the interrogation room and meet Kevin and Vernon in the office area, where Vernon is picking up the keys to the safe house.

"Joe, let me speak to you in private for a moment. If you're going to speak to the Governor, I have a little something you might want to know, " Kevin says.

I walk with him a few steps away from the others and the secret that he reveals to me is overwhelming.

"Kevin, that is a serious accusation, don't be bullshitting me." Kevin has never been one to lie to me. The information he's revealed, will be my ace in the hole in convincing the Governor to release the hit on him.

"Kevin, are you positive?"

"Joe, my girls talk to me all the time. We have no secrets and that's what she told me. Think about it. It makes since. If he's her step-father, then what I say is true, " Kevin explains.

We join the others who are looking on curiously. I give Vernon the, "I'll fill you in later look." Agent Chase just stares at us.

Vernon orders as he and Kevin head for the door, "C'mon, pimp daddy. Let's get a move on."

"Don't do anything that I wouldn't do, " Kevin warns with a contemptuous smile.

Vernon says as he slaps Kevin in back of the head, "Mind your manners."

"Man, you gonna get enough of putting your hands on me, " Kevin says with a sinister smile. "See you later, Agent Chase."

"Whatever!" she responds, rolling her eyes at Kevin.

I state as I go to the phone, "It ain't even like that." Agent Chase sits across from me and goes through the crime-scene photos from the forensic team, ignoring Kevin as he makes flirting faces.

Vernon grabs him by the shoulder. "Let's go, fool, " Vernon says as he pushes Kevin out the door.

"We need to pick up some dominoes on the way. If I got to stay with you, we need to be doing something constructive. "If you push me one more time, I'm going to have to forget you're my elder. Joe, call me in the morning and let me know what the Gov says. Tell him I really didn't know that was his daughter. I'm sorry."

I respond as the odd couple disappear into the hallway, "Yeah, Kevin, whatever."

Cheryl gestures at her watch. "So, what was the big secret?"

"If I tell you, I'd have to kill you."

"Oh, so that's how it's going to be? I thought we were a team?"

I put my hand up. I dial my home number and Nia answers on the first ring.

"What's up, cutie?" I ask, trying to contain my smile.

"Daddy, where you at?"

"I'm at work, sweetheart. What you doing?"

"Riding my pony Uncle Vernie got me. Momma readin' a book. When you commin' home so we can play?"

"We'll have to play tomorrow. Daddy has to work late. Put Mommy on the phone, please."

"You gonna bring me some candy home?"

"Yes, I always do, don't I?"

"Yeah. I love you, Daddy."

"I love you too, baby. Let me talk to Mommy."

She asks like a professional receptionist. "Okay, can you wait a minute, please?"

"Yes, sweetheart, but hurry up. Daddy has to go."

I can't help blushing, because I can just imagine Nia's expression and demeanor. Cheryl continues looking through the pictures of the slain prostitutes.

"Joe, how'd it go today? I thought I saw you and Vernon on the 6 o'clock news?" Sierra asks.

"Hi, baby, yeah that was us. They found another body. Look, they're sending me to Jeff City tonight to talk with Governor Brush. It was his step-daughter that we found today. I won't be home until tomorrow. I don't want you worried about me, okay?"

"Baby, I'm sorry to hear the bad news about the Governor's daughter.

Give him our sympathy. Is Vernon going, too?"

"Nah, I'm going with one of the other agents on our team. I'll fill you in when I get home. We need to get on the road."

"You guys be careful. There'll be leftovers in the fridge. I also was planning to wear that special night gown you bought for me for our honeymoon to celebrate your assignment with the FBI. I never slept with a G-man before, " Sierra seductively whispers so Nia can't here.

"Hold that thought and I promise it will be worth the wait."

"You know I will, Joe. I miss you baby. I love you and be careful. I'll see you tomorrow."

"Sierra, I love you too. Kiss Nia for me, " I respond smiling as I hang up the phone.

Chase inquires, "That was the missus, I presume?"

"Yes, that was my wife and my daughter, Nia. I don't like for them to worry about me. I check in when I'm gonna be late."

"Well, that's sweet. We better hit the road and since you're the considerate one, you can drive." Chase gives me a wink and a crooked smile, while grabbing her purse and folder of pictures.

"I can see this is going to be a long trip, " I say, laughing as I grab the keys and directions to the governor's mansion.

nine

WE'VE BEEN ON HIGHWAY 50 FOR ABOUT AN HOUR ON OUR
way to Jefferson City, Missouri. KPRS, Hot 103 Jamz blares out the current hits over the radio and mixes in some old school jams as we journey
the two-lane highway. "Beauty's Only Skin Deep, " by the Temptations is
playing and we sing along with the chorus. It has been a fun ride. Agent
Chase and I hit it off pretty good.

Agent Chase asks as she turns down the radio, "So Johnson, how long
you been married?"

"A little over two years. It's been great. We adopted our daughter, Nia
a little before that. What about you? You seeing anyone serious?"

"Not in the last fourteen months. The last guy I dated, couldn't deal
with me being an agent and moving all the time. I think he was also intim-
idated by my independence. He wanted me to give up my career. I figured
if he really loved me, he would accept me as I am. I never asked him to
give up his job. You know what I mean?"

I smile. "You have to respect each other's room for growth. I'm sorry
it didn't work out. You seem like you would be quite a catch for the right
man."

"You know, Joe, you can be a real sweetheart. Sierra is a lucky lady."

"I'm the lucky one. I was in a relationship with Tracy Jackson, the reporter for Channel 7 before Sierra, and that was a romance headed nowhere. I wasn't close to being happy. Then, I met Sierra and my romance is in full effect, " I confess with a rapper's hand gestures.

We both laugh. Wild Cherry's song, "Play That Funky Music White Boy, " comes on the radio. I do the snake and imitate playing the air drums, while Agent Chase plays the air guitar as we speed down Highway 50, about twenty minutes away from Jefferson City limits.

"...Lay down and boogey,
and play that funky music til you die..."

At 9:40 we pull to the front gate of the Governor's Mansion. I push the speaker button to announce us.

A male voice comes over the loud speaker. "May I help you?"

I look into the video camera mounted on the post and display my badge. I announce with authority, "FBI Agents, Johnson and Chase, to see Governor Brush."

"They have retired for the evening."

"Sir, this is of great importance and concerns the Governor's daughter. I suggest you open the gate, wake the Governor and First Lady, and announce our arrival."

The iron security gates immediately open and we proceed up the long red-brick road to a circular drive. A lush green lawn surrounds the drive with a lighted fountain with a ten-foot-tall bronze statue of children playing in the middle.

The Governor's Mansion is three levels and made of orange brick with white cement borders and cornerstones. It is a magnificent structure with three huge windows on each floor facing the drive.

We park in front and are met at the huge kissing oak doors by the butler.

"Come in. I'm Alfonzo. I've notified the Governor and First Lady of your urgent news. They'll be down directly. I've been instructed to have you wait in the parlor. If you'd kindly come this way."

Agent Chase and I follow, taking in the refined decor of the Renaissance Revival. The vaulted ceilings look to be about seventeen feet high. A hand-carved walnut stairway winds gracefully from the inlaid parquet floor.

On a massive wall hang assorted pictures of former First Ladies of Missouri. The place is full of rich Victorian colors and furnishings.

We enter the double parlor and sit in two large chairs facing a couch that could easily seat six people. Agent Chase and I look at each other with disbelief at the extravagance of the mansion.

Alfonzo leaves and closes the door as Governor Tom Brush and his wife Jaunte enter. The Governor is a big man with an ugly face he doesn't look hospitable, as he and the Governess enter in their pajamas and robes. The Governess seems more friendly, smiling as she enters the room.

"What is the meaning of disturbing our rest at this hour, " the Governor snarls with his hands in his robe pockets. "What kind of trouble has Courtney gotten into this time?"

"I'm FBI Agent Johnson and this is my partner, Agent Chase. I think it is best if you were seated."

The Governor shouts, "Look, you come here in the middle of the night like bandits, then you proceed to give me orders in my own home. If you have information about our daughter, out with it, man!"

I state. "We found your daughter in the Missouri River this afternoon. She was murdered. We're very sorry."

A long silence follows. The Governess looks at us and blinks uncontrollably. She looks at the Governor, Her pretty face turns to a scowl and she begins to shake.

Agent Chase rises to aid Jaunte Brush, if needed. The Governor looks at her, then turns his attention to us.

"It was that pimp, wasn't it? He killed my baby girl, " he accuses with tears in his eyes.

The Governess rises abruptly and knocks over a vase that crashes to the floor. We jump.

"Tom, don't you dare! Don't you dare shed a tear for her. You're responsible for this!" She screams as she storms out of the room.

I nod to Agent Chase to follow her. I get up and close the door. "Is there anything you can tell us that might help with the case?"

"What do you mean? She was a wayward girl trying to find herself. We thought she'd grow out of it, " the Governor explains while pouring a double shot of bourbon as his eyes dart around the room suspiciously.

"That's a funny way of growing out of it, turning to prostitution. Is that normal behavior to you?"

"Don't be ridiculous, Agent. I don't know what had gotten into her. That pimp probably drugged her or something. Hell, I don't know. But, he will pay God-damn-it, believe that."

"That would be a problem, Governor. Are you sure you don't have a clue as to why she would leave all this? Living in this beautiful mansion and being the Governor's daughter. Most people would die just to spend a night here. It doesn't add up. Was she in some sort of trouble or something like drugs, alcohol, or did she have a mental disorder? Anything you can tell us would be something."

The Governor takes another drink and slams down the glass. "None of the above. You delivered your message, Detective. I think we would be better served if you were out arresting that pimp of hers."

"Let me give it to you straight, Governor. We have a known hit-man, Dennis Forest, in our custody. He claims that you paid him to kill Kevin Wine and he'll testify to that fact. Did you know that is a felony and that could end your career, Sir?"

The Governor fumbles with the empty shot glass. "Look, I don't know any Forest Dennis or whatever his name is and you got some nerve coming in here threatening me. I can have the State Troopers come in and have you arrested."

"Sir, I'm with the Justice Department and we are aware that you have a contract out on Kevin Wine as we speak. I'm really sorry about your step-daughter, but Kevin did not realize who she was. Now, either you can take the hit off of him tonight or we can bring you in and charge you with conspiracy to commit murder."

"You don't scare me. I'm connected farther than you can believe. So you just do it, if you think you got the balls. Your pimp friend has about as much chance of staying alive as a Black has at winning an Oscar, " the governor states puffing out his chest with an arrogant smile.

"Well, there's one other thing, Governor Brush. Kevin says that Courtney confided in him about a family secret. He says that Courtney not only accused you of having relations with her, but there is a child that she bore for you. Kevin knows the whereabouts of this child. All we have to do is order a blood test. How will that affect your political ambitions?"

The Governor turns red with anger and walks to face me. "You threatening me, Agent?"

"No, Sir. But if anything happens to Kevin, you can kiss this mansion goodbye and all your political aspirations. Kevin will never bother you again and your secret will be kept that way, I promise."

The Governor and I stare each other down. His anger turns to fear. His facial muscles relax and his original color starts to return. I know that he is the only person with something to lose and he understands it, too.

The Governor inquires perspiring profusely, "How can I know that you can be trusted?"

"I am an Officer of the Law and working for the Justice Department, Sir. You have my word."

"What about Kevin?"

"Kevin just wants to be left alone. He has a very short memory and wants no trouble with you."

The Governor fixes another drink and swallows it in one gulp. He walks to the phone that sits atop a Victorian walnut desk and dials a number. "It's off!" he states into the receiver and hangs up. "If Kevin isn't the killer, who is?"

"We're working on it. We will find this guy. I promise you that, Sir."

Agent Chase emerges from another entrance that is embedded in the bookcase. The sound of it closing startles me for a moment. The Governor jaws start to tighten again.

"I'll leave my card. If you have any questions or anything that you feel will help in our investigation, Governor, please use it. We'll see our way out. Once again, we're sorry about your daughter, " I state as we exit the parlor and meet Alfonzo, who escorts us to the exit.

Once in the car, Chase rolls her eyes, as if I won't believe what she has to say.

We find our way to Nikeya Street in Jefferson City and look for the Embassy Suites.

"Johnson, you won't believe what Jaunte Brush told me. The reason that Courtney left was because Governor Brush had made sexual advances toward her daughter, when he was drunk. Jaunte said she kept quiet about it because it would have been a political disaster for him."

"She's probably right."

"The Governess has been taking Zoloft for her depression and guilt. She talked about their hard road in getting to office and how Governor Brush took her in with child. This was after her first marriage to an abusive husband, while Brush was a representative in St. Louis. Jaunte said she felt torn between her obligation to him and her daughter."

"From one abusive situation to another. Great choices the Governess makes."

"When Courtney decided to leave, she felt that everything would get back to normal. Can you believe that?" Agent Chase asks as we pull into the Embassy Suites parking lot, which is full. We find a lone spot toward the back of the building.

"Chase, he succeeded in his sexual advances toward his step-daughter. Remember when Pretty Kevin pulled me to the side to talk to me? He told me that the Governor and Courtney have a baby boy. She left to save her mother from the shame of it and the Governor's political career. Kevin's mom has the little boy. Courtney made Kevin promise not to let the

Governor have anything to do with the child. That little boy is saving Kevin's life. The Governor agreed to take the hit off Kevin."

"What hit?" Agent Chase grabs my arm and questions.

"Before Vernon and I came to your department, Kevin had apprehended Dennis Forest, a hit-man sent by the Governor to kill him for pimping his step-daughter. We got him to confess and he's in lock up at the county jail for attempted murder."

"That guy is connected to several murders, isn't he?"

"Yes, but none of them stuck. He agreed to take the fall for this one, after Kevin beat the shit out of him with golf balls."

Chase asks scratching her head, "Golf balls? That's illegal, and you guys participated in that?"

"Not exactly, " I say biting my bottom lip. We weren't actually on duty. Our transfer to the FBI was official. We just happened to stop by Kevin's at his request. This guy had got off on murders and now he will do five to ten. He didn't want a lawyer and signed a confession. Case closed."

"So, what do we do about the Governor?"

"What do you suggest we do, Agent Chase? All we have is hearsay. Do you think a jury will believe the word of a known pimp or a government official? You're smart. That will be easy. Forest won't testify against him because that would be like signing his death certificate. Look at some of the Governor's contributors. He's connected to the mob, Chase. We got what we want for the moment. The Governess will do the rest with time."

Chase folds her arms, "What do you mean by that?"

"I'm talking about a mother's love and a woman's intuition. She will put two and two together. She's a smart lady. You see what she did to that expensive vase? Her conscience will get to her and she will ruin him. It's only a matter of time."

"This place sure looks crowded. It must be a convention in town or something, " Chase says as we exit the vehicle and walk to the entrance.

At the door, a middle-aged doorman meets us. He looks like he gave up exercising five years ago, dressed in a tight fitting, black and red uniform. His gold name tag reads, Smith.

He inquires graciously as he greets us, "Welcome to Embassy Suites. Any bags this evening?"

"No sir, " we answer as he holds the door open for us.

We haven't stopped to pick up anything for our overnight trip.

"Enjoy your stay, " he states looking at us over the rim of his glasses as we approach the front desk.

The night clerk's a lady in her mid-fifties, who uses too much make up and way too much perfume, acknowledge us. She asks with a cigarette-stained smile, "Good evening. Do you have reservations with us?"

"Hello, and I'm afraid we don't Ma'am, but--" She says, her smile turn to a regretful frown. "I'm sorry but there's a Pork Convention in town. We're booked up for the evening. You probably won't find another hotel within fifteen miles of here."

I display my FBI identification and bad attitude. "As I was about to say, I'm Agent Johnson and this is my partner, Agent Chase. We're with the FBI and are here on assignment. We would really appreciate if you could put us up for the night. I realize we don't have reservations, but this has been a very long day and we don't want to be up all night looking for a room. So, if you can check and see if you have anything, that would be fine with us."

"Sure, sir, just give me a minute to look at the computer, " she says.

Her fingers rapidly dance across the keyboard. She bites on her lipstick-red bottom lip and occasionally glances at Agent Chase and me, smiling.

My eyes begin to water from the strong scent of her floral perfume.

She looks up triumphantly. "I have one corner suite, but it's a handicap-accessible room. It's the only one we have left. That won't be a problem will it?"

Agent Chase and I look at each other with tired eyes and a expression of surrender. "No, " we say in unison.

We charge the bill to the Justice Department's corporate account and accept the keys to the much-appreciated room.

We stop to get two cans of soda and chips, then enter the room.

"What are you doing?" I ask.

"I'm laying on the bed. You can go get comfortable in that recliner, " Chase orders, never looking up.

I get up and head toward the recliner, frustrated and jealous as she sprawls atop the king-sized bed. I take off my Smith and Wesson .45 and shoulder holster and unstrap my silver-plated 9mm automatic from my ankle holster and place them on the TV stand.

"Good idea." Agent Chase too disarms her weapons.

I can't help blushing, noticing the similarity, when she unstraps a 9mm from her ankle as well. She says as she places her weapons on the night stand and falls back onto the bed, "Can't be too careful."

"Just like a woman to take advantage of a man's chivalry. I do all the driving and you get all the comfort. That's just typical, ain't it, " I say as I sit on the uncomfortable recliner, hoping to appeal to her feminist, independent side.

"What you saying? That I'm ungrateful and women always have it easy and don't appreciate men?" She sits up on the side of the bed facing me.

I smile on the inside at how quickly she took the bait. Now, I try to reel her on for my fifty/fifty shot at getting the bed without laughing and revealing my sinister plot. "Yeah! A real woman would at least be considerate enough to flip a coin for the bed. That's what a fair woman would do."

"Okay, Johnson. You flip and I'll call it, but we'll use my quarter. I don't want you trying to cheat me. I don't need any favors, Mr. Man, " she responds as she digs in her purse for a quarter.

"Best two out of three. That way you can't accuse me of cheating."

She agrees as she hands me the quarter.

"Call it in the air, " I order. I flip the coin high.

Chase yells, "Tails!"

The coin lands in the palm of my hand and I lay it across the back of the other to reveal the tails end of the coin. Agent Chase jumps up and down clapping confidently.

"Yeah-yeah. Don't eat your apples, before you check for worms, Chase. We still have two more flips, " I remind her.

"You the man, get to flipping."

"Call it in the air, " I yell as I flip the coin for the second time.

"Heads, " she yells with exuberance.

I slowly show the silver coin atop the maple skin of my hand.

"Tails! We're even." I announce as I start to do the cabbage patch and hum "That's the Way Love Goes, " by Janet Jackson.

"Who eating apples now, punk? I'll flip this time, " she states and snatches the coin, turning her back to me. She says looking over her shoulder, after rubbing the coin between her fingers and letting it fly, flipping it into the air, "Call it in the air, sucker."

I can't help noticing the way her sexy, plump, behind is fitting her suit pants as she stands with her back to me. "Tails!" Comes rolling off my tongue, revealing my subconscious thought aloud.

She catches the quarter in her hand and slaps it against the top of her golden-brown skin. She slowly turns around and shows me the outcome of our debate. The quarter has landed on tails.   I start singing "Celebration, " by Kool and the Gang as I jump into the air and land in the middle of the bed. I say with a victorious smile, "Mine, all mine."

Agent Chase's bottom lip sticks out. She sits slowly on the recliner and places her face in the cup of her hands. "Congratulations creep, " she grumbles.

I start to feel sorry for her, while she displays that lost-puppy look with sorrowful big eyes. "Look, I know you're not a sore loser and to show my gratitude for you being a good sport, I want to share in my good fortune, " I declare as I pull a pillow and toss it at her. Then I throw the top spread to her, which lands on her, making her look like a manmade ghost.

"Who's the sucker now, Chase?" I tease, chuckling.

She sits under the cover and does not move. I give in to my compassion, remove the spread from her head, and try to straighten her hair. "I'm sorry, Chase. You can have the bed. I was just fooling with you."

She removes the spread. "No you won, even if you are a creep. I'll sleep on the recliner."

"Look, I suckered you into the bet. I knew if I went after your feminist side, you would agree to the challenge. So we entered into an agreement under false pretenses. You win. I'll take the recliner."

"I'm a big girl. I fell for it. I'll suffer the consequences. Do you mind if I shower first or does the winner get all the privileges?" she asks with a stern, yet provocative smile.

I reply feeling somewhat guilty, "No, you go ahead. A hot shower should feel good after the long day we've had."

"Thank you." She grabs a hanger from the lowered coat rack that a person in a wheel chair could easily reach and enters the bathroom, closing the door behind her.

The room is wider than usual, with two peep holes, one three feet lower than the other. Pretty cool. People in wheel chairs have to be safe, too. I take off my socks and water shushes from the bathroom.

I close the blinds, turn out the lights, and turn on the TV to see what's happening in Jefferson City. Nothing interesting. The community calender channel, it has nice mellow jazz playing, so I leave the yellow and blue background screen on and listen to David Sandborn as I lay across the bed with my arms behind my head and watch the messages scroll across the screen.

"Johnson! Johnson! You can take your shower now. Sorry I took so long. I was trying to use up all the hot water, " Chase says as she awakens me.

She has a towel wrapped around her with a knot in the middle, revealing her cleavage. As she sits in the recliner, she applies lotion to her upper body. Her legs fly open unexpectedly when the chair suddenly reclines, as she tries to lotion her legs and ankles. She has on underwear under the towel.

She shrieks. "I forgot this was a recliner. You gonna help me up or what?" she asks with her hands over her face. "So did you enjoy your eyeful, Johnson? Yeah, I saw you!"

I blush, shrug, and help Chase up, smiling uncomfortably for getting caught looking between her lovely, sexy brown legs. She holds onto my hands a few extra seconds before letting go. I go into the bathroom, looking back at her as I close the door.

"Dog!" she shouts at me from the other side of the door.

The hot pulsating water on my shoulders and chest feels great. I get out, dry off, and wrap the towel around my waist. Agent Chase is in her recliner wrapped in the bedspread eating chips and drinking soda.

"Nice jazz. At least you're good for something."

"Can I borrow your lotion? You know ashy skin attacks a black man in a matter of minutes, " I ask while getting my soda and chips and sitting on the edge of the bed.

"Sure, the lotion's on the night stand. You look good for an old man, Johnson. And hair on your chest, too? You're just a girl's dream aren't you?" she says with a devilish smile.

"I don't know who you're calling old, Ms. Missy?" We both laugh. "You know you can have the bed. Really, I was just messing with you. I know how uncomfortable that recliner is, " I state as I lotion my face, arms, and legs. Then I attack my refreshments like I haven't eaten in a week.

Chase comments as she turns on her side and closes her eyes, "I'll be okay. Thanks for the offer though."

The revelation that her towels are on the floor beside her startles me, as my mind wanders under the cover. Sierra and Nia come quickly to the front of my thoughts. What the hell am I doing? After turning off the TV with the remote, I crawl under the sheets of the bed.

"Goodnight, Agent Chase."

Goodnight, Agent Johnson."

I grab the two remaining pillows and find a comfortable spot. I lay awake, somewhat restless. A single ray of moonlight invades the blackness through the curtain and Chase thumps in the recliner fidgeting.

I lay still and concentrate on my breathing and try to push the adulterous thoughts out of my head. It feels like I'm about to hyperventilate from the excitement of being in the dark with Agent Chase, half-naked.

My temperature is steadily rising and so is my nature. No matter how hard I try, her essence and the scent of her fills me. This is my first night working as an FBI Agent and to risk that on sexual desire is crazy.

Chase still fidgets in the chair and slowly moans as tho she's having a bad dream. My body responds to her every movement and sound, like a needle on a seismograph.

Minutes creep through the restless night, like a slug through wet grass. I think of the suspects that I reviewed in the folder. The postman, store clerk, taxi driver, and Pretty Kevin. Something didn't fit. I'm anxious to question each of them. Kevin couldn't have anything to do with it. I grew up with the guy.

Chase continues to move around on the recliner. I smile at her pride and think of offering her one last chance to trade places and suddenly, she throws her spread across the bed and climbs in. I try to hide my surprise.

"That chair is unbearable, " she says in a soft tone.

"Did you want to change places?" I feel like I should move, yet want to stay.

"We're adults, Johnson. We can handle ourselves."

We remain still, each not trying to stir emotions or provoke sensual thoughts. Minutes pass and I un-expectantly feel her soft fingers touching the hairs on my chest. She places her knee and thigh on top of mine. She edges closer to me, and I'm aroused by the feel of her firm breasts upon my shoulder.

I impulsively take her in my arms and we kiss to the glow of the renegade beacon of light that spies on our forbidden embrace. Our hands explore each other's body with slow tantalizing detail.

"Joe, I don't normally do this, but you excite things in me that I haven't felt in a long time. You drive me crazy." Chase whispers in my ear as she slowly kisses my ears and neck.

The moist warmth of her tongue and kisses entice my body. The towel that covers my lower half has disappeared, just as mysteriously as her panties. I feel the warmth of her sexual desire against my thigh and the sense of urgency is met by the strength of my erection as our passion pushes us to the point of no return.

It feels so right. I hold her soft hair in my hand as I caress the back of her head; yet so wrong, as my hands slowly flows down her back to partake the full bounty of her buttocks.

Chase begins to pulsate and sway back and forth against my erection. The wet of her ecstacy can be cascades against me. I yearn to feel me inside of her and satisfy her every need. My entire body tingles as she takes hold of my manhood to insert me into the depths of her passion. My conscience takes hold. I pull away from our climactic course.

The vision of Sierra fills my mind. The realization that she is at home in bed alone, trusting that I'm doing the right thing is too much for me to bear and snaps me back into reality.   "Chase, I'm sorry. I can't do this." I slide from underneath Chase and lay facing her, somewhat ashamed. "This is wrong. I have a wife and daughter at home who love and trust me. I could never look them in the eye. This has gone too far."

Chase drops her head.

I take her face into my hand and look her in the eyes. "You are very desirable and beautiful and under other circumstances, I would make this the night we would always reminisce about, but I'm a married man. She doesn't deserve this and neither do you. You're more than a one-night stand or an affair Chase, and I respect you more than that. I'm just as much to blame as you and I have to admit, I've been thinking about having you to myself most of the night. I'm sorry and I hope you understand."

"Johnson, I need to be the one apologizing. It's been so long since I've been held by someone I respect and admire. I see so much in you I want for myself, yet I know you belong to another. I've been attracted to you ever since you first walked into our office. I understand what you're doing and I respect that. It won't happen again. I just got caught up in the moment."

"No problem. Friends?"

"Friends, " Chase answers.

"Do you want me to take the chair?"

"If you could just hold me, it would mean a lot to me, Joe."

I pull her close and kiss her forehead. This is the first time she has called me by my first name. I smile and squeeze her a little tighter. We remain locked in warm, forbidden, solitude, until sleep comes and carries us into the next morning.

ten

A WEEK HAS PASSED SINCE WE'VE TAKEN OVER THE CASE. Pretty Kevin is out of police protection and we have finally gotten through all the information the previous investigators have gathered. Agents Smelly and Li are re-interviewing the missing women's families, while Agent Chase, Vernon, and I set up interviews with the suspects. Gathered in the meeting room at our location on Benton Boulevard, we are all seated as Agent James calls us to order.

"People, I trust you had a restful Sunday, and I apologize for having you work on Saturday, but the killer is still out there and at least four women are still missing. This is a beautiful Monday morning and hopefully a good start to a productive week."

Agent Li shuffles his reports. "At least we didn't find anyone killed this weekend."

"That's right, no other bodies have shown up, so maybe our killer is dormant as a result of our activity. We're going to break into teams. Johnson and Brown, I want each of the suspects re-interviewed. Squeeze the shit out of them if you have to. Somebody has seen this guy. We need new leads, " Agent James announces as he stands.

Agent Smelly adds, "If we had more on this guy it would help."

"Chase, I want a profile on this guy and you have twenty-four hours to compile it. Li will be at your disposal for any data collection and cross sectioning of similar cases in the four-state area. Maybe this guy drifted into our area. Agent Smelly and I will stick with the family members and be the liaison between the coroner's office and forensics."

"So we'll meet in a week, right?" Agent Chase asks.

"No, I want to increase our meetings to three times a week. Monday, Wednesday, and Friday's. We'll meet at 8 o'clock in the morning. Now, I don't want any of you talking with the press. Direct them to me. That shouldn't be too hard, " Agent James states, smiling, knowing we just tolerate them as part of the job.

To our surprise Captain Wayne enters the office with a package in his hand. "Excuse me, Agent James, your office told me I could find you here. I have a letter addressed to Johnson and Brown that came to our office. I think it will have great bearing on this case."

Captain Wayne hands the letter enclosed in plastic to Agent James, who surveys it meticulously, looking for any signs that could reveal the sender.

The Captain gives us a small acknowledging smile, yet does not look us in the eyes as usual. This is the first time I've seen him with a tense and totally professional disposition, letting me know that something is seriously wrong.

Captain Wayne continues, "This guy is some kind of wacko and has it in for you two guys. Be careful, fellas. This guy is watching. Agent James, I took the liberty of having our lab boys give it the once over and made it top priority on their list. You will have their findings by this afternoon. One thing we do know is that it has a Riverside, Missouri postmark on it. I informed the postmaster at Riverside that you'd probably be sending somebody over."

"Thank you, Captain, I see where your men get their diligence, " Agent James states, shaking the Captain's hand.

"Well, I better get back to my office. If there is anything else I or my department can do, we're at your service. Good luck, " Captain Wayne bids farewell as he gives Vernon and me a wink of confidence and exits.

Agent James hands the letter to us to read, then we set it on the table for the others to review, as we try to decipher what the note is trying to say to us. The letter reads:

> *...There's a darkness living deep in my soul,*
> *i still got a purpose to serve...*
> *So let your light shine, into my home,*
> *God don't let me lose my nerve...*
> *Johnson & Brown,*
> *One floats and three hopes!*

Agent Smelly says as he snaps his fingers, as if trying to summon his memory, "This sounds familiar. It's the lyrics to a song."

We all look on, waiting for his memory bell to chime, and ponder the words that are pasted to the letter.

Agent Smelly's blue eyes light up and a big grin spread on his large face. "Santana!" he shouts. "Those are the lyrics to the third track of the Supernatural CD, 'Put Your Lights On.' I bought it a month ago. It's a great disc. Santana plays excellent guitar and really outdoes himself on this project."

"We believe you, son, good job." Vernon says. "Now, just calm down and let's get back to this message. Santana could almost be mistaken for Satan, if you think about it."

Chase sides with Vernon. "You could be right. Santana also put out the song, 'Black Magic Woman.' There may be other titles like that too. This murderer seems to be tormented. I've gone over the case files three times, comparing him to other serial killers."

"What other traits can we look for?" Agent James asks.

Agent Chase explains, "We can assume by his elusiveness that he is intelligent. He's probably a white male in his mid to upper thirties. He's had some medical training. Maybe the military? He uses a little 'I' when he refers to himself, signifying insignificance."

Agent Li asks, "So what is his connection to Joe and Vernon?"

"This guy is very methodical in his murders. He is daring the two of them to capture him. It is evident that he respects Joe and Vernon's skill and intelligence by naming the two of them. You might want to check into any other cases you guys had."

Vernon and I look at each other. I don't recall any sex-related murders we've worked. I am impressed with Agent Chase's take-control attitude and her knowledge in profiling.

Agent Chase continues, "We can assume that he's a sadistic, twisted, sexual predator and he's more than likely having an internal struggle with right and wrong. The forensic reports states that the victims had vaginal abrasions inflicted after death. Our man is a necrophiliac. His spirituality is in serious conflict."

"Wait, are you saying that this dude is having a good vs. evil conflict? You actually think he has religion?" Vernon asks.

"Yes, but in a twisted kind of way. He probably thinks he's saving his victim's from themselves and their promiscuous lifestyles. More than likely, he was sexually abused as a child."

I say, "Excuse me, but why do you think he's putting the prostitutes in the river?"

"Something about him and the river is ritualistic, maybe he had a traumatic experience and survived. He feels connected somehow. He more than likely lives within a thirty-mile radius and works in the Northeast district. He blends in and is a person you would least expect. Looking shy and withdrawn, but his power comes in controlling."

Agent Chase's eyes are dazed and she stares off like she's in a trance. She looks around the room as if bringing us and the present back into focus, as we all sit astounded. I see why Agent James brought her aboard. She is definitely a valuable asset to our team.

Agent Li jokes as we all laugh to ease the tense reality. "So, Chase, when you gonna open up that nine hundred number?"

Chase blushes.

"Excellent analysis, Chase. Let's follow through on that. I want you to ride with Johnson and Brown and see if you pick up any vibes on the suspects they question. All right, people you have your assignments. He has three victims and we need to find them. Time is against us. Let's be careful."

Vernon, Chase, and I meet at the coffee pot and grab a couple of Kansas City's famous Lamar's donuts. We pour ourselves coffee to begin our sure-to-be long day.

"Vernon, you need to stop playing with that phone and paging me, dude. You're worse than a kid with a walkie-talkie."

"Joe, it's so cool that I can just push a button and get you. This wireless stuff is all right. You know I didn't have a lot of toys when I was a kid. I made my fun acting like I was Speed Racer. I would pretend to drive this car, sitting in a old refrigerator cardboard box that a neighbor had thrown out. I painted black wheels on it with some old shoe polish and used a broom stick and a plastic chitlins' top for a steering wheel, " Vernon replies as we walk to the car laughing.

Chase adds, "Vernon, I bet you walked thirteen miles to school in the snow and rain too, huh?"

"How'd you know? Damn, that mind stuff really works. Stop reading my mind, girl, " Vernon jokes as he opens the passenger door to my vehicle for her.

I just stand outside the SUV with my hands full as they sit in the unit looking at me. Vernon opens his back door, thick eyebrows raised, and shrugs. "Boy, you coming or what?"

"Why y'all think I have to drive all the time? My name ain't Alfred. Maybe I want to ride sometimes. Either one of you ever think of that?"

Vernon looks at Chase as she straps on her seatbelt, then closes her door. He does the same.

"Y'all a trip. I have to drive Ms. Daisy and her son, Pookie, around all day. This stuff is gonna change and change real quick, " I state as I put the last of what's left of my donut in my mouth and balance my coffee, maneuvering to open the driver's side door.

I mock as I start the engine, "Oh, at least let us get the door for you, Joe. Can I hold that hot coffee for you, so you won't burn yourself while you buckle up? That's the least we can do."

"At least, let me get the door for you, Joe, " Chase repeats.

Vernon adds, laughing, "Can I hold that hot coffee for you, so you won't burn your sensitive-ass self?"

"That's the least we can do, " Chase replies, completing the mockery as she and Vernon high five and crack up laughing.

"Shit won't be so funny when I drop your asses off at the next corner, will it?" But I finally give in and share in the humorous moment.

Chase questions after calming down, "So, who we calling on first, Joe?"

"I figured we'd see the store clerk, Frank Scott. He gets off at 2 in the morning, so he should surely be home now. He lives off Van Brunt Avenue and twenty-fifth Street." I work my way through heavy morning traffic. I turn on the "Tom Joyner Morning Show" on K-107 FM.

We pull in front of Frank's brown and white two-story house. The houses' outside, looks ugly and dilapidated. The love for a good-looking home is as suspect as Frank is.

The yard is shoddy, full of dandelions, crab grass, and patches of dirt. A dirty barbeque grill sits on the porch, in need of some wood work. Assorted lawn chairs are sprawled about the porch. We all look at the structure with a hint of contempt. It is sad, because it needs paint and yard work, it could be a nice place.

Chase comments, "I hope the inside isn't as bad as the outside."

"Don't be surprised if the door is answered by a roach or a rat, " Vernon replies with a grin as he unwraps a cigar.

We open the doors and before we get out, we are contacted by two-way radio on my Nextel phone.

"Johnson, Brown, and Chase. The Lansing Police have discovered another body in the Missouri River. Report to Moore Ferry Road, thirty miles East of Lansing, Kansas off Highway 45. ASAP!" Agent Smelly announces.

"We're on our way, " I respond.

We climb back into the vehicle and do a u-turn to get to the I-70 West turn ramp. As we drive by the unkept house, I see someone peering through the front curtains.

"We'll be back, buddy, you're not getting off that easy, " I state, looking in his direction as Chase sets the portable police light on top of my vehicle, so we can make time through the morning rush hour traffic.

We arrive on the concrete landing of West bank in the outskirts of Lansing, Kansas. Agent Li is waiting on us and we proceed to the deserted muddy and weedy portion of the river where the body was found.

We travel through thick brush into a clearing that leads to a loose rock embankment that falls into the river. It's tricky getting down the steep incline. Vernon follows Li down the loose rock, and I assist Chase, who is having a little rougher time, because of her medium-heeled shoes.

I say halfway down, "I hope we catch this killer soon. This guy is ruining my shoes."

"I heard that, " Vernon agrees as we reach the bottom and proceed to the watery embankment.

The forensic team and coroner have already arrived and are taking clothing and fingernail samples.

"Union Pacific railroad personnel found her this morning while doing their routine track inspection." Agent James says. "Her arms and legs have been recovered in two different locations up stream. It seems like our guy is getting more aggressive. Look at the strangle marks on her neck."

The young lady of the evening came to rest under a railway bridge. Nude, her right side against the embankment, she looks to be in her mid twenties. Her water-dulled brown eyes are slightly open and one has been pierced by a splinter of loose wood. Her once-permed black hair has matted and become a net for algae and loose twigs.

I put on rubber gloves and reach down to move her face to get a better inspection of the hand marks on her neck. A baby water moccasin slithers from her open mouth.

"Jesus Christ!" I yell and jump back, kicking the snake toward the water.

"I hate snakes. That was gross, " Vernon says as he loses his breakfast of donuts and coffee on the rocky embankment. "Be careful, Joe."

I proceed more cautiously, turning her head, not wanting any more surprises jumping to greet me from the water-swollen cadaver. The body is in worse shape than the others we had seen in the photographs. Probably because it has traveled farther in the river.

The woman had an athletic build, the form of her chest and defined abs, even in her swollen state. A Tweety Bird cartoon character tattoo smiles above her right breast. There're numerous lacerations and abrasions upon her body.

Chase states, "Poor kid. It tears me up to find these women like this. I can't help but think of their families."

"If we don't catch this guy soon, there will be more, " Smelly says. "From our interviews with family members, it seems that most haven't had contact with these women for several months and some, even years. That's why they come up missing without notice. The pimps don't report them missing for fear of being arrested and they can have a replacement in a couple of days. The families don't report them because of shame and embarrassment or the families don't know they're missing. They get used to not hearing from them for a couple of months. Some families wouldn't even talk to us. It's pretty dis-heartening, the only people these women have to turn to are ones who manipulate them. Prostitutes are easy targets."

Vernon questions, "We are aware of four women missing, now we are down to three. Where could he be keeping them?"

Chase turns in her chair, "I think it would be underground. Kansas and Missouri are known for tornadoes and there were a lot of bomb shelters built in the 1950's in this area of the country. People figured if we were bombed, the Russians and Japanese would aim for the middle of the country and divide it in two. The heart of America is also known for its multitude of underground missile silos."

Agent James stands. "Good point, Chase. Li, get on the computer and give me a map of a forty mile radius of bomb and tornado shelters around the Independence Avenue area and I want that information on the Santana note. Agent Smelly, you get the reports from the coroner. Find out if her condition is consistent with the other victims. Then, stay with the families and question some of the Independence prostitutes' pimps. Bring a couple of Kansas City Officers with you."

Agent James turns to us and orders, "Johnson, Brown, and Chase, proceed with questioning the suspects we have listed, but step it up. If you can, I want them all questioned today. Let's put some fire under this guys' feet and see if anyone dances. He knows about us; let's see if we can find something out about him. Get on it!"

We return to Frankie Scott's junky front porch and knock on his door. He peers out of the chain-linked door in dingy white and maroon boxers, black silk socks, and yellow t-shirt. He looks as much in disarray as the inside of his house, which is visible from the partly open door.

I announce, "FBI, Frankie. We got some questions."

"Why don't you guys leave me alone? I answered all of your questions," Frank whines behind the door.

"We have a few more, Frank. You got something to hide?" Vernon asks.

Frank rebuttals, "Naw, but I do got neighbors and you know how rumors get started. And every time you show up, the press ain't far behind. Know what I mean?"

"Well, if you let us in, we wouldn't attract so much attention." Chase says with a diplomatic smile. "You seem like a reasonable man. The sooner we get in, the sooner we leave."

Frank closes the door, unchains it, and invites us into his dirty home.

He says as he pulls scattered clothes off chairs so we can sit, "Excuse the house. I wasn't expecting company."

He proceeds to wrap empty beer cans, a half-eaten hotdog, nachos, and peanut butter cookies in yesterday's newspaper. The cornflakes he was eating when we arrived already show signs of sogginess.

The house is small and quaint, but sturdy. By the dust on the furniture, months have passed since he cleaned anything. The smell is putrid, but contained by the cinnamon-scented candle burning on top of the TV.

He returns and sits in front of his languid cereal and proceeds eating, slurping the milk from his spoon and chewing with his mouth open. An apparent drop-out of charm school. "What you want to know?" he questions between bites as a soggy flake clings from his unshaven chin, waiting for an opportunity to fall on his food-stained shirt as did some of last night's meal.

I interrogate, "What are your connections to the missing women and do you have any idea who might be doing this?"

"A lot of women come into the store at night for coffee, cigarettes, condoms, gum, and stuff like that in between their hustle. We chat and have a few laughs and that's how I get to know them. They come in all the time. I'm sure you know by now that I obtain the service of a few of them on regular occasion, but at least I ain't out here raping nobody, " Frank explains his hands fidgeting with his shirt.

"Don't get defensive on us, Frankie. We're not here to judge you, " I reply. That's exactly what we're here to do.

Vernon asks, "Have you noticed any suspicious-looking people in the store?"

"Have you been on Independence at night? Shit, everyone is suspicious. Give me a break." Frankie smirks nervously as he sets down his spoon on the dirty table and sucks the remaining milk out of the bowl.

Vernon stomps on the floor and we all jump. He says with no expression, "Roach!"

Chase and I look around for any unsanitary invaders. Something was bothering me before, but I couldn't put a finger on it. "Frank, there is a way to get us out of your hair for good, " I say to Chase and Vernon's amazement.

"I'm listening, " Frankie responds with the corn flake that hung to his chin sitting proudly on his bulging stomach.

I explain, "If you submit to a lie-detector test Wednesday and pass, we can take you off our list and not bother you again. You can get on with your life and we can proceed with our investigation."

"If I do that, I'm in the clear?" Frank inquires as he paces the floor.

I respond, "Yes!"

"Okay, I ain't got nothing to lose. I'll be there. Just name the time and place, " he states clapping his hands.

I answer, "Meet us at the Federal Building Downtown on eleventh Street and Locust at 11 o'clock."

"I'll be there, but you might want to check out some postal employees, the girls told me they pay well, " he says as we rise to leave the untidy confines of his hospitality.

Agent Chase offers as we exit the house, "Thank you for your time and cooperation, Mr. Scott."

Frank closes the door with no response.

"I never noticed that no one had been given a lie-detector test, " Agent Chase states as we pull from in front of Frank's home.

"Probably because it's inadmissable in court, " Vernon responds.

"But, it will let us know who's being honest. If we get a negative test, you can bet that person is connected somehow, " I say as we pull in front of Pretty Kevin's home.

My cell phone rings and I answer, "Johnson here."

"Johnson this is Postal Inspector Hines. I thought you might want to know that we have the names of a couple of postal employees who have been known to have used the services of some of the prostitutes in your case. We even caught one employee having sex with one of the girls in a postal vehicle."

"And those names would be?"

"I thought it might be better if we met in person. I understand there's a sizable reward being offered for information leading to the arrest and prosecution of the person responsible?"

I pause and say a small prayer to control my anger. "Yes, there's a reward, Inspector Hines. When would you like to meet?"

"At your earliest convenience."

"Well Inspector, I'm doing field investigations at the moment, but I should be done in three or four hours. Give me your number and I'll call when I'm done."

"Of course this is off the record, right Agent Johnson?"

"Yeah right, Inspector Hines."

He gave me the number and we hang up. I give Vernon and Chase the look. They heard the conversation as I switched the phone to speaker after Hines informed me of who he was.

"That snake bastard, we can have his badge for that, " Chase says.

I respond, "Not until we get the information we need. Until then, we play along."

Pretty Kevin's home is the opposite of Freddie's. It is well kept and the landscaping is superb. We ring the doorbell and Kevin greets us, holding a young boy. The child looks to be about fourteen months. He is chubby, with royal blue eyes and blond hair. He must be the bastard child of the Governor and his step-daughter.

"Hey guys, come on in. Joe, you must of known I was cooking pork chops today? Timmy and I were just finishing the dishes. Hey, Agent Hollywood, I knew you couldn't resist me. Welcome to my humble abode, " Kevin says as he ushers us inside.

"That's Agent Chase to you."

"You'll warm up to me, you just need to get to know me better. I'm a real sweet guy. Ain't that right, Vernon?" Kevin asks.

"Yeah, you're about as sweet as a dill pickle and twice as ugly, " Vernon teases, as he plays with the young toddler.

Chase rolls her eyes and stares at her nails.

He looks in my direction. "Vernon's just jealous of me; Joe can back me up."

"My name is Bennett and I ain't in it. Look Kevin, we need to talk. You got a minute and somewhere we can sit?"

"That's cold, Joe, I thought you were my friend. C'mon, we can go into the living room." We follow him into the open area that is well furnished in leather and red oak fixtures.

Little Timmy climbs into Chase's lap.

"See, little Timmy knows a good-looking lady when he sees one, too." Kevin winks at Chase. She rolls her eyes again and focuses on the child.

"Kevin, ease up, this is serious. We found another body today. Did one of your girls have a Tweety Bird Tattoo somewhere on her person?"

Kevin's dancing eyes become watery and his body slumps, the wind let out of his sails. "Yes, Sheila 'Sweet T' Thomas. She had a tattoo above her right breast and on her right buttock. She loved that cartoon character. Especially when he would say, 'I thought I saw a putty cat', it would crack her up. She would raise her dress to her Johns and flash her Tweety panties at them. She wouldn't get undressed until they used that line. She was silly like that. I can't understand why this sick fuck is killing these woman. Did he cut her up, too?" Kevin struggles, never looking up.

"Yes, " I answer.

Vernon and I look at each other. Kevin is shaken up pretty good. For a pimp he seems to genuinely care about his girls.

He asks desperately, "Joe, have you heard anything on my lady, Cherry Chavez?"

"No, Kevin, nothing as of yet. Maybe he won't kill her, because she's pregnant. We're trying to find her before anything happens to her. You can believe that. One thing I've noticed is the victims have tattoos. Do all your girls have tattoos?"

"Yes, but what does that have to do with anything, Joe?"

I explain, "This seemed like more than a coincidence to me."

Chase hands Timmy to Vernon as she checks her folders. She stares at my, blinking occasionally. I smile at her.

"Most women with high visibility on the street get tattoos. The men think it's sexy, " Kevin says.

I interrogate. "Kevin, you said you had mutual funds, medical insurance, and saving accounts for all your women. Do you have life insurance on them as well?"

Kevin stares at me with fury in his eyes. "Yes, I have insurance on them and I'm the beneficiary on the policies. What you trying to say, Joe? That I killed the women for the insurance money?"

I don't like Kevin's tone, "I don't know, Kevin, you tell me. How much are the policies for?" I ask keeping the indifferent, but stern look on my face as the tension between me and my childhood friend mounts.

"Two hundred and fifty thousand dollars each."

I explain, "You have four women missing at two hundred and fifty thousand dollars each, which means you look to gain a million dollars. With the additional ten thousand each from their savings account, that's at least a million and forty thousand reasons to kill them. That's the way our department and the insurance company will look at it. This is going to put you at the top of our list. I'm trying to give it to you as straight as I can."

"Well, you sure as hell can say you did that, friend."

Vernon and Chase both rise. The child struggles from Vernon's grip and idly finds his way to Kevin's legs, where he is picked up.

I inform him, "Kevin, you can clear your name by submitting to a polygraph test tomorrow at 1 o'clock. I'll want to talk to your other two ladies, too."

"I'll make them available to you, but I won't take no lie-detector test. I don't do well on them things. I won't help you set me up, Joe, " Kevin states.

"Is that what you think this is, Kevin? You came to me for help, remember? You're a suspect. Did you ever once think of how that makes me look? I helped you anyway. Who's being the friend here?"

Kevin's dark brown eyes fill with water. Why is he reluctant to take the polygraph?

He walks over to the couch, sits, and hands Timmy his bottle of juice. "Polygraphs make me nervous. I was almost fired once at my job as a bank teller. The place got robbed and they wanted to make sure the tellers weren't in on it. I was the only one who failed the damn thing, and I was innocent. They let me take it again and I passed, barely. I don't know. I have to think about it. A lot is on the line if I fail and it's not your ass they want. It's mine."

"Know this, Kevin. I can't help you, if you don't take it. The ball's in your court. You can play or sit on the bench and let this thing play out. I always thought of you as the kind of person who liked to be part of what affected you." I signal Chase and Brown that it's time to go. "Thank you for your time. By the way, I admire what you're doing for Courtney."

"Anytime, friend, " Kevin states with no expression, that lets me know that we have worn out our welcome.

He never takes his eyes off me as he and the child follows us to the door, then closes it behind us.

Vernon states as he shivers in his seat, "Damn, that was a cold exit."

Chase asks, "Well, that was one way of getting his attention. What brought on the money issue?"

"The number-one reason for murder is greed, " Vernon responds. "Joe, you were kind of rough on him. Shit, I don't even like the guy and felt sorry for him."

"I've known Kevin all my life. I wish to believe he has nothing to do with this, but I would never have thought he'd be a pimp. I can't let my emotions get in the way."

Vernon rubs his eyebrow and smirks. I'm sure he's thinking of how I met, Sierra. Emotions were the only reason I'm still with her today. I trusted my heart and instincts on her, but with Kevin I am just not sure.

When we get to my car the phone is ringing. Agent Li is on the other line.

"Joe, Agent James wants you guys back here pronto. We received another letter."

"On our way, " I answer and hang up. I fill Vernon and Chase in on the way back to our command post.

We enter the back of the building as usual and once inside the meeting room, we see the same type of note sitting in the middle of the table.

Agent James looks worried as he grabs the back of his neck. "This just arrived from your department. Your captain says the forensic team received it Saturday. They ran tests and released it to us this morning. No prints were found. Just like the other one, nice and neat. He used Elmer's glue and recycled paper. They established that the letters were cut out of assorted magazines, due to the ink, color, and paper quality that they tested from samples. Take a look and see what you can make of it."

ROXANNE,
YOU DON'T HAVE TO PUT ON THE RED LIGHT...
THOSE DAYS ARE OVER,
YOU DON'T HAVE TO SELL YOUR BODY TO THE NIGHT...

JOHNSON & BROWN
TWO FELL IN THE WATER...
ONE WAITS FOR SLAUGHTER...
THAT LEAVES MOTHER WITH CHILD...
THEIR DEATH ON YOUR HANDS,
AS YOU STAND BY BEGUILED!

"He's challenging us, Vernon. He's laying the responsibility in our lap and he's right. We're no closer to him than the other guys. The song is by the rock group, 'Police.' Someone was playing that song, not too long ago. I can't think of who it was. He is definitely fixated on the prostitutes from the lyrics. He's trying to tell us something through music. Shit!" I bang my fists against the table.

Agent Smelly says, "Johnson, if we weren't close, why would he be sending the messages? We have to be on the right track."

Vernon adds, "Joe, he's right. We'll get this guy. He's just messing with our minds. He's gonna slip up and we'll be there to catch him."

Agent Chase stands. "What we have here, gentleman, is a time clock. He's letting us know that there is a timetable for his next murder. Two in the water are our latest victims. He wants us to know that he plans to kill another and that he has Kevin's girlfriend, Ms. Chavez, and he knows she's pregnant. What we need to find out is when and where. He wants us to be puzzled and to stand around. That's why he says that we're beguiled. He thinks he's deceiving us, but we're on the right track. We need to keep pursuing our leads."

My frustration is not helping our situation. The team wants this guy just as bad as I do. I feel a new found energy and I'm determined not to let this guy get inside my head.

I say. "There's a record store down the street. I'd like to go in and see if we could listen to these songs and maybe pick up on something. After that we can see the other suspects. Agent James, we're setting up polygraphs for the suspects tomorrow afternoon, can we make that happen?"

"Yes, Agent Li will see that it's set up. Joe, we don't want this guy to get off on a technicality, so play this by the numbers. If you're too close to this case, dismiss yourself."

"The truth will do the rest and I can handle this case. I won't make it personal, " I reply.

"Joe, understand that truth and justice won't convict a person in the court of law. Evidence and proof is what prevails, " Agent James says.

How true. I have always had trust in my gut instincts. The key to our case is in the music.

Chase, Brown, and I depart our base of operations and travel four blocks to the Brown Fox Music Box record store that sits in the middle of the block of storefront businesses on Independence Avenue, between

College and Indiana Street. It is a quaint establishment with rows of stacked albums, CD's, and cassettes.

Numerous musical group posters adorn the walls: Prince, Michael Jackson, Fleetwood Mac, The Police, The Time, Santana, Barry White, Mariah Carey, the Crusaders, Quincy Jones, and Earth, Wind, and Fire.

The heavy reggae bass of Bob Marley's song, "One Love, " is playing on the loud speakers. The rhythmic beat is in harmonious pulsation with a heartbeat and before we know it our heads are like metronomes.

We walk to the brown, braided-haired, pale woman at the front counter. The thin lady, who looks to be in her early forties, has her nose, tongue, and eyebrow pierced. Her loose-fitting, tie-dye T-shirt gives way to her unrestrained, fully developed breasts, which jiggle freely with each movement. Assorted colorful tattoos cover her body. Her courteous smile looks warm.

"Hey, how you doing? My name's Julie. Can I help you find something?" she asks, leaning slightly forward on her forearms.

Vernon states, "Nice place you got here, Julie. The speaker system sounds great. This is the first time we've been in this store. Bob Marley, right?"

"Yeah, man, he's the greatest. We got his new-released CD's from Sony Records two days ago. I'm not the owner though. I just help run the place. Mr. Bryant will be right back. He just ran to the store for a second."

"Is it possible to hear, 'Roxanne,' by the Police and 'Put Your Lights On,' by Santana?" Agent Chase asks, retrieving the songs and titles from her notepad.

"Sure, you guys have taste in soft rock, huh? I would have picked you guys for R&B, jazz, or blues, " Julie states, sizing us up.

I tease, "Are the clothes that obvious?"

"You guys look straight enough, " she responds with a wink. The pierced, free-moving girl replaces Marley with the Police. We listen to Sting belt out the lyrics with a soulful, coarse falsetto. From one extreme to the next, Julie plays Santana's, "Put Your Lights On, " after that. The vocalist, Everlast, is dark in his delivery with music that gives thoughts of a subliminal exorcism. The music raises the hair on my neck. The message is creepy and insightful at the same time. And I begin to see the sick side of our serial killer all the more.

"We'll take both please, " I respond as she returns Bob Marley's 'Stand Up,' to the store's sound system, which immediately rejuvenates the atmosphere.

As we are paying for the music, a medium-built White male, about six feet and one hundred and eighty pounds, enters with a couple of plastic grocery sacks. He looks at us as he approaches and smiles.

"That was good timing. This is the owner, Mr. Bryant. Marvin, this is the first time they have been in the store. They're interested in soft rock today. Hopefully they'll come back for their music needs, " Julie says with a smile.

She graciously hands me my receipt and change, then walks back toward the front to help a customer who waits patiently at the counter.

Mr. Bryant sets down his bags and shakes each of our hands. "Please come by anytime. If we don't have what you need in stock, we can order it and have it within a week. You know they're even putting the old stuff on CDs these days. Re-mastering is what they call it. Isn't technology wonderful?

"I'm getting used to it, but I still prefer my LP's, " I respond.

Mr. Bryant smiles and nods. "We also have assorted things here for your home and listening needs. Headsets, cleaners, racks, tour t-shirt, jackets, and caps. I give a handsome discount to law enforcement. All our posters are twenty-five percent off and we do framing as well. We have futon's downstairs that we deliver for an extra fifteen dollars. We also have scented and flavored oils for intimate times, " Mr. Bryant says as he gives us a nudge with his elbow, while raising his bushy eye brows.

Vernon asks, "What fragrances?"

I state before Vernon can head to the back of the store, "Maybe next time, Vernon. We need to get moving."

"There's all the main fragrances like lemon, strawberry, banana, choco-late, bubble gum, grape, vanilla, you name it. Next time you come in, I'll let you sample some, " Mr. Bryant says as he lifts his bags off the floor. I notice several boxes of Kotex feminine napkins inside.

"You're a better man than me, Mr. Bryant, " I say. "I remember when my mom would have me go to the store to get sanitary napkins for my sis-ters and I would just fuss and fuss. I would be so embarrassed."

Vernon frowns up. "My wife still sends me and I'll never get comfort-able. It seems like everyone looks at you funny. I remember one time the damn tag fell off the package and the stupid teller called for a price check over the loud speaker. Man, I crawled out the place."

All the men laugh, while Chase shakes her head in disgust. "It's a force of nature, gentleman. I bet you don't cringe when you buy toilet paper. You guys are so immature."

"Actually, my little sister has started her cycle, " he explains. "My mom called and asked me to pick some up for her. I'm dropping them off on my way home. I'm sorry if you thought we were being insensitive."

Chase rolls her eyes at us on her way to the exit. "No problem."

"Thank you for your time and I hope your sister is all right, " I state as we follow Chase to leave.

eleven

WE ENTER THE OFFICE OF CEDRIC BARNES, POSTAL MANAGER of the Northeast Station. Chunky and balding, he looks to be in his late forties and hasn't shaven in a couple of days. Dandruff dusts the shoulders of his dark suit jacket and more falls every time he moves his dark head.

His office is cluttered and there's a half eaten Big Mac hamburger on his desk with a large french fry container and drink. The container holding the cool liquid perspires so profusely that it wets the papers on his desk. Either he doesn't care or doesn't notice.

We show him our identification. He looks at it and and then at us and jumps from his chair shaking our hands, like he doesn't get much excitement in his job. We do not want to draw attention to the carrier, Willie Reed, so we decide to give a bogus reason to the manager for wanting to talk to him.

Mr. Barnes asks, his mouth still full, "How may I help you?"

"We're interested in talking to Willie Reed, " Agent Chase answers looking the manager up and down, shaking her head with a half smile.

The manager gives us a suspicious gaze with a hint of nosey intrigue. He wipes his mouth of Big Mac special sauce with a paper napkin. "What did he do? Do I need to contact the Postal Inspectors?"

"That won't be necessary, " Vernon says. "He works the neighborhood around Independence Boulevard where there have been numerous disappearances of females and we want to know if he noticed anything suspicious. You guys are in the area daily and know who belongs in the neighborhood and who doesn't."

"He left for his route about an hour ago. You should be able to find him around fifteenth Street and Smart Avenue, " he answers, finally noticing his drink and wet desk. He quickly grabs a hand full of paper towels and applies them to the wet surface, then turns back to us. "Is there anything that I can do? I'd be glad to be of service." The special sauce hangs at the corner of his thin mouth.

"Not at this time, sir, " I reply as I hand him a business card and we thank the kind unblushing gentleman with the cluttered office and continue our search for postal carrier, Willie Reed.

My pager goes off as we head down Independence Boulevard. It's home, with 911 attached to the end. I pull out my cell phone. Chase and Vernon listens intently, while we continue to scour the neighborhood for our suspect.

"Sierra, is everything all right?"

"Joe, Tracy Jackson just called asking questions about one of the prostitutes who was murdered and asked if there was a connection with the Governor. Then she starts asking questions about your friend, Kevin. How'd she get our number anyway?" There's a long pause.

"I honestly don't know, sweetheart, but I'll find out, " I respond, trying to ease the tension rising through her silence.

We both know she can't stand the woman. Something about a woman shooting at someone you love can lead to a fire wall of un-forgiveness.

I ask, "What did you tell her?"

"Nothing. I told her she needed to talk to you, but I wouldn't give her your number and asked her not to call our home again. The heifer just hung up on me. I know how you hate the media and you know how I hate her. So I figured it best if you handled the situation, before I have to snatch the bitch's hair out of her head, " she says, trying to control her anger. I can feel her displeasure coming through the phone.

"That won't be necessary, sweetheart. I'll take care of it. She doesn't realize how volatile a situation she's walking into. She can ruin people's lives if she gets too close to this. I'll fill you in when I get home. Just relax, I'll take care of it. Kiss Nia for me and I'll see you tonight. I love you with your mean self, " I tease as Chase looks away from me, putting her hand to her forehead and returns to surveying the neighborhood as I turn onto Smart Street.

I like Chase, but my heart belongs to Sierra. She realizes it also by the expression on my face. She looks back up and winks at me.

"Joe, you know I don't play. By the way, I miss you. I'll see you when you get home. I'm making peach cobbler."

Peach cobbler is my favorite, and leads to us making gratifying love every time. I like showing my appreciation for thoughtful acts.

I reply blushing to no avail, "Well, keep it hot for me, boo."

She blows me a kiss through the phone and we hang up.

"That was sweet. That must have been Sierra?" Chase says with a warm understanding smile.

Vernon eyes dart between Chase and I as he scratches his head, trying to analyze Chase's interest.

"Yeah, we got a problem. Tracy Jackson is onto the Governor and she's asking questions about Kevin. She's about to blow this whole thing."

Chase states, "She can't report anything unless she has the facts."

Vernon says, "Tracy will do what she wants. She's just interested in the story and if she breaks the one on the Governor, it will surely make head-lines."

"Tracy will do it, so we need to talk to her and let her know the rami-fications of her actions, " I respond.

"She seems like she's a responsible and rational reporter. Give her the benefit of the doubt, " Chase says.

I reply, "She just called my home and questioned my wife about the case. Is that normal? I know her and have a pretty good idea what she's capable of."

"Chase, he knows what he's talking about, " Vernon says. "Tracy almost ran over the guy and tried to shoot his balls off after they broke up. How rational and responsible is that?"

Her smile turns to a frown as Vernon's comment changed her impression of Tracy in one sentence.

"Okay, we'll talk with her and see what her story is, besides being a scorned lover, " Chase says as she pokes me in the side.

I yell, "Holy shit, there's Willie!"

The carrier is dressed in his ash-blue uniform with black shoes and mailbag swung over his shoulder. The slender, freckled-faced, dark-brown-haired man, with a goatee peers through his sunglasses and spots us.

Willie continues saundering sorting through mail as he goes up the block inserting it into the postal boxes. As he comes from the fourth house our eyes meet and I nod as we inch after him in our vehicle.

I pull to the curb and Vernon gets out. He approaches carrier Reed as he looks on eyes darting between Vernon and our vehicle. He licks his lips as he looks around quickly.

"Excuse me, Mr. Reed. Can I have a word with you?" Vernon asks as he reaches for his ID.

Postman Reed thrusts his bag into Vernon's chest, knocking him across the bushes that line the front lawn of a house. Vernon lands in the grassy yard as Agent Chase gets out to help him. I follow Willie Reed to the corner where he jumps in his postal jeep and takes off going North on Smart Avenue.

I back up. Chase and Vernon jump in the car. I step on the gas. The postal jeep turns onto Prospect. As he gets to the circular turn on St. John's by the John F. Kennedy Memorial Monument, I hit his back left fender, flipping the jeep and sending mail flying all over the street.

The postman jumps out and heads for the steps leading to a wooded area adjacent to the back of the concrete memorial. I give chase. Vernon shuts off the engine to the damaged jeep, which is leaking gasoline. He ropes off the scene.

I pursue the suspect down the steep dirt hill with Agent Chase close behind. Mr. Reed heads for a ravine that leads to a sewer tunnel. Agent Chase and I sprint behind the evasive postman.

The guy is fast, but I gain ground by cutting across a path that heads off the tunnel. Before Willie Reed can enter the sewage entrance, I dive across the small creek and tackle him. Chase prances upon the fallen carrier before he can react, puts him in a thumb lock, and cuffs him.

I ask, winded and panting heavy along with the suspect, "Why did you run, you dumb shit?"

"I don't want to go to jail. I can pay back the money for the food stamps I stole, " Willie pleads.

I explain, "Fool, we weren't chasing you for food stamps. We're the FBI. We wanted to talk to you about the prostitutes who disappeared in this area. We know you've had relations with a number of them."

The Postman breaths heavy and profusely sweating. "Please man, I don't know nothing. These cuffs are tight. Let me go man."

Chase informs him, "Sorry, we can't do that. We have reason to believe that you are involved with the disappearance of several prostitutes. That charge is much more serious than stealing food stamps, Willie."

The thin carrier breaks down crying. "I had sex with some of them, but I ain't killed nobody. You can't pin that on me!"

I remind him. "When you were questioned before, you had no alibi. If you can't account for your time and no one can vouch for you, I think we can get a jury to believe you had something to do with it. Your credibility will be shot, once they find out you stole food stamps, assaulted a Federal Agent, damaged Postal Property, and resisted arrest from a law-enforcement agent, Willie."

"C'mon brother, cut me some slack. What can I do?"

"Either you can take a lie-detector test to clear yourself, or go down as the killer, " I say. "Either way, your career as a Federal employee is through. As I see it you are looking at jail time or death row. Do you see where I'm going with this?"

"Okay, I'll take the damn lie-detector test. I didn't kill no prostitutes. Please, can you loosen these cuffs, " he begs as he puts his face in the dirt.

"You promise you won't give us any more trouble?" I ask as he nods in pain.

I motion for Agent Chase to loosen the handcuff's grip. She puts her knee in between his shoulder blades to secure his submission, and loosens the cuffs around his wrists.

We get the postal carrier to his feet and make it back up the hill. The police have already started roping off the area with crime-scene tape and postal personnel are collecting the mail from his jeep. Vernon and two Postal Inspectors meet us.

"Detective Johnson, we meet again. I'm Inspector Hines. We met briefly at the unfortunate event at the Pershing facility and spoke on the phone. Agent Brown informed us that you were trying to question Mr. Reed regarding some killings?"

Vernon has learned a long time ago how to deal with these type of individuals. He brings situations he feels he'll lose his temper on to me. He cuts his eyes at the inspectors, giving me a heads up that they have an unreasonable request.

"That is one of his problems." I say. "He just admitted to stealing food stamps from the mail. We will have the police take Mr. Reed downtown. You can question Mr. Reed there."

"Well, actually he should be in our custody due to the damage to the mail, stealing food stamps, and damage to postal property, " Inspector Hines says raising his nose in the air, arrogantly while wiping his glasses with his handkerchief.

"Look, Inspector, I don't have time for this. Your carrier avoided our questioning, assaulted our agent, and we gave chase. He's in FBI hand-cuffs and that makes it an FBI collar. Don't show up here looking for handouts without putting in the work, " I say as we push pass the Inspectors with our prisoner and hand him over to the police with specific instructions on what to do.

I wave Inspector Hines over to where we are standing away from the other inspector. "Here's what's going to happen. You're going to tell me the names of the postal employees right now or I'm going to put your ass in jail for unlawful conduct and bribery of a Federal Agent. How's that for a reward, asshole?"

The inspector looks around at Chase, Vernon, and I, weighing his options and realizes that I am dead serious as Vernon and Chase place themselves on either side of him. "You have Willie Reed, the other suspect is Cedric Barnes."

"Thank you, Inspector, and never call me again. You lucky I'm letting you keep your job. Now get out of my face, " I order.

Inspector Hines adjusts his tie and scurries back over to his partner.

We climb into our vehicle and wave bye to the two inspectors turning red with anger as we drive away.

Vernon phones into our command post and reports on our progress to Agent James. James gives us permission to proceed with our course of action.

We decide to stay our current course and get with Cedric Barnes later. He never showed up on our previous list, so we feel the case will be weak and time be better spent on our current suspects.

Amir Mohammad is our last suspect to see. It is close to 2 in the afternoon and we can catch Tracy before she goes into the studio for the 5 o'clock news. I head toward Southwest Traffic way and Channel Seven Station, where Tracy works. Vernon puts the Police CD back in and plays, "Roxanne."

"Joe, we've heard this song before. Doesn't it ring a bell?" Vernon asks.

I think hard as the chorus rings with a hint of deja vu. I think back to

Niecie's Restaurant and Pretty Kevin pulling up in his Cadillac. I see his blue FUBU sweat-suit, gold watch and necklace. I see his handsome smile and hear the music from his car stereo. Vernon and I look at each other wide eyed.

We shout in unison, "Pretty Kevin!"

"Vernon, it has to be a coincidence, " I state.

Vernon and Chase frown at me. He explains with a fatherly tone, "Joe, you have to admit that's one hell of a coincidence. The same song Kevin has playing in his car when he asks us for help, just happens to be the same song the killer uses to bait us." He puts his hand on my shoulder and gives me a half smile. "Joe, we'll hate to think it's Kevin. He's a likable guy, even with his controversial occupation, but all serial killers are likable. They fit into society very well. It's the dark side we don't see that make them so sinister."

I bitterly respond, "Yeah, I hear you, but Kevin wouldn't kill anybody."

Chase places her hand on my shoulder. "I bet you would never of thought him to turn out being a pimp. Kevin seems to thrive on money, and greed can make a man do strange things."

"Kevin wouldn't kill for money, Chase, it don't make sense."

Chase says, "Joe, we're talking about a million dollars. There's a thin line between sanity and insanity. We all have that little voice that wants to run over the idiot who's walking in traffic or wishes something bad would happen to the driver who cuts us off. It's the morality, discipline, and stability that keep us from crossing that line." She grasps my forearm in support, while her eyes fill with sorrow.

"I grew up with the guy and I know his family. Kevin could not kill a person. He's not a serial killer. Fuck that!" I snap, backed against a wall.

I stare ahead at the road and remember basketball, dominoes, and tennis games with Kevin. I recall the good times hanging out in the neighborhood, chasing girls, and the college days hitting the fraternity and sorority parties.

I recall the expression on Pretty Kevin's face when I confronted him about the polygraph test and how he looked at me with betrayal. Bile fills my throat at the thought of putting Kevin behind bars. Am I being played? What if he did in fact do the killing? How will it look to my team? Will they think I was covering for him? My instincts tell me to trust my loyalty. The cop in me says bring him in. I continue to drive, but Vernon won't let it go.

"Joe, we got to bring him in. If Tracy breaks this story, then we're doing him a favor, because people will hunt him down for sure and I know you don't want that. You have to trust me on this one, fella, " Vernon says with fatherly conviction.

I reluctantly nod. Chase looks on, but says nothing. The rest of the ride is quiet after I shut off the CD.

We sit in the waiting area of Channel 7 as the receptionist calls Tracy over the loud speaker to report to the front lobby. We stand around saying little.

The view off the glass-enclosed waiting area reveals the rush-hour traffic on Highway I-35, already starting to form as people make their way to their homes, bars, gyms, and other things normal folks do when they get off work.

Tracy appears from behind the 'Personnel Only' door. "Hi Joe, I'm on the air in forty-five minutes. What's this about?" Then she notices Vernon and Chase. "Hi Vernon, and this would be?" She gives Chase an arrogant once over.

"Tracy, this is Agent Chase. We need to talk, " I state as Chase returns her snobbish glare. She leads us into a room with two large mirrors. We sit at a table while Tracy excuses herself.

I wait until she leaves, go up to the first mirror, pull a dime out of my pocket and place the dime's edge against it. There's a space in the reflection, which tells me it's a mirror. I do the same to the second mirror but there is not a gap between the dime and the reflection. The dime's edges touch in the reflection.

"This is a two-way mirror. We're probably being recorded." Vernon and Chase rise at the same time Tracy returns to the room. Her face is red and she can't look anyone in the eye.

"I should have known better than to try to fool you, Joe. Sorry about that, " Tracy says with no conviction.

"No problem, " I reply as I take her by the arm, usher her out of the mirrored room and into the women's bathroom adjacent to the waiting area. Once inside, Chase checks the stalls. We're alone and Vernon locks the door.

"Tracy, enough of your bullshit. Let's cut to the chase, shall we? If you proceed with your questioning and stories on Kevin and Governor Brush, you'll be in so much shit the Tidy Bowl Man won't even want to come around you. Not only are you playing with fire, but you're on the wrong track and about to start a public panic. I promise when we break the case, you will get the exclusive story."

"First of all, you guys are holding me against my will. Second, if I wasn't on the right track you wouldn't be here. Third, I know that four of the missing prostitutes are Pretty Kevin's hookers and Courtney's the stepdaughter of Governor Brush. Word on the street is he has a hit out on Kevin."

"Okay and your point would be?" I ask.

Tracy takes a step back, tilts her head and narrows her eyes, like she's tasted something bitter.

"Now, why would Courtney leave home if there wasn't something wrong there? It doesn't add up. A little money can buy a lot of information. There's one more thing, " Tracy states.

"What is that, Tracy?" I ask?

"I don't owe you shit. This is the story of a lifetime and it's mine. So, let me out of here, before I have all your badges, " she orders trying to walk through us.

Agent Chase steps in front of her, daring her to try to leave. Her half-smile, the way she tilts her head, and stares Tracy down is so cold, it even has me apprehensive.

Tracy stops in her tracks. "Call off your female pit bull, Joe, " she demands.

Chase stands her ground, never taking her gaze off Tracy and folding her arms, blocking Tracy's path.

"Tracy, if you go with this story a lot of innocent people will be hurt. You owe me, Tracy. I did not reveal our settlement in your assault case. Would you have this position if I would have? Let us solve the case. You'll get an exclusive and no one will be harmed. Tracy, please don't do this. You'll set our case back months if you go with this story, " I plead, placing my hand on her shoulder and looking her in the eye.

She looks away and pushes my hand off.

Vernon states, "Slow your roll, girl, and calm down. Now, if you want to be in the middle of a defamation-of-character lawsuit, drag your station in it, and end your career, that's up to you. You talking about going after the Governor and that would be right up Pretty Kevin's alley. He'd love for you to bring down the Governor and after he wins his defamation-of-character case he'll surely file against you, he'll live off you and this station for the rest of his life. You'll be the laughing stock of this town and who will hire you after that? A lawsuit will ruin you financially. It'll cost millions and I'd hate to see your pretty little self down and out."

Tracy stands there, arms crossed, face flushed red, and her anger shows as her eye brows converge to the middle of her face. She's pissed. She turns to me abruptly. "Joe, if you screw me on this, I will get even. Jesus, I can't believe I still have feelings for you, " Tracy states as she stares at Chase.

"Thanks, Tracy. You're doing the right thing and if you need to get in touch with me, use my pager. Don't call my home, " I order.

She looks at me and shakes her head, turning to Agent Chase. "Do you mind?"

I give her the okay and Chase moves to let Tracy through.

"Bitch!" Tracy mutters just loud enough to be heard as she exits the bathroom.

Chase states, "Joe, you can't trust that heifer."

"I know, but she can't say I didn't warn her. She has a choice to make. It's her life. Let's go find Mr. Mohammad."

We exit the bathroom and station. Vernon shakes his head and puts an unlit cigar in his mouth. "You really know how to pick em' Joe."

Chase smirks, as tho she's fighting back laughter.

"Whatever, Vernon. Don't forget, Mr. Fine as sixty-nine, you tried to pick up at the Pink Oyster, " I say.

Vernon grumbles and Chase leans closer, wide-eyed, mouth open with surprise.

Chase teases as we proceed in the vehicle toward I-35 North, "Say it ain't so, Vernon. I've always seen you as Mr. Manly."

"Joe, why you always pulling that out your ass? You never quit do you?"

"What happened, Joe?" Agent Chase asks as Vernon rolls his eyes, folds his arms, and bites down on his cigar to prepare to hear his comical exploits for the twentieth time.

I reveal laughing with Chase, while Vernon frowns and sits back in his seat with an attitude, "We were at this club called the Pink Oyster looking for a couple of suspects. We didn't realize it at the time, but the place was frequented by gay patrons and this gorgeous transvestite approached Vernon. They got to dancing and just having a good time. Vernon got off the floor, sweating and blushing and ready to put in for 'Mac Daddy of the Year', when I made him aware of the guys Adam's apple. Vernon turned red as a cherry."

"It was dark and it didn't happen like that. Why you always adding shit into the story?" Vernon looks at me and I wink at him and he can't help blushing. "That boy sure could dance though, " Vernon declares as he joins in the laughter.

We pull in front of the four-story, brownstone apartment building where Amir Mohammad lives. There're people scattered on different balconies. They stare at us as if they know we don't belong around this part of town.

This is a section-eight building and we probably look like rent collectors or someone from the health department, but it ain't the end of the month and we ain't giving out flu shots. By the way that we're dressed, they probably have deduced that we are the police. We get out the car and enter the four-story structure.

There're three nappy-headed, little boys playing catch with a Nerf football in the hallway. They are probably all brothers, judging from their ages of about six, eight, and nine and the resemblance. I intercept a pass thrown by the chubby kid of nine.

The young man says, "Nice catch, Five-O."

"I played a little ball in my day. Why do you think we're cops?"

"Well, y'all don't look like dealers, and I see the bulge under your jacket, " the boy replies.

Chase and Brown blush. This little guy is very bright.

"Hey kids, I have a dollar for the first person who can tell me where the cab driver Amir Mohammad lives."

The kids look at each other, then run toward me screaming "2-M!" they shout in unison.

"It's right up there, " the middle child explains, pointing us to the door of Mr. Mohammad's apartment.

"Thanks kids, here's the money I promised." I reach into my pocket and get two dollars for each of them and send them on their way.

We proceed to Amir's apartment and knock on the door several times. No answer.

"He must have gone to work already, " Vernon says.

I look amazed sarcastically, and shake my tilted head, like a duffus, "Do you really think so, Vernon?"

Agent Chase bursts out laughing. "You guys are crazy. Y'all never stop do you?"

Vernon and I look at her like we don't know what she's talking about. I stick a business card in the side of the doorway and we leave.

The sky is getting dark as we drive around the Northeast district looking for our taxi driver. He works for KC Cab Company. It'll be quicker finding him on the street rather than talking to his dispatcher. We want to avoid another auto pursuit.

We spot the red and white cab at Flapper's Chicken on Truman Road and Jackson Boulevard. Amir sits on the hood of his cab, eating a three piece and a biscuit as we block in his vehicle and approach him.

He continues eating unalarmed as we identify ourselves. A robust man in his late forties, he has very dark skin and his teeth are yellow. Amir's dark hair is short and he is neatly shaven.

His pants and short-sleeved jean shirt are heavily starched and the creases look like they could cut you. His black army boots shine like the eyes of an alcoholic. We know he has been to prison by the tattoo adorning his right forearm. The crescent-moon tattoo with the star in the middle is one color, black. The crude, bold outline is the work of a prison artist.

"Amir Mohammad, I'm Agent Brown. This is Agent Chase and Johnson. We would like to ask you a few questions?" Vernon displays his badge.

"So, what can I tell you now, that I didn't tell you before?" he asks as he spreads strawberry jelly on top of his biscuit, then devours the whole thing.

Agent Chase says, "I noticed in your juvenile file that you did jail time for sodomy against your next door neighbor."

He stops chewing, swallows, takes a long look at us, smiles, and takes a drink from his soda. "Me and Sally were playing doctor and things went a little too far, but it was consensual. Her daddy just freaked when he walked in and caught us. What can I say?" Mohammad shrugs.

Vernon and I look at each other with surprise at Chase's depth of research.

"I also know you changed your name in prison from Franklin Spears to Amir Mohammad. Why was that?" Agent Chase asks, even surprising

Amir.

"I found Allah. You have to affiliate yourself with a group in order to stay alive in prison and the Muslims were a safe enough group. I learned some things about myself, changed my diet, did my time, and got out. Why y'all still messing with me?" he asks, shifting from side to side.

Chase continues, "Did they know that you were in jail for statutory rape?"

Amir takes out a tooth pick and starts fishing remnants of his chicken dinner from between his teeth while eyeing us. "No, you get moved around so much that your history has a way of getting lost."

"Look Amir, you can get us out your hair for good if you submit to a polygraph test. If you pass, you can consider us ghost, gone, smoke, outta here, you know what I mean?" I ask taking a toothpick out of his shirt pocket and placing it in my mouth.

I glare at him.

We bitterly stare at each other.

Finally he spits the toothpick from his mouth. "When and where?"

I do the same.

"Tomorrow, 1:30 at eleventh and Locust at FBI Headquarters. It should take about an hour if you pass, " I reply.

"When I pass, " Amir corrects me as he takes a bite out of his apple pie with a mocking smile.

I smile at his confidence and we proceed to our vehicle as I prepare myself for one of the hardest things I'll ever have to do: arrest Kevin on suspicion of murder charges.

When we arrive at Kevin's home, he's reading the newspaper. By the way he frowns up and heavily sigh, I can tell he is agitated to see us. The way I glare back at him, he can tell this isn't a friendly visit.

"Why the grim face? I had the girls call your office and they said you hadn't returned yet. I did what you asked, so why y'all here again?" Kevin asks as Vernon and Chase position themselves on either side of him. His eyes get dark as his face gets red and he stares at me cold.

I can barely look him in the eyes. "Kevin, due to new information in the investigation, we need to bring you down to the department on suspicion of murder in connection with the missing prostitutes."

I feel as though I'm going to throw up, and about as yellow as a back-stabbing coward emotionally. But I have a job to do.

"Joe, do you really think I could do something like this?" Kevin questions, his angry eyes searching my face.

His lip quivers with anger, a single tear rolls from his eye. Vernon moves toward Kevin, taking out his cuffs. Kevin steps away, putting us all on alert.

I demand, "Kevin, cool out and let Vernon do his job."

"Joe, you're the friend I grew up with. If I'm going to be put in hand-cuffs, I want you to do it. You take me in, partner!" Kevin states, putting his hands behind his back.

Chase looks at me and Vernon lowers his head. I take out my hand-cuffs, look at them, and then Kevin. I walk behind him and put on the cuffs and walk him out to the vehicle as Vernon locks the door to his house.

It has to be one of the longest eight miles I have ever driven. I occasionally look up, only to find Kevin staring at me misty eyed, and shaking his head in disbelief. Kevin chose his profession, and I chose mine. We are both responsible for the consequences that come with our decisions. In my heart, I know Kevin is innocent. But, my detective mind has reasonable doubt. Vernon, Chase, Kevin, and I ride in total silence with only the thoughts of innocence and guilt on our minds.

Agent James enters the interrogation room, joining me, Chase, and Vernon. Kevin, wordlessly leans his chair up against the wall with his hands behind his head.

"Mr. Wine, my name is Agent James. You are here on the suspicion of murder in the case of the Independence Prostitutes. I'm sure you have already been read your rights, but I need to ask again, do you want an attorney present?

Kevin set his chair flat on the ground and looks at Agent James. "I don't need no damn attorney."

"I see. Well, is there anything you'd like to tell us?" Agent James asks picking up a note pad and sitting on the edge of the table in front of Kevin.

Kevin gazes up at the ceiling, then directs his attention to Agent James. Looking around the room at each of us he answers, "Yeah, I'd like to tell you all to kiss my Black ass." Kevin bursts out in a roar of laughter.

Agent James jumps at Kevin, pinning him in his seat with one hand and grabbing him by his scrotum with the other. Kevin's eyes water and he bites his lower lip from the pain. We all step toward them, but let the situation play out.

"Look, asshole, this ain't no fucking game. You be straight with me and don't be wasting my time. You get your attitude together, mister, I don't play." Agent James releases his grip and pushes Kevin into his chair.

Kevin coughs and tries to regain his composure. We all sit shocked, never having seen Agent James lose his cool.

"Fuck you! Is this what you brought me here for?" Kevin asks as he continues to gather himself from Agent James' attack.
"I told you I don't know shit and that's what I mean. If Joe feels that I'm guilty, then I'm willing to do the time. I owe him for getting the Governor off my ass, but I don't owe you shit and if you ever put your hands on me like that again, it will be the last thing you do." Kevin says, standing and trembling from pain and anger.

Agent James lunges for Kevin, but we grab him before he can make contact.

"Let me go. Lock this prick up! When you decide to talk, I'll decide to listen." Agent James storms out of the room.

I shake my head. "Kevin, what the hell was that all about? Don't hang your life on what I think."

"Joe, you bring me in here to get jumped by some damn fool and accuse me of killing my women. What else I got to lose, huh?" Kevin asks as tears stream down his boyish face.

I say nothing as I take Kevin's arm and lead him to the holding cell. My heart is confused and full of despair. Chase and Vernon sit at the table silently, both dismayed at what transpired.

We walk down the faintly lit corridor to the holding cells. Kevin hesitates before entering. "Joe, I'm sorry I got you into this. No matter what happens, dude. This is on me and I accept that. This is all so jacked up, man. I never killed anybody in my life, Joe. You got to believe that, dude." Kevin enters the cell and has a seat on the metal bed.

I close the cell door behind him. I just stare at him. I try to muster up something to say, but I am lost for words. I give Kevin a small smile, wink for reassurance, then return to the office area feeling sorry for my friend and myself.

When I get back to the office, things have calmed down and Agent James seems back to normal. He decides we'll go over all the information in the case. Agent Li, Smelly, Chase, James, and I each take a suspect and discuss the pros and cons of their statements.

What did each have to gain or lose? We work well into the night with tireless effort, until fatigue, stress, and too much caffeine finally takes hold of us and Royal James sends us home with hopes of a progressive morning.

The drizzle slowly falls from the night sky onto my windshield. I stretch my neck from right to left and ease the tension. When younger, I always had this thing, I'm not sure if it is intuition or a premonition, but I could always tell when things were about to go to shit and I'll be damned if I'm not feeling that sensation right now.

I shake off the butterflies in my gut. I drive my car, appreciating the sure handling on the wet streets on this blistery evening. As soon as I reach to turn the radio on, my cell phone rings.

My senses are going crazy and I don't recognize the number in the caller ID. I feel nervous and awkward. Something tells me not to answer it, but I go against my better judgement.

"Agent Johnson."

"I'm ready to turn myself in, but only to you, Detective, " the raspy voice says on the other end.

Is Vernon or one of the guys playing a joke on me? This does not feel like a joke. My hair is standing on the back of my neck.

"Who is this and how did you get this number?" I ask as I pull the car over to the side of the road, stunned by the chill in this man's voice.

As my adrenaline starts to kick in and mix with anger, I listen to the windshield wipers as they slowly glide the wet buildup to one side, then the other.

The headlights from the ongoing traffic radiates against the wet glass. I try to divert all my skills into my ears, trying to listen for a clue about the location of this killer. I reach across the seat for my personal cell phone to put a trace on the call.

"Detective, don't even waste your time trying to trace this call, because I'm using a scrambler on the phone."

I look around to see if there's anyone looking at me. How did he know what I was about to do?

"Are you somewhere I can see you?"

"You disappoint me, Detective. Why are you asking such stupid questions? None of that matters, now does it?" He takes a long pause, breathing slowly in and out.

The rain looks black as it streaks down my windows. I can't help feeling like it is symbolic of the tears that all the dead women have shed.

"No, " I answer, afraid he will hang up.

"It took you long enough to answer, maybe that's why it's taking you idiots so long to find me. I'll be at the abandoned warehouses in the stockyards. I will be watching and if you have someone with you, one of the bitches dies. You got fifteen minutes to get here or the deal is off."

He hangs up as I turn my car around and speed toward the stock yards, located downtown by the river's edge. This is probably a set up, so I call Vernon as I swerve through traffic as fast as I can.

I explain what happened. Traffic comes to a stand still. An eighteen wheeler has flipped over, striking a van and pushing it off the shoulder. There're five or six emergency vehicles on the scene and it begins to rain harder.

"Joe, how in the hell did he get your number? You know it's a trap and it'll take me at least twenty minutes to get there. Just hold up until we meet, you don't want to go in there alone. Most of the buildings have been condemned and it's not safe."

"Shit Vernon, I don't know how he got the number, but this is the closest we've gotten to this bastard during our whole investigation. I got to go, Vernon, " I explain as I pull into oncoming traffic, honking my horn and flashing my light.

I display my FBI badge at the traffic officers and let them know that I'm on an emergency case. They allow me to pass and get back into my appropriate lane, after warning me to be careful.

"Joe, I don't like this shit at all, you taking chances, dude. Remember what the Captain said, " he reminds me.

"Well, that means you need to move your ass then, don't it? Just look for my car. Don't leave me hanging, Vernon. I'm out." I hang up the cell phone as I speed down the twelfth Street exit ramp, leaving a spray of water in my trail. I pull onto Gennesee Street where the buildings are. Vernon will contact Agent James and will get here as soon as he can. I pull onto the deserted and badly lit street with one minute to spare. A flash beckons with an eeric flash in the second warehouse, third-floor window. The red-brick buildings were constructed in the early 1830's. They were mainly ice houses, furniture storage units, and sewing-machine shops.

The city wants to revitalize the stockyards and they're even considering a new, state-of-the-art basketball arena that will seat eighty-five thousand fans. So the abandoned buildings were condemned and the city took over the property rights. It's been five years since the take over and nothing has become of the stockyard renovation project.

I park in plain view on the isolated street and check both guns to make sure they're off safety and ready to use. I turn my pager and phone on vibrate, so not to draw attention to myself, should they ring while I'm in the building; making me an instant target.

I inch with caution into the dark building. I climb up the flimsy stairs, using my flashlight attached to my gun to light my way through my dark journey. My shoulder caresses the staircase wall as I ascend.

No wonder the building is condemned. Gapping holes allow me to see outside into the dark night and into the adjacent building that is saturated like this one with broken windows and exposed wood beams. Only the faint glow of the lonely street light penetrates these walls. Thank God it has stopped drizzling. I get that feeling like in a movie when the music starts and you know something bad is about to happen. I tense up.

"That's right, Detective, come on up and get me, don't be scared, " the killer says, trying to taunt me.

"I'm on my way. Just wait right there, " I respond, unable to see him. I take the stairs, two at a time.

He gives out a hearty, raspy laugh. "You like playing cat and mouse, Detective?"

He's really starting to piss me off. I'm one floor from where his voice is coming. I slow my pace and catch my breathe.

"I don't like it as much as Big Bubba is going to like your ass as his cell mate. A little hint for you; don't eat the cupcakes on cup cake night while you're in jail. That's how they pick out their punks for the evening, " I reply. I have a half flight of stairs left to climb.

I hear the clop-clop of the killer's footsteps as he takes the stairs toward the roof. I hurry my pace, gun aimed forward and ready to fire as necessary.

"Catch me, Detective, so I can shove that cupcake up Big Bubba's ass. Neither you, nor him scare me!" He bursts through the door leading to the roof.

Fresh air relieves my lungs from the chalky, stale, damp, musty stench of this building when I reach the roof top, seven stories off the ground.

A wooden two-by-four plunges into my stomach. It knocks the wind out of me. I fall to my knees. The killer places a gun to the side of my neck. The cold steel presses against my skin. Anger and pain causes any fear I might have to take second place to my senses.

"This would be too easy, " the killer says as he kicks me onto my side and takes off running across the roof top.

I get up mad as hell and give chase. The buildings have to be about four and a half feet apart. The killer never breaks stride. I can't get a good look at his face. His trench coat flaps behind him as he takes flight, leaping from one dilapidated rooftop to the other.

I jump as well, barely landing on my feet, but catching my balance as I continue my pursuit. The loose gravel on the tops make it difficult to get good traction, but I keep the killer in sight and gain on him.

I am in arm's reach when he jumps for the next building. I dive in mid air and grab him around his waist. We land on the third condemned building's roof and crash land. The roof gives way.

We plummet to the next floor, landing with great force. I am temporarily stunned as most of the debris falls on top of me. Luckily we land on old painting tarps stored on this floor. The killer gets up dazed and staggers his way to the stairs. I try to shake off the pain, attempting to remove the plaster and loose boards that have fallen upon me.

Vernon calls out to me from the second building's roof top. I gather myself and walk to the window.

"Vernon! Secure the front of this building, our man is on his way down!"

Vernon turns and vanishes. I find the stairwell and run down, two stairs at a time. I don't hear the killer's footsteps anymore. When I get to the bottom entrance, Vernon has his gun pointed at me.

I scream, "Whoa, Partner!"

"Got damn it, Joe. You need to signal somebody or something. I thought you were the killer. He never came out, " Vernon says, pulling his gun from the direction of my chest.

"Let's go through this building and make sure he's not in here. He had to go somewhere, if he didn't come out here."

We search the warehouse for an hour. No sign of the killer.

"Shit! He's gone, " I state as Vernon puts his gun away.

He throws his hands up and shrugs his shoulders in disgust. "Joe, you can't be running off by yourself, dude."

"Vernon, I followed procedure. I called you for back up and what else was I supposed to do? How many chances do we get like this?" I sit on the curb.

Vernon snatches a cigar from his jacket pocket and places it in his mouth, frowning, "You're supposed to wait! We are each other's back up. You don't do shit without me, Joe. Don't run off and leave me, ever again. You got that?"

Vernon is my older partner and probably right. "Yeah, Vernon. I won't let it happen again."

Who is the killer and where is he at this moment? He got away this time, but I vow not to let this happen again. Vernon calls Agent James and reports the incident and the results of tonight's chase.

I can tell by the way Vernon's face contorts and he pulls the phone away from his ear that Agent James is not pleased. Vernon gets off the phone, we shake hands, and I get in my car for my drive home.

While driving, I think about what Kevin must be thinking. Can he possibly be the killer or have played some critical part in this murderous escapade? The postal employee Cedric Barnes comes to mind. As disgusting as he was, I can understand why he'd have to pay for love, but he just doesn't fit the serial-killer characteristics. I just can't see his angle or where he would fit into this puzzle.

My mind wanders into the record store and what music the killer might be listening to. Then I go back over the chase in the warehouse. I remember the embarrassment on the store owner's face when we noticed the Kotex in his bag and how my sisters would tease me when Mom sent me to the store for them to 'assist Mother Nature,' in her monthly visit.

The prostitutes must know him and feel secure enough to go with him. What about the killer's notes? Is he watching me right this minute? I check the rearview mirror, a simple precautionary procedure I dismiss for the sake of not giving in to paranoia.

The street on my block is calm and gives me a sense of pleasure and reassurance. I pull into the driveway and enter my home, disarm my weapons, put them in the lock box, go in Nia's room and kiss my daughter as she sleeps.

The hot shower I take eases the pain of my fall. I dry off, lotion, and put on my pajamas. Downstairs, I enter into the scented-candle-lit living room and find Sierra fast asleep on the couch.

Baby Face's 'I Said I Love You' is playing on the radio. Love After Dark with DJ Greg Love is on. We often relax to the jazz station 106.5 FM. Sitting in the adjacent chair from Sierra, I marvel at her beauty and how at peace she makes me feel.

Her curly hair and her warm complexion of caramel-hued skin entices me. The smell of the cucumber-melon lotion she applies after a long bath arouses me. The teddy she wears under her see-through robe is snug and makes me envious of the way it embraces her curves.

Her angel face wears a slight smile as it rests on top of her hands. I blush at one of her slippers, which has fallen off of her foot that is suspended from the couch. I gaze at the plumb shape of her breast and cleavage. Desire fills my lungs, pushing the air right out of my body, forcing me to pant with excitement and reach within to gain control.

The flicker of the candles send shadows dancing across her body like tiny ballerinas in an Alvin Ailey production. The ecstasy of the moment, the music, shadows, scents, and visions invade my essence.

She is making love to my mind and soul in her sleep or am I caught in the rapture of her dream unsuspectingly? Whatever the case, I am grateful for the moment, grateful that I married Sierra, and so grateful that she loves me as much as I love her.

Her thick brows and eyelashes tremble and slowly open. A smile forms. Our eyes meet with exotic explosion and she rises to greet me as I stand for her embrace. We don't say a word, but let our emotion-filled kiss speak for us. She slowly undresses me and sits me in the chair as she reveals what the teddy holds. Then, she straddles me.

We don't speak one word as the shadow ballet, passionate scents, songs of love, and orgasmic moans fill the moments of darkness. The moments turn to minutes and minutes, to hours. Complete in sexual satisfaction and our love, I take her in my arms, carry her to our room, and lay her on our bed.

AT 2:30 IN THE AFTERNOON, WE MAKE SURE WE ASK ALL THE suspects about their whereabouts last night and all the suspects have completed their polygraph tests. As we get their results they are excused, except for Willie Reed who is held over for pick up by the Postal Inspectors.

Amir Mohammad, Willie Reed, and Frank Scott's tests have all come back negative. The administrat of the polygraph test, Professor Flo Jordan, looks over Kevin's test results, scratching her cinnamon-colored, short black haired head with her pencil, dumbfounded.

Agent James asks, "Professor Jordan, what were the results of Mr. Wines' polygraph?"

Professor Jordan is a small woman, pretty, very professional, and the best in her field. She has been contracted by the FBI for the last six years. She flips through the chart while looking over her wire-framed reading glasses, and runs her fingers through her curly black hair.

She looks at us, then at Kevin, who sits on the other side of a two-way mirror at a desk in an adjacent office, playing with a radio that sits on a desk.

"This is the strangest thing I have ever seen. This guy is borderline. Absolutely borderline. I have no conclusive evidence if he is telling the truth or not."

"Why is that, Professor Jordan?" Agent James asks.

"I've gone over these charts four times and I just can't say. Some people just don't do well on these things, but if I were to give my own opinion, I would lean toward him telling the truth. He wasn't perspiring, fidgeting, trying to avoid eye contact, or any of the usual things a guilty person does while taking the test. He could be a detached, cold-blooded murderer, suppressing his feelings, but I doubt that. This is the first time I've run across a true borderline, " she states, sighing heavily.

We all stand and look at Kevin. I finally open the door, and we enter the room where Kevin is listening to a sports talk show.

Kevin turns off the radio and studies my expression for any clues. "Well, if it isn't Judas and the five hypocrites. How did I do on the test?"

"The test was non-conclusive, Mr. Wine. You are what we call in the profession, 'borderline,'" Professor Jordan explains.

Kevin, becomes agitated. "So, did the test say I lied or I'm telling the truth?"

"We can't say. Your results point in both directions. That's the best I can tell you, " Professor Jordan responds.

Kevin explodes, "Is the machine broke or what? How can I be telling the truth and lying at the same time? That don't make no damn sense. What kind of game are you people playing? Joe, can't you see they're trying to set me up? I told you fools I don't do good on those fucking tests!"

"Calm down, Kevin. If you're innocent, you have nothing to worry about, " I state.

"If? Fuck you, Johnson. Instead of you guys finding my women, you're in here wasting time trying to pin this shit on me. I been putting up with all this and you won't even back me, you back-stabbing bastard. Take me to my holding cell and kiss my ass, Joe!"

Vernon escorts him to his cell. Everyone looks at me as I walk to my desk and begin going through the case files to see what we had missed, my only solace. We're back to square one by process of elimination. Kevin is our sole suspect.

Could Kevin be working with someone and getting paid to provide his trick with females? I know how he loves money, but does he have the capacity to be that much of a criminal.

I am not convinced he is our killer and apparently, Agent James isn't either or he would have Kevin sitting in a federal penitentiary, instead of here. Chase sits across from me, but respects my space after what has just occurred.

We both continue our search for missing pieces that might lead us to our serial killer. The killer is still out there, and the clock of death is ticking for the two women we assume he has in captivity. It's time to turn this guy's sense of illusion into a reality. We are close, maybe too close, to see things for what they truly are.

twelve

ANOTHER DAY PASSES. WE'RE NO CLOSER TO THE KILLER than when we began. Kevin remains locked up as our primary suspect and our friendship hangs by a thread. Everyone is tense. We're all pulling at straws trying to look into an angle we may have missed.

Agent Li bursts through the door, just as the phone rings.

"Joe! You got to see this."

"Hold on, Li, let me get this, " I reply picking up the receiver.

The employees in the Fairfax Industrial Park in Kansas City, Kansas have discovered another body. Our seventeenth victim.

I have to admit, I feel like a failure. This guy is too smart for us. I sit back in the chair and rub my eyes.

"What's up?" Agent Smelly asks as he enters.

"We got to roll. Another victim's been found in the Fairfield District, " I announce as everyone pauses to reflect on our ineptness.

The only good thing is that it will put Kevin in a good light. He could not have killed someone while in our custody.

Agent Chase says as she grabs her purse and we file out of our command post, "Jesus Christ, this guy doesn't quit."

I ride with Smelly, Li, and Agent James in the white suburban, pondering the notes that the killer left for us, all musical ensembles. How much of the profile that Chase discussed matches this guy's personality?

"Agent Li, what were you going to tell me before we got the call?" I ask.

"I have a list of thirteen people who were dropped from medical programs with surgical skills in the Kansas City area, " he answers as he hands me the list.

I browse down the names. One looks familiar. I circle it and ask Li to find out when and why this guy was booted from the medical program. It might just be coincidence, but I wasn't going to take any chances. The killer has one hostage left. No, she's pregnant--make that two.

I start to realize how Kevin must feel. In his own way, he was trying to help the women he exploited. Even in the negative profession, they would come out financially secure. They'd be in a better place than when they came to him. Three of them now dead and the one he loves with child is in peril, beyond our control.   Maybe him wanting to be locked up is a way to cope in solitude and reflect on the consequences of such a scandalous profession. Is he taking the blame for their demise? I don't know. When one is alone and in silence, demons of past thoughts and indifference stir in echoes of remorse, indecision, and guilt.

We pull off I-70 West Highway, into the Fairfax District, and proceed to the big muddy river. When we get out of the vehicle, television crews are being held back from the crime scene by the police. I nod to a couple of the officers I recognize.

The twin city police department's of Kansas City, Missouri and Kansas often cross paths. We also have friendly competitions of softball, basketball, clothes, and food drives to help the unfortunate in our immediate communities.

I pass the three fishermen, who are giving their stories, probably for the fourth or fifth time. We like to interview people several times to see if their story stays consistent. Each fisherman talks to a different detective, then, we switch detectives on them, always keeping them separated so we can make sure their stories are consistent with each other's. When interviewing a person, sometimes the witness is the actual culprit of the crime. Our job is to make sure the facts fit the situation.

The forensic team is numbering evidence bags as the coroner wheels the just-discovered body toward us. When they get to us, we ask them to open the black body bag.

The seventy degree temperature has already had an effect. The smell of raw chitterlings multiplied by fifty is the stench of gases and secretion released from the body. It is almost unbearable. The foul stench has us reaching for anything to cover our noses. I use the sleeve of my sports jacket to block the nauseating gases that bring water to my eyes. The sister is a red-bone. Light in complexion, with reddish-brown hair and freckles to match. She looks to be in her upper-twenties, one hundred and twenty pounds. Like the others, she is very attractive. Her hair is straight and long, falling just over her shoulders. She must have fussed with it regularly.

"Her name is Jennifer 'Red' Braxton, " Chase informs us.

Vernon asks, "How do you know that?"

Chase leans forward with pen in hand and moves the corpse's red hair away from her neck, revealing a gothic tattoo with her name inscribed. The body is not as decomposed as the others, but is slightly swollen and blue in spots. Her arms and legs although amputated, stay close to the body, like loyal pets, not wanting to be abandoned, although detached. Did she watch the others die?

Is the killer out there watching us at this very minute? Watching our every move amongst the curious onlookers drawn to tragedy, like sharks to blood. None really wanting to help, just being nosey, gathering information at the victim's expense to say they were part of the action. Like a reporter, wanting to give every tiny gloomy detail, the feeling of being in the know or having privileged information that'll make them the big shot around the coffee machine. People who dreamed of being a man or woman of the law, but for some reason never fulfilled their dream.

"Law enforcement!" I say aloud to the surprise of our team, looking at Vernon and Chase to make the connection I just realized.

Vernon asks, "Joe, you all right, man?"

"The Red Fox Music Box? The owner, Marvin Bryant? He offers law enforcement a handsome discount?" I nod to Chase and Vernon, trying to get them to see the connection as Agent James, Smelly, and Li look completely clueless.

Vernon rubs his chin and frowns getting it. "How in the hell could he know we were law enforcement?"

Chase finally catches my thought. "When we never announced that we were."

I question, "Yeah, how the hell is that?"

"If that's all you got to go on, that's weak." Agent James responds. "You and Vernon have been on the news and in the paper before. I think you're reaching for straws."

I say with a wink of an eye, "That's all we got is straws, and remember it was the straw that broke the camel's back."

Agent James squints his eyes as he rubs the back of his neck. "Check it out and we'll finish up here. Take Brown and Chase with you. Is it anything you need for us to do?"

"Yes, I need Agent Li to check into the Q. M. Bryant on the list and see if this is our man who was kicked out of medical school and why."

Agent James nods to Agent Li.

"I'm on it. I'll phone you with the results, " Li states as he exits the crime scene.

At 11:34 Agent James gives us our directives and informs us to proceed with caution. This is not much to go on, but at this point nothing is making sense. Before we can depart for Vernon's vehicle, Agent James's pager goes off and he dials.

He puts up his hand for us to wait. His eyes get wide and his face becomes long and agitated.

"We have another note at your captain's office. Meet me there in fifteen minutes. You can visit the record-store people after that. This guy is messing with us and I don't like it. I can't keep the press off this much longer and Joe, your friend, Tracy Jackson, is breathing down my neck, threatening to report on some information about the Governor and Kevin Wine. We can't have that happen. Can you talk to her?"

"We've already done that. We better have a contingency plan if she does shoot off at the mouth. She's aware of the consequences if she does decide to talk, " I say, sighing heavily.

Agent James, Chase, Vernon, and I head for Captain Wayne's office as Smelly finishes gathering information from the crime scene.

At headquarters we give salutations to our fellow detectives as we head toward Captain Wayne's office. He gives us a warm welcome, but he gives us a long depressing stare. Captain Wayne has not smoked in twelve years, yet he has a Kool cigarette between his fingers and the smoke floats above his head.

He snuffs it out and directs us to the note the killer mailed, which like the others has been enclosed in plastic by the forensic team. This note is different from the rest because it is worded completely in red-inked cut-out letters. We circle the Captain's desk and read.

Street life, and there's a thousand parts to play
street life, until you play your life away...
When the crescent moon reaches the midnight sky,
the two will have a life expectancy of a dragonfly,
committed to the waters of the river wild,
both will die mother and child,
if you don't, their death is on you...
in the music you'll find the clue.

We look at each other with anger, frustration, curiosity, determination, and kinship, bound together in the quest to solve this puzzle. We are all being played like five-dollar hookers, cheap and reckless. I have received no further phone calls from the stranger since that night at the warehouse.

Vernon puts an unlit cigar in his mouth. "The song is 'Street Life' by the Crusaders. It's been referred to as a pimp and prostitute serenade."

"A dragonfly has a life expectancy of twenty-four hours, " I state as everyone looks at me wondering how the hell I know this. "I watch the Animal Kingdom on satellite. You get all kind of interesting information, " I answer, easing their looks of amazement.

"He references music twice in this note and all the other notes are music related, " Chase says. "It would be more than a coincidence for a record store owner to have access to this knowledge. It makes sense that we should look at him as a suspect. Pretty Kevin has been in our custody all this time, so that would count him out." She winks at me with a slight smile. Thanks God she's now in Kevin's corner.

"Captain Wayne, do you happen to have yesterdays paper?" Agent James asks.

"Yes, I have it here in the trash." The Captain hands Agent James the newspaper.

Agent James quickly dismantles the paper, until he comes to the sports section of the Kansas City Star and flips to the back page and scrolls down to the Almanac, which lists the moon phases. He looks at his watch and then looks up slowly with a frown.

"The moon was crescent last night, people. It is now 1:10 in the after-noon, giving us less than eleven hours to find this fool. You guys get to the record store and see what you can find out. Captain, I need some help with manpower. We need to have men stationed at different points on the Missouri River. Maybe we can keep this guy from going there. See if we can get Alvin Brooks from Crime Busters to make a radio announcement warning citizens not to go around the river for the next twenty-four hours, that will help.

"We could give Mike Carter and KPRS radio station a call for help, " Captain Wayne suggests.

Agent James smiles and places his hand on the captains shoulder. "Great idea, give him a call for a public service announcement. He's real good about giving free air time for community alerts and public safety. I'll also get with Joe's friend, Tracy Jackson, to do some spots for television. That will give her something to do and hopefully keep her out of our hair long enough to apprehend this guy. Let's get on it, people!"

We depart as Captain Wayne and Agent James pull out a map of the area and plot their strategy to secure the river.

We head toward I-70 East, make a left on Prospect Avenue, and turn onto Independence Avenue. When we enter the store this time, our FBI badges hang from the chest pockets of our suit jackets.

Julies puts her hands to her face surprised. "Oh, wow, you guys are Feds. Damn, how cool. Glad you came back, y'all looking for some new sounds or what?"

"Julie, we're really here to see your boss. Is he in?" Vernon asks smiling.

Julie explains, placing some CD's on the store counter, "Nah, he called in. Said he wasn't feelin' too good. He said he was up late with a stomach virus."

"That's too bad. Will he be in at all?" Chase asks.

"It's hard to say. He's usually a stickler about coming to work. This is only the second time he has ever called in since I've been working here, " she answers as she digs in her ear with the butt of her ink pin.

I question. "How's Mr. Bryant's little sister doing?"

"What sister? Marvin don't have no sister. He's an only child. Marvin don't even have parents. His dad killed his mom, and then killed himself. Marvin's a loner. He doesn't even have a girlfriend. I think he's gay. I thought about giving him a little nookie, once or twice. I hit on him a couple of times and he blew me off like a fly about to land on his sandwich. I wish he had a sister, maybe the guy wouldn't be so introverted, " Julie says as she twists a couple of her unraveling braids.

We all look at each other. Why would he lie to us for no apparent reason? He knew we were cops. My hair stands on the back of my neck and my stomach knots up as I survey the record store. I can't believe what we have discovered. In the North, South, and East corners of the store are posters of Santana, The Police, and the Crusaders. I point to them. Chase and Vernon both jolt to attention. How did we miss this the first time in the store?

Vernon questions, "Julie, would you have an address for Mr. Bryant?"

"Yeah, he stays in a trailer park about twenty minutes from here in Parkville, Missouri. What's this all about? Marvin's not in any kind of trouble, is he?" Julie has finally realizes we're not here on a social call.

"We don't think so, " I reply. "We need to talk to him, to see if he can help us out on this case we're working on. If you can get that address for us, we'd really appreciate it."

She moves to her address book behind the counter as I page Agent Smelly to meet us at the record store. He tells me that he's with Agent Li and has some critical information for us. They are three minutes away.

"Here's the address, " Julie says, handing it to Agent Chase.

"Have you ever visited his home, Julie?" Vernon asks, touching her hand.

"Jesus, yes!" She starts to shake and her eyes swell up with tears as her hand go to cover her face.

Vernon takes her by the shoulders and smiles as he probes further, to help calm her. "Is there anything unusual about the place?"

"No, but he stays on top of a storm shelter. There was a tornado warning once and he took me down there. He keeps food, water, and medical supplies. He's a survivalist, you know? He thinks the world is gonna be a big disaster in the year 2005. I told him he was nuts, but he said 'better safe than sorry.' Go figure, " Julie replies, wiping the tears from her face and cracking a small smile.

"How did you guys get to the underground shelter from the trailer?" Chase asks.

"He has a trap door under a throw rug in his kitchen that has a staircase leading to the shelter. You would never even know it was there by looking from the outside."

We could easily be walking into a trap. The killer will have the advantage of knowing his surroundings.

"Can you describe how it looks there in the shelter? How many rooms does it have and is there another exit besides the kitchen?" I ask. Even a small animal that lives in the ground will have more than one way to exit his burrow.

Julie answers, "We were just in the front part of the shelter. I saw other doors, but we just sat on the steps, listened to the weather station on the radio, and drank wine he had stored down there. As soon as they lifted the tornado warning we went back upstairs. We were only down there for about thirty minutes."

Agent Li and Smelly arrive and motion us to them at the front of the store.

"Julie, could you excuse us for a moment and remain where I can see you?"

I like Julie, but I'm not sure about her. She agrees and starts thumbing through a current issue of Rolling Stone, with Ice Cube on the cover. We walk toward the front of the store and congregate with our fellow agents, keeping Julie in sight.

"Johnson, Quincy Marvin Bryant wasn't kicked out of Kansas Northern University Medical School, " Li begins. "He dropped out voluntarily, so he wouldn't be brought up on charges. He made a deal with the dean of students, Emma Meadows, that if he received psychiatric attention he wouldn't be charged. It seems that Marvin liked late-night rendezvous with the female medical cadavers."

I look up in shock, "You gotta be shittin' me."

"Yeah, he dropped out of school after that and that's not all, Cedric Barnes was a student as well. He was allowing Bryant access to the cadavers. He was a janitor at night as part of the work-study program to help pay his medical-school bills. He was forced to drop out as well. They later exonerated Barnes and he was cleared of all wrong doings, but he never went back to school."

"So how'd Bryant get caught?" Vernon asks frowning while getting a cigar out his jacket pocket.

"A janitor caught him in the act and reported him to the dean. This guy gives new meaning to a late-night booty call, " Agent Li states, blushing.

"So Joe, why did Bryant have all the Kotex in his bag and do you really think Barnes is connected?" Chase asks.

"Think about it. If he did kidnap all those women and is hiding them away, at some point he would have to do something about their menstrual cycle. Thus, the need for feminine napkins, while he had his victims detained before he killed them. I don't think he's working alone. The Postal Manager, Barnes might be sympathetic to Bryant's sexual needs."

The way we all look at each other wide-eyed and gazes darting around to each other emphasizes that me we are at a critical phase in this case.

"There was something about that guy I chased in the stockyards, " I state. "I just have this gut feeling that more than one person has their hand in this, call me crazy, but I haven't been able to shake this feeling."

Agent Li shrugs his shoulders. "Joe, that could have been a coincidence."

"Like it was a coincidence that he had my cell number too, huh?" I ask.

"Look people, it's almost 3 o'clock, " Vernon says. "It will take us at least two hours to get back to headquarters, get armed, prepare to take this guy down, arrange for back up, and still get a search warrant. That will only give us so much daylight. We need to hurry up."

We all concur.

"Agent Smelly, " I begin. "You stay with Julie to make sure she doesn't tip off Marvin or in case he shows up here. We'll page you if we need you on the premises. Contact Judge Evelyn Cole and let her know we need a search warrant A.S.A.P. Inform her that it's on the grounds of kidnaping, murder, and rape. She'll know what to do from there. Let us know when you get it. Then drop off Julie for safe keeping and meet us with the warrant. We'll keep Agent James in the loop. Agent Li, you come with us, " I order as we leave the record store with a little over eight hours remaining to get to the Independence prostitute killer.

Time ticks against us, stress engulfs us, and death looms ready to consume the life of mother and child.

It's 6:15 PM we have Marvin's ugly trailer under surveillance. It is covered with rust spots. We park about three hundred yards away in a wooded area. Through the wide-lensed binoculars
I see Marvin darting around nervously. His small shaggy head looks all over the place as he moves things hurriedly inside the trailer.

Agents Li, Chase, Brown, and I wait in Vernon's suburban, listening to Sean Tyler on 107 radio station and the late great Grover Washington Jr.'s 'Mr. Magic'. Vernon and I listen to Sean's show regularly on our stakeouts. The brother is a good friend and throws down with the old-school hits.

We are earnestly waiting on the search warrant from Agent Smelly. He has paged us to let us know he's on his way. All the lights, except for one, go out in the trailer. Dusk embraces the horizon and we all would feel better attacking this guy with daylight left. Oh well. We have less than six hours left and the killer must be headed for the underground shelter where he is holding Cherry Chavez, Pretty Kevin's pregnant girlfriend.

At 6:48 Agent Smelly gets to us with the search warrant.

"What took you so long?" I ask.

He answers with an angry frown on his face. "The Judge was in conference with the Governor when I got there. I don't know what they were talking about, but she wouldn't see me until they were through."

"I wonder what that was all about?" I say bitting my bottom lip. "We're sitting here trying to catch the killer and they're talking shit and holding up our bust. Sorry, it's not you. It's just that time is running out and I would feel a whole lot better if we prevented at least one death."

We pull the cars further off the road and signal Agent James by walkie-talkie that we are about to proceed into the killer's domicile. The reinforcements are positioned five hundred yards away and ready to come in, if needed. No activity has been reported on the river, so we must assume that Ms. Chavez is still in the custody of the killer.

We gather outside the cars and go over our tactical plans. We all put on our FBI lettered bullet-proof vests and arm ourselves with assorted rifles, flashlights, and guns. The trailer is just beyond the steep ridge of the thick trees. We journey up the gravel road and stop about one hundred yards from the dilapidated mobile house our killer calls home.

"All right, Smelly and Li, you guys work your way around the back of the trailer and hold your positions there. Watch out for booby traps. This guy is a survivalist and might have prepared for company, " I warn the anxious agents as they begin to proceed toward the back of the trailer through the shrubs and sparse trees.

"Brown and Chase, once inside we'll split up and canvas the trailer, then I'll proceed into the cellar with you guys coming behind. Vernon, you take up the rear. Let's be careful down there. It'll probably be dark, but don't use your flashlight unless it's necessary. You might as well paint a target on your back. Let's be alert and watch ourselves. We need to locate Ms. Chavez before he has a chance to do anything to her, then get the killer. Remember, this guy is dangerous, so proceed with extreme prejudice."

After signaling Agent James to come forward, we carefully proceed toward the trailer, trying to stay out of clear view of the lighted window. The crickets and other nocturnal insects' harmonious songs pulsate with each step we take. The night air is crisp and the crescent moon, an illuminating white.

Something glimmers. I pull Agent Chase backward from her forward step, and motion for Vernon to stop and look down. A trip metal wire is strung between two trees with an explosive device at its base on the right side.

I radio the other agents and warn them of the un-seen dangers that await. We cautiously step over the trip wire and proceed toward the rusty white trailer with aluminum trim.

The trailer, set upon brick blocks, looks to be about forty feet. Agent Chase and Vernon place themselves on either side of its front door. I reach for the knob. Locked. I look at Agent Chase. She motions me aside.

I take her place on the left side of the door. She reaches inside of her pants pocket, retrieves a gadget, and inserts it into the lock. She twists the door knob open. As she is about to open the door a trigger clicks. A string is attached to the inside of the door.

I quickly tackle Chase as the door flies open to the roar of a shotgun blast. Vernon moves inside the doorway, gun drawn, with a flashlight and laser scanning to shoot anything that moves. Chase smiles, nods, and gives me a thumbs up.

Agent Chase and I gather ourselves and go to Vernon's side, armed and ready. None of the light switches work. We canvas the three bedrooms, living room, and bathroom area by the glow of our flashlights. No sign of the killer.

In the kitchen we move the carpet that reveals a trap door just as Julie had said. We open the trap door and before any of us proceed down the stairs, I go into the living room and grab two pillows off the couch and the box of baking soda sitting on the counter. Vernon pours the white powder into my cupped hands as Chase shines her light down the narrow stairwell. I rub my hands together letting the fine powder float down the dark stairs revealing the blue security laser beams.

Yet, another trap laid by the killer. I toss one pillow down the stairs then another as the sudden whisks of darts shooting across the path of a would-be intruder. Our flashlights reveal that the pillows now look like porcupines napping.

I travel down the stairwell first and signal to Chase and Vernon that all is clear. They proceed down the wooden stairs. We shine the lights on the opening revealing two corridors that run parallel to each other.

The place is cool with the musty smell of earth and acrid rubbing alcohol. We split up in order to search the place thoroughly. An explosion outside shakes the ground beneath us. Agent Li and Smelly must have come across a trip wire and ignited the explosive. We can only hope and pray that they are alive and well.

Vernon says, "Okay, Johnson, we need to split up. I'll take Chase with me and we'll take the right side and since you're left handed, you can take the left."

"This place is much bigger than we anticipated, so be careful, people. Please notice everything. This guy is tricky and we don't know what he's capable of. Just watch yourselves and come back in one piece. I'll see y'all on the other side, " I state as we nod and proceed our separate ways.

In the left corridor I come across a wooden door on the right side. I swing the door open wide and count to five, then enter with the laser and white light of my gun leading into the dark room like a seeing-eye dog. My heart beat and breathing have increased, but my nerves are calm. The room has bunk beds with shackles at the feet and head of each post. I pull back the covers. Different colored strands of hair lay on each bunk. Some of the females have been here.

A faint mumbling sounds and I follow it out of the room two doors down. An illuminating light creeps from the bottom of the doorway. I shut off my light. A muffled whimpering comes from the other side of the door. The butterflies in my stomach let me know that the killer is on the other side.

I hit my distress signal on my phone, kick in the door, and burst into the room gun raised and ready to fire. My red laser beam finds the back of Marvin Bryant's head. His pants dangle from his left leg as he lay on top of the naked, Cherry Chavez in what looks to be a makeshift operating room. It seems that I caught the killer in the act of rape. Her wrists and ankles are bound by white linen to the four corners of the metal table. The killer freezes, hunched atop of the woman.

"Marvin, get your hairy ass up slowly, turn around, and raise your hands, " I order.

Marvin slowly pulls himself off his pregnant victim. He turns around, revealing a .38 pistol in one hand and in the other, a scalpel to the throat of Cherry Chavez. She is gagged by a leather strap around her mouth. Her tear-filled, swollen eyes show her excitement to see me, and a fear of death.

She lays there exposed, semen running down her thigh from Marvin's extraction. Her right arm shows an IV, attached to a clear liquid suspended by a metal stand. Her stomach shows protrusion from pregnancy. Her breasts are bruised from what looks to be suck marks. Her arms and legs have markings that look like lines for amputation. The stainless-steel saw and assorted medical tools on the table at her side indicate that Marvin is getting a quickie before the operation.

Marvin stands, smiling with confidence. His pupils are dilated and he is giddy. His body is pale and sparsely covered with blond hair. He stares directly into my eyes and doesn't seem embarrassed or bothered that he is exposed, his pants clinging to one ankle.

"Late as usual, I see. I hope your ribs are feeling better. That was a nasty fall we took together." He smiles.

I ask as he mockingly stares at me, "Where did you end up that night, you didn't stay around so I could have had the pleasure of whipping your ass."

"Wouldn't you like to know? I ain't telling you anything. So, what do we do now, Detective?" he asks with a sinister grin.

"You give up, you sick fuck, or you die!" I try to think of something to distract his thoughts and buy me some time. "I heard your coward father killed your mama!"

"The bitch deserved it and my father was no coward, " Bryant states. His hand balls into fist around the scalpel. "He wasn't a coward the way you were, when I held my gun to your neck that night."

I get the sense to rush him and beat him to death, but fight the urge and focus on trying to get next to him

"You're the coward, not my father!"

"Nah, I wasn't scared, more pissed than anything else."

"For your information, my father loved my mother. He trusted her. The Post Office had him working six days a week, ten to twelve hours a day."

"Right, it must be a postal thang. Yeah, it's starting to make sense now. Kill your woman, because you're working too many hours. He really sounds like a stand up guy."

Marvin says with hate flowing from his words, "My father was a good man! You watch your mouth when referencing my dad, ass-hole!"

I look at Cherry and he takes a quick step closer to her, like an animal protecting its territory.

"Whoa fella, don't get excited, " I say, shaking the gun, reminding him with the red beam of my infra-red sight that I'm armed.

He freezes and stares at me. Cherry lays her head back on the gurney and closes her fear-filled eyes. He's kept her alive this long with me here and with him talking, she is in no imminent danger.

"So, Bryant, why did your dad kill your mom?"

He shifts his attention back to me. "He did it for me. My father was a postal clerk on the graveyard shift. He would be gone all the time. I was fourteen years old and my mother would force me to have sex with her. This went on for two years, before my father came home early from work one night and found us in bed together."

No wonder the guy is all messed up. But, the dead people thing. I can't wait to hear about that.

"I'm sorry about that, Marvin, but that still doesn't give you a reason to kill. I'm sure your father knew it wasn't your fault."

"Well, his actions led me to believe otherwise, Detective!"

"So, what about having sex with dead women, what is that about? Would your father approve of that?"

Marvin face turns red and his lips quivers. "The day my mother was killed, I was stricken with grief and all alone. I managed to escape the boy's shelter they placed me in and found my way to the funeral home my mom was brought to. I loved her one last time, that night. I liked it, no, I loved it. Thus my appetite began. My father abandoned me. I was all alone, you can understand that, can't you?" he asks as his eyes search my face for some emotion.

"Bryant, I think you're one sick dude. I feel sorry for your father for having spawned such a pathetic son. He seems to have been the victim of your deeds and now you even crap on the memory of his last name."

"You don't know shit, Detective. My father hated me for what happened. He beat me up and threw me out the house. He killed my mother and himself that same day. I try to help women see their sinful ways and purge them of their transgressions, " Marvin explains.

"Sure I get it, you play priest and exonerate them, right? You purge them of their sins by raping, amputating their limbs, and killing them. You were kicked out of medical school for having sex with dead women. Were you purging them, too? As I see it, you're just some perverted sick shit, who's too much of a punk to own up to his own sins. You just project them onto others. You're more fucked up than your mama was."

I keep the gun's beam locked on his blond, head, waiting for him to raise his hand from Ms. Chavez's bloody throat. I try to think of anything that will distract him from killing the girl and buy some time for Chase and Vernon to reach the room.

"What would your mother think of you, now?"

Marvin Bryant's face muscles tighten and he scowls. "You shut your fucking mouth about my mother. You don't know shit about her! I haven't killed anyone, you fool. You don't know shit! Yeah, you're clever, but not that clever. I had to leave you idiots clues like a grade-school game!"

I respond, "So, that means you wanted to be caught and so you are. Your father was caught in an ugly situation. He made a bad decision, you don't have to do the same. Let's end this here. Don't cop out like your father did."

"You shut up! My dad was no cop out. I'm sanctifying souls. Enough of this bullshit, I want out of here, now!" Marvin screams as he places the scalpel deeper into Cherry's throat, causing blood to slowly fall from the cut. He aims the gun at me with tears rolling down his face.

Chase and Vernon appear in the door way, both aiming at Marvin. He looks at them eyes crazed and darting between us.

"Look, Marvin, we can get you some help, " I say. "Please give up. This is over. Let the girl go. You've killed enough already. What you're doing has no justification. C'mon man. I don't want to have to kill you."

Marvin explains calmly, "I will leave this place today or she dies."

"I don't think so."

I think back to another hostage situation where Officer Rico, a rookie cop, was killed when we pursued a killer into the Research Medical Center morgue. The killer shot him in front of my face. I hesitated, when I had the shot. I swore to myself that I would never let that happen again.

I refocus my aim in the middle of Marvin's forehead as he pushes the scalpel deeper into Chavez's throat and pulls the hammer back on his .38 pistol. As a small flow of blood escapes from the incision by the scalpel on Cherry's throat, I fire three times, each bullet pushing Marvin further from Pretty Kevin's woman's pregnant body.

Chase runs to free Cherry. She covers the terrified woman's naked body and frees her from her linen and leather bondage. Vernon and I go to Marvin, kneeling down to assess his injuries as his mouth moves.

He whispers as we get closer to him, "I didn't kill anybody. You got the wrong guy." Then he collapses.

The last gasp leaves Marvin's bloody, bullet-torn body. The bullets struck him once in the head and twice in the chest. Marvin dies with a frown on his face as blood flows slowly from the head wound.

"Joe, did you give the man a chance to raise his pants? Damn! A man should never be caught dead with his pants down, Jesus Christ, " Vernon says.

"Well, we don't have to worry about his limp dick, dead ass snatching any more women, " I state as Captain Wayne, Agent James, paramedics, and other FBI and police crime-scene personnel enter the room.

Agent James rushes into the room looking to see if any of us are hurt. "Johnson, is everyone okay?"

"Yes, we got our man and Ms. Chavez is alive. How's Li and Smelly? We heard the explosion."

"They were shaken up a little bit, but they'll be fine. You guys did a great job. We need to meet outside in fifteen minutes, " Agent James commands as Captain Wayne gives us a head nod of a job well done and walks with Agent James, canvassing the crime scene.

I state, "Agent James, you might want to have someone bring Pretty Kevin down here. I'm sure the reunion will be good for him and Ms. Chavez."

"Pretty Kevin is outside waiting in one of the units. We picked him up on the way out here. I'll make sure you guys get three weeks off with pay after this is wrapped up, " Agent James states.

Agent Chase, Brown, and I answer, "Yes Sir!"

I dial Tracy Jackson's cell number and give her our location, honoring the promise about an exclusive.

After touring the subterranean shelter where the killer held the seventeen prostitutes, we climb the wooden stairs and walk out from the kitchen into the open dirt lot surrounded by trees. The lot is filled with law-enforcement personnel and their vehicles. We walk over to the ambulance where the paramedics strap Cherry Chavez in. Pretty Kevin is sits beside her, holding her hand.

I walk over to him and reach to shake his hand. I apologize looking Kevin in the eyes, "Sorry about getting rough with you, dude."

Kevin hesitates, jumps out of the ambulance, and embraces me with tears falling from his eyes.

"Thank you, Joe. For saving Cherry's life and being a true friend. I was the one who put you in a compromising situation where you had to question my character. But you did your job and that's all I can ask. You're still top man in my book, Detective." Pretty Kevin and I shake hands.

Kevin thanks Vernon and Chase before he climbs back into the ambulance and departs for the hospital.

Agent Li and Smelly approach us from the crowd, lightly bandaged.

Agent Li says, smiling, "Hey, next time you guys get to take the back."

"That's for sure, " Agent Smelly exclaims as we all laugh and hug.

Agent James approaches us with Captain Wayne. "Okay, people, great job. We have enough evidence down there to put a lid on this case. Our streets are safer tonight. You guys did an excellent job. I'll need a final report on my desk in twenty-four hours. Joe and Vernon, I've been authorized to offer you two a position with the Federal Bureau of Investigation, " Agent James informs us.

Vernon and I glimpse at each other and the anticipation on Smelly, Li, and Chase's face. We have worked together well. Captain Wayne looks away, shoving his hands in his pockets. I stare at Vernon as he puts an unlit cigar in his mouth and shrugs.

I say rubbing my neck, "Agent James, we love Kansas City and our department. Our Captain is one of the greatest reasons we have to stay. He watches out for us. We just made Sergeant and life is good. We'll stay in Kansas City for right now, but thanks for the offer. It was great working with you all."

Vernon affirms, "Yeah, it was cool."

"I knew you'd do the right thing, " Captain Wayne says with a wide toothy grin. "Vernon give me one of them cigars, " Captain Wayne says. He unwraps it, places it in his mouth, and waves goodbye while strolling to his car.

"Well, the offer stands if you guys change your minds. We'd love to have you. The press is here and like Ricky says to Lucy, I got some s'plainin' to do, " Agent James says while shaking our hands, before he walks toward the press.

We all shake hands and agree to meet at the office to finish up the reports and close the case.

Agent Chase pulls me to the side as we excuse ourselves. "Joe, you don't have to be a stranger. We can always be friends, " she says.

I tease, smiling, "That's cool, I'm glad everything worked out all right and no one was seriously hurt. I really had a great time working with you. You have to promise that Sierra and I will get an invitation when you get married."

"You can count on it, " Chase replies and softly kisses me on the lips. "See you at the office and that was a friendship kiss. It didn't mean nothin', so stop looking at me like that."

I state, "Girl, you gonna get both of us killed. Sierra don't play that."

I follow her towards Vernon's vehicle, when I'm stopped by Tracy and her camera man.

"Let's get on with this interview Joe, " Tracy demands.

"Yeah, so we can be done with it. You know how I hate the press."

"Well, the faster you talk the faster we can be done. Who was your friend?"

"Don't worry about it, let's get on with this."

Tracy gives me an evil look but once the camera starts up she is immediately transformed into Ms. Congeniality. It takes thirty minutes to complete her questions. I take off the clip microphone and head toward Vernon's vehicle.

Tracy shouts, "Call me sometime!"

"Whatever!" I exclaim, 'in your dreams' sarcastically in my thoughts.

My pager goes off. I pull out my cell phone and dial the unfamiliar number that flashes across the screen.

"This is Johnson."

"Joe, this is Pretty Kevin." He's talking at a rapid pace. "Dude, I just talked with Cherry and she says Marvin Bryant didn't work alone. There is a guy who picked them up and brought them to Bryant's place after stungunning them. He was the killer. Marvin just supplied the place and raped them. I got the guy's address, 915 East Fifth street. Joe, I'm on my way there and I just hope you get there in time to keep me from killing this dude."

"Kevin, don't do anything stupid. Let us handle it. Stay with Cherry, she needs you." I wave to try and get Chase's, Vernon's, and the other agent's attention.

"Joe, this guy killed my girls. Cherry and the baby are safe. But, I always promised my girls I would protect them and I didn't. I owe this guy, big time." His voice breaks.

Li, Smelly, Chase, and Vernon surround me and can tell by the expression on my face that something is terribly wrong.

I explain as the agents look on inquisitively, "Kevin, don't do this. You don't need this kind of trouble and you don't know what this guy is capable of."

"Fuck that, Joe. He don't know what I'm capable of!"

"Kevin, just calm down, tell me who this guy is?"

"He works for the post office--some guy named Barnes and after I finish with his ass, he'll be singing the postal blues."

Kevin hangs up. I hate it when people do that. "Shit!" I yell.

"Joe, what's the matter, partner? What was that all about?" Vernon asks, taking a cigar out and placing it in his mouth.

"Cedric Barnes was helping Marvin Bryant. Cherry told Pretty Kevin he was the one that picked them up, stun-gunned them, brought them to Bryant's place, and killed them."

"Who in the hell would have thought that?" Chase exclaims. "So Bryant must have done the amputating. We went over the suspects at least fifteen times." She runs her hands through her silky black hair.

"Kevin gave me the name. We got to move because Kevin is on his way there and I'm afraid he's about to do something crazy, like kill the guy."

We all rush to our vehicles and take to the highway. Chase and Vernon ride with me, Li and Smelly follow as we speed on the freeway, heading to Barnes' address that Kevin gave me. I phone Agent James and he tells me he's on his way to meet us there with back up.

"Joe, why do you think he did it?"

"Chase, at this point, I'm worried more about Kevin. But, it seems Bryant and Barnes were both in medical school. They both had sick sexual appetites. Some things can't be explained. Hopefully Barnes can fill in the blanks of the whole story."

"If Kevin had not given us a name, Barnes would have gotten away with this, " Vernon says. "What kinda postal freak are we dealing with?"

I reply, "The worst kind, Vernon. A perverted serial killer."

We pull off Benton Boulevard and turn onto Fifth Street and go down three blocks. A car flashes its lights on and off. We pull our guns and approach slowly. We shut off our lights and pull up to it, putting our weapons away. He gets in the back seat with Vernon.

Have we gotten here too late? Li and Smelly approach. I roll down the windows so they can hear what Kevin has to say.

I turn around and look at Kevin for an explanation.

"Kevin, you didn't do anything stupid, did you?"

"Nah, I got too much to lose and I've lost enough already to last me a lifetime. I just been casing the joint. The ass hole is in there. I've been seeing his shadow move around the house. It took everything inside me not to rush in there and kill this guy, Joe." Kevin's eyes swell from anger.

I respond as Agent James joins us, "You did the right thing, Kevin."

"What the hell is going on here, Kevin?" Agent James asks.

"Some postal dude named Barnes is in there, " Kevin says. "He's friends with Bryant. Apparently he was a janitor at some medical school that Bryant attended. He and Bryant got kicked out of school for some weird freaky shit that involved dead people. When Bryant worked one summer for the postal service, he was recognized by Barnes. He was going to blow the whistle on the guy, but Bryant threatened to kill him if he told. Bryant and Barnes worked out a money deal to keep his mouth shut and get him the prostitutes when he needed them."

My mouth falls open at this bizarre story and the others all look just as amazed, never considering Barnes to be part of the equation. He was never questioned in the initial investigation, either.

I say, "He would know the area well. Barnes is the manager at the Northeast Station, so he would have access to the prostitutes. How do you know all this Kevin?"

Pretty Kevin positions himself in the seat so that we all can hear his response. "Bryant and Barnes were going to kill all the women, so they felt free to talk in front of them. They didn't think any of them would live to talk about it. Thanks to you guys, Cherry did."

Back up arrives and we gather outside of the car. Bullet-proof vests are passed out and we discuss the plan.

Agent James begins, "Captain Wayne, your men can secure the parameter, front, and back of the house. I'll have my men come in thru the back of the house and we'll need your battering-ram officer to assist my team in entering the front of the domicile. We don't know how many people are in the house, so let's be sharp. I want a clean sweep, until this guy is apprehended. Consider this postal pervert armed and dangerous, but let's take him alive if we can. Understood?"

Everyone nods.

Kevin says to Agent James, "I want in on this."

"Sorry Kevin, but you're a civilian and I can't be responsible for your safety. Stand down, " Agent James orders.

"Look, James, you owe me. You've roughed me up, had me detained for murder, and have been treating me like shit since I met you. This guy has destroyed my life. I just want to see him go down. You can give me the satisfaction of that, can't you?"

Agent James rubs his head as he looks at the Captain who shrugs. "You're too close to this, Kevin. I don't need a time bomb with me, waiting to explode."

"If I was going to kill the guy, I would have done it long before you got here, " Kevin states.

Agent James looks at Captain Wayne again and shrugs. Agent James looks at me and I give him the nod.

Agent James orders, "Get him a vest."

"Search him, Johnson. Kevin, keep your ass in the rear and keep your head down. I'm doing this against my better judgement. Let's get in position!" Agent James orders.

We surround the two-story house with tan vinyl siding. Officer Sanchez, who has the battering ram, Vernon, Captain Wayne, Agents Li, Smelly, Chase, Pretty Kevin, and I climb the concrete stairs. When we reach the porch, Officer Sanchez, gets the nod from Agent James and bursts through the wood and glass doors, assault weapons drawn.

The shattered door hangs from its hinges. Glass covers the oak floors and cracks under our feet as we run from room to room. We cover the downstairs in minutes and meet at the foot of the stairs.

We take the stairs in pairs. Vernon and I lead and Chase makes sure Kevin brings up the rear. We go from bedroom to bedroom. No sign of Mr. Barnes.

We stand in the middle of the second floor hallway baffled. A latch sits on the ceiling in the right corner of the hallway, attached to what looks like an attic door. I direct the others' attention to the latch.

I get the shotgun from Agent Chase and reach up and tap on the attic door.

Agent James orders, "Barnes, give it up. We know you're up there. The place is surrounded. You were involved with Marvin Bryant in the prostitute killings. Come out and you will not be hurt!"

A single shot blasts. We all take cover to the extremities of the hallway. Everyone's guns aim for the attic door. A loud thud sounds above our heads. Vernon helps me snag the latch and a fold-down ladder opens with the door. I get a pocket flash light from Vernon and ascend the wobbly wooden ladder into the attic.

In the dark and musty room the acrid smell of gunpowder fills the air. I canvas the room full of boxes, trunks, and old furniture. I find the light switch and turn it on. The single bulb cast shadows as it swings from its fixture. Partially exposed legs extend from behind an old sofa.

"I think I found him!" I yell down as Vernon climbs through the hole into the attic.

We approach the exposed legs with guns aimed. Sprawled across the floor is Barnes. He shot himself through the roof of his mouth. The bullet looks to have exited the top of his head. Blood spills from his hair and the top part of his skull is exposed.

"Well, I guess we'll never know the whole story now, " I say with a heavy sigh.

Captain Wayne, Chase, and Pretty Kevin join us. They look on at the dismal sight. Kevin shows no emotion, turns and descends the ladder.

"The poor guy has had a rough couple of days. Make sure he gets back to the hospital, Joe. You're through here, " Agent James orders.

I find Kevin in his Cadillac with his head against the steering wheel. I tap on the passenger window. He unlocks the door and I get in.

I let a few minutes go by, then break the silence. "Hey buddy, you doing okay?"

"I've been cheated. These guys had a quick death. They didn't suffer like my girls, Joe. I have to make the arrangements for their funerals and try to contact the families. None of this is going to be easy. Cherry will be out of it for quite some time, but I'll be right there by her side, " Kevin explains.

"Kevin, if you need me, I'm here for you, dude."

"I know you are, Joe. Thanks for everything. I need to get out of here, man. My woman's waiting on me. There's nothing left for me here."

We shake hands and I watch Pretty Kevin's blue Cadillac turn onto the isolate Benton Avenue and drive, its red tail-lights giving a lonely glow, until they disappear into the night's haze.

thirteen

"THEY'RE HERE!" NIA SCREAMS AFTER A THIRTY-FIVE minute wait in the bay window facing the front of the house. She has been restless all last night, waiting for the arrival of her first cousin, who's really her nephew, and her Auntie Diamond, who's really her sister.

I follow her to the door and go outside to help Diamond and little Raymond get their things from the silver Lexus 400 LS.

Diamond is a spitting image of Sierra, except for a mole above the right side of her lip and thinner eyebrows. She has her sister's brick-house body and excellent taste in clothing. Her cheer has been lost since Raymond's death. Yet, she's looking good and smiles when she sees us.

"What's up, sister? I see the art business is treating a woman good. Give me some love, girl, " I tease as Diamond gives me a hug and a kiss on the cheek.

Little Raymond and Nia do the same thing, then Nia gives Diamond a big hug and kiss as Raymond Jr. hits me in the leg and runs off with Nia laughing.

"You know a sister be surviving. Y'all ain't doing too bad, either. My sister told me about the BMW Roadster you bought for her. Go on with your bad self, " Diamond teases, slapping me on the back while Nia and Raymond play tag in the yard.

I whisper devilishly, telling a full-blown lie, "I just picked it up. She got to make the payments, but don't tell her that until I leave."

"So, where is my sister at?" Diamond inquires with her well-manicured hands in the air.

I explain, "Uncle Ashford came in last night and she's helping him with some gifts he brought for the kids."

Her hands fly to her face with excitement, "I can't believe Uncle Ashford is here. I haven't seen him in three months. Little Raymond will be so surprised. It's so cool that he came all the way from St. Louis to take care of his great niece and nephew. It's really a blessing having someone on Raymond's side of the family involved with Nia and Raymond Jr. He is the only living relative of Raymond Tyler that we know of, and after Raymond's death, Uncle Ashford insisted on being part of our family, so he could spend time with the kids. They are his only link to Raymond and his family's bloodline. He is so sweet." Diamond says, misty eyed.

I ask, smiling, "Okay, enough of that. You bring your dancing shoes?"

"Yeah man, we gonna kick it at Vernon's party. I heard about you and Gertrude. I was scared to death. Y'all made national news. I'm surprised Sierra haven't made you quit yet, especially after that serial-killer thing. Postal people just goin' crazy. I don't know how you do it, Joe. But, you good. You be solving them cases, brotha. I'm always braggin' on you."

"Well, thank you, sister. But I'm part of a big team and my partner, Vernon, always has my back. It means a lot to hear you say you're proud of me. I'm proud of you, too. We just two bad individuals, ain't we?"

Diamond responds with a high-five hand clap, "You know it!"

"Little Raymond, dude, how you gonna just hit me and run? Come here and give your uncle a hug, boy."

"Un-Unh!" Raymond replies as I playfully chase him and Nia in the front yard.

Uncle Ashford and Sierra appear at the front door. Diamond and Sierra scream with joy and run to each others' loving embrace as they always do, overjoyed to see each other. Uncle Ashford walks up and joins in the family love being passed around.

It is 2 in the afternoon by the time things get settled down from the excitement of Diamond's and Raymond Jr.'s arrival. We sit at the kitchen table enjoying wine coolers, sunshine, a cool breeze, conversation, and each other's company.

Nia and Little Raymond team up to put their Sesame Street big-piece puzzles together.

Uncle Ashford is a small framed man, with dark skin, gray hair, and a loving smile. "When them two kids get together it's like they been playing together everyday. It really makes me feel good that y'all took me in as family and let me be a part of their lives."

Sierra and Diamond say in unison, "You are part of their lives!" Then start laughing at their two-part harmony. This happens frequently.

Uncle Ashford laughs hard.

"It's a twin thing, " I explain.

"What we're saying, Uncle Ashford, is that you are our family and the kids too, " Sierra says, smiling as she and Diamond grasp his wrinkled hands. They all smile misty-eyed.

Uncle Ashford states as he pulls his hanky out and wipes his nose in an effort to fight back his emotion, "Y'all all I got in the world and it means so much to me."

"We love you, Uncle Ashford, " Diamond states.

I tease, "We'll see how much he loves us after taking care of the treacherous two tonight. He'll probably have his bags packed when we get home from the surprise anniversary party. You bring your Geritol with you, Uncle Ashford?"

"I don't need no wonder drug. Just a whole lot of patience and love, " Uncle Ashford says as he gets down on the floor with the children to help with the puzzle.

I join in the fun, putting pieces in the wrong places on purpose, so the kids can correct and help me in finding the right spot. Uncle Ashford and I also steal their cookies when they aren't looking.

I WALK INTO THE KITCHEN AND DIAMOND AND SIERRA ARE all huddled up at the table, laughing loud.

"What's all that noise about?" I ask hearing all the commotion.

They abruptly stop their conversation, like I should not hear what they were talking about and look very suspicious. "I was just telling Diamond that you need to be getting ready to go pick up Vernon. It's almost 3:15 and you have to get him by 5 o'clock, " Sierra reminds me giggling.

I look suspiciously as the two of them sit up straight faced and blushing like they just got caught breaking something.

I tease, raising the brow of one eye, "I know y'all up to no good, and being the detective that I am, I will get to the bottom of it."

I kiss Sierra and give Diamond another welcome-home hug, then head upstairs to get showered and dressed for the evening's big bash.

I PULL UP TO VERNON'S TWO-STORY, LIGHT-BROWN-COL-ORED home as he kisses his wife goodbye and heads for my car.

Vernon gets in the car in his tan suit with brown pinstripes and brown Stacy Adams wing tips. His shirt is brown silk with a lighter shade brown tie. "Oh-wee, look at you all dressed up, got your hair cut, looking as sharp as a mosquiter's tweeter and you smell pretty too."

"That's right, I got on my Old Spice and lookin' twice as nice, " Vernon says, laughing as he slaps me five on the Black hand side. "Shoot, look at you. You lookin' like one of them Catholic boys on prom night. Dressed all in black and ain't givin' no slack. My partner's dressed to kill. Don't hurt em', Joe, they can't take no mo'." Vernon laughs at my black Armani suit and matching button-down silk shirt.

Like Vernon, I'm wearing my black Stacy Adams shoes. We both fall out laughing as we drive off to Vernon's unsuspecting surprise party.

Vernon asks, "So, how you been enjoying these last few days off, buddy?"

"Well, Uncle Ashford and Diamond are in town. So I've been busy with Nia, little Raymond, and entertaining family. It's been real cool, " I answer as we drive around town. I want to kill a little time before we pick up Pretty Kevin.

"So, how's Diamond and Uncle Ashford these days? Has Diamond visited her mom yet?"

"Nah, not that I know of, but she's doing good and Uncle Ashford is in heaven with the kids around. That guy has so much energy and he's good with the kids too."

"Joe, you don't mind if I ask you a question do you?"

"Nah, mu-cha-cho, what's up?"

"Where the hell we going? The awards ceremony is supposed to be on Forty-Seventh and Main at the Marriott. We all the way over here by Sheraton Estates."

"I told Pretty Kevin we'd pick him up and go shoot some pool afterward. He was still kind of sore about us putting him in jail. I figured since we got the night to ourselves, we could act a fool and do the fellas thing. Do the ceremony, then slide over to Jesse Jack's Pool Shack and play some eight ball.

Vernon puts an unlit cigar in his mouth. "Awe, hell naw! I didn't get all dressed up to go to no damn pool hall with a pimp. Shit, this ain't the Player's Club. We can go listen to some jazz at Three Black Cats on Eighteenth and Vine, but I ain't 'bout to go to no pool hall. Y'all must be outta y'all's freaking minds to think I'd go for some shit like that. It was your idea to put him in jail. I don't owe Kevin shit. Let's make that perfectly clear."

"Vernon, why don't you calm down, you old fart? You know you like Kevin. So, stop putting on the act. We can do Three Black Cats, if that'll make you happy. You always got to have things your way, but I'll get even with your grouchy self, " I promise as we pull in front of Kevin's house.

Kevin has on the same suit as Vernon, but his is brown with tan pin-stripes and he has a brown cane with a gold Rottweiler top.

"Evening, gentleman. Vernon, nice suit. I see hanging with me for a little while had some positive advantages. You acquired some taste. You almost look as good as me, " Kevin jokes as he settles in the back seat.

Vernon says, laughing, "What you need a cane for? You still haven't got over that ass whipping I put on you in the park?"

Pretty Kevin laughs with him. "Yeah, that's it, Vernon. I'm going to let you have your fun tonight since you fly boys are getting honored and all. So have your fun, brother. Tonight's your night and I wouldn't spoil it by pimp slapping that cigar out your mouth, " Pretty Kevin states as we all bust out laughing.

"Good one. Okay we'll have a truce tonight, " Vernon says as he and Kevin shake hands.

I ask with concern, "Kevin, how's your girl holding up?"

"She's seeing a psychiatrist, but other than that she's coming along. We plan on getting married at the end of the year. We don't want the baby being no bastard. I'm giving up the player's life and settling down and buying into the plastic business with Celeste and Marquitta. Listen up, fellas, this boy's going straight!" Kevin says throwing his hands up in the air like he's made a field goal at a football game.

"I'm proud of you, dude, " I say. "You're doing the right thing, Kevin."

"Kevin, you're a bright young man. I wish you all the luck in the world. I know you will do good son."

Kevin looks at both of us and nods his head as he smiles. "I want to thank you guys for everything. It meant a lot to me that you guys came to the funeral for the girls. That was real cool, fellas. I won't forget it."

"What are friends for?" Vernon states as me and Kevin look at each other, smiling.

Kevin responds, "You all right with me, Vernon."

"So, Joe, what type of award do you think we'll get?" Vernon asks as we pull into the parking garage at the Marriott.

"Well, the FBI has money, but it'll probably be a plaque and a medal or key to the city or something like that. I don't know. We'll see, " I respond as Kevin and I do the "Cabbage Patch" dance to the musical rhythm of the R & B group, Lakeside's 'Raid' played by DJ, Tony G on the radio. We park, turn the music up, get out of the car, and all start dancing in the garage. Even Vernon starts shaking his booty to the music. We laugh and have a good time until the song goes off.

Ballroom A sits atop the hotel with a beautiful view of the Plaza and the night sky. Kevin and I smile at how we are pulling this thing off. We ride up the elevator and outside the closed doors of Ballroom A is a sign that reads, 'Federal Bureau of Investigation Awards Ceremony'. Agent James gets up from the cushioned gold chair in the corridor and comes over to greet us. Yeah, he's in on it too.

"It's about time you guys got here. They pushed the ceremony back an hour. I knew you guys would be late and didn't want you to embarrass me. I have to admit, you all look sharp. Well, let's go in and get ready. You guys calm?"

Vernon complains, "Just a little apprehensive. But, me and Joe are always on time, Royal. You be trippin', man. We wanted to be outta here by 8. You messin' up our plans, damn."

Kevin says, laughing, "Don't mind Vernon, Agent James. He just got up on the wrong side of the house this morning." We all chuckle along.

"Kevin, I never apologized for the way I treated you during the inter-rogation. I'm sorry, man, " Agent James says as he extends his hand.

"Don't worry about it, it's all ready put behind me. I was surprised your hand could fit around my family jewels, " Kevin says, laughing and taking James hand and shaking it.

"Yeah, right!" Agent James rolls his eyes. We all get a good laugh out of it.

I look at my watch and get the okay sign from Agent James. "Well, Vernon, my man, let's do this and get our 'proper's' as MC Hammer would say.

We enter the dark ball room and are greeted with "Surprise!", as the lights come up to a room full of people. The room is decorated with "Happy Twenty-fifth Anniversary" balloons and party favors. The DJ kicks on the music and the party begins.

Sierra and Diamond come over and usher us to the front table where Gertrude gives Vernon this big kiss. The crowd applauds and cheers Vernon and Gertrude as they are seated at the head table, adjacent to a champagne fountain and a table full of food provided by Smoke Me Baby Bar-be-Que and Karen's Delectables.

To the left, a five-tier, white and yellow anniversary cake, has a small black couple at the top and stairs connecting the other tiers of cake and a champagne fountain flowing from the stairs, which lead to the center where it fills the glass number twenty-five. It is absolutely beautiful.

I motion for the crowd to settle down, so we can get started. First up is Vernon's and Gertrude's Pastor, Valdez O'Neil.

"Brothers and sisters, friends and family. What a beautiful day God has made. We are here to share in what God has truly shown to be a blessing. A couple who despite the troubling times, has been able to stay together in love, romance, devotion, and spirit for twenty-five, silver-lined years. Ain't God wonderful? Can I get an amen?" the preacher asks.

"Amen!" the crowd says in unison.

"I don't want to get long-winded, but I married these two, twenty-five years ago and it makes me feel good that I could be a part of something so lovely. So as I end, may the grace of God continue to bestow the love and spirit upon the both of you and protect and keep you in good health and happiness and the people said, " the pastor pauses.

"Amen!" the crowd again responds.

The preacher shakes Vernon's hand and kisses Gertrude on the cheek.

"Watch it now, Reverend, " Vernon says to his aged pastor as the crowd erupts in laughter.

As the evening continues Gertrude's mom and dad, Captain Wayne, and Agent James all give sentimental toasts to Vernon and Gertrude. I walk back up to the podium. "My wife and Gertrude have been best friends since the first time they met. Vernon has been like a brother to me. And even though I hate to admit it, he's taught me everything I know about police work. He has shared some of his life secrets and has had my back too many times to count." I raise my champagne glass for a toast.

"I love you guys and I've prepared this song just for you, " I give the DJ the sign to put on the musical demo tape of Larry Graham's "One in a Million."

...and life showed compassion, and sent to me a stroke of love called you... A one in a million, You!

"Okay, it's about that time, y'all. Let's get the soul train line jumpin' and the music pumpin', " I yell as the crowd takes to the floor with Vernon and Gertrude leading the way. The DJ put's on Cameo's song, "Candy."

We eat, dance, celebrate, and party hearty. I'm sitting at the table with Diamond, Sierra, Chase, Li, Smelly, and Gertrude when Vernon strolls over from talking with some of our detective buddies from the precinct. He motions me to come with him.

"Excuse us, please, " I pardon.

"Walk to the bathroom with me, dude, " Vernon says.

"What up, man?"

"Damn Joe, you invited everybody. I never thought Hilda would be here. He's all dressed up and has a date, too, " Vernon gripes.

"Vernon, Hilda is our friend. We wouldn't have cracked Raymond's case without him. So he's a transvestite. What he does is his business. That doesn't reflect on his friendship with us, does it?"

"Naw, he's cool, but guess who I ran into in the hallway?" Vernon asks as he leads me over to where Ebony Dupree is seated, nervously playing with a glass of wine. She gets up to greet me as we embrace.

"Mom, how you doing? How'd you get here? Does Sierra know you're here?" I ask, flabbergasted that she's out of prison.

Ebony comes up and hugs me and look very fit, firm, and beautiful. "I got an early release from jail yesterday. I went to your house and Uncle Ashford told me where to find you all. So here I am. I hope I'm not crashing the party. I was released on good behavior and the letter you and Vernon wrote to the parole board didn't hurt either. This will be a surprise for Sierra and I hear Diamond's here too, " Ebony states smiling, but her hands are shaking nervously.

I respond, "Mom, you're family. You could never crash a party. You look radiant, Ebony."

Her hour-glass figure in the blue sequined shoulderless gown has Vernon and me staring hard. Her hair falls around her shoulders and I can tell from where Diamond and Sierra get their beauty. I give Ebony a hug and we lead her inside to the party and over to the table where Sierra and Diamond are sitting.

Sierra's hands fly to her mouth and her eyes are as wide as silver dollars upon recognizing her mother. She gets up excited, runs, and gives her a hug. Diamond remains seated and the tension in the immediate area starts to rise.

"Mom, when did you get here? You look so good. I'm so happy to see you, " Sierra says warmly, while embracing her mom.

Ebony eyes fill with tears. "I got out yesterday. I was released on good behavior. I'll be on probation for three years. I'm home and looking forward to making up for lost time with my family."

All the attention is on Diamond now, and no one knows how to proceed.

"Diamond, you're looking very beautiful this evening. It's been so long since I've seen you. Can't I even get a hug?" Ebony asks her daughter.

We look on helplessly.

"Mother, it's good to see you and I'm glad you're out, but I just need some time to handle this. I didn't expect this. Please forgive me, " Diamond states as she gets up.

As she walks away we all sit down, not knowing what else to do. The party is still kicking and no one really notices what's going on at our table.

"Mama, don't let this opportunity pass. Y'all need to talk. C'mon, Joe, let's go after her, " Sierra demands as Ebony and I follow her out into the foyer, where Diamond sits by the fountain. Ebony sits down next to Diamond, while Sierra and I stand near for support.

"Mama, I don't know if I can ever forget what happened between us. I still wonder if Raymond would be alive if it weren't for you?"

Ebony clasps her hands together and reaches for her daughter, "Diamond, I don't want you to forget, but I do expect you to forgive. Yes, I was wrong for sleeping with Raymond, but remember we had something before you. Raymond was also sleeping with men, not just you and me. I can't change what happened, but Raymond was no saint. He was going to try and suffocate me. I'm sorry I killed him, I did my time for the crime and I'm still paying for it. I don't want to lose my family, Diamond. I'm here and I love you. Just give me a chance. That's all I'm asking."

Sierra says, "Diamond, Joe and I are expecting twins and this is the first time I've been pregnant. I'm going to need you and Mom to help me get through this. C'mon, girl. You got to get over this."

I ask, numbed by the new information and ready to jump with joy, totally forgetting the problems at hand, "You're what? Twins? I'm gonna have twins?"

"Calm down, baby. Yes, we're having twins. I'm two months pregnant, " Sierra explains as she helps me sit down on the side of the fountain.

I'm suddenly feeling faint.

I ask to nobody in particular, "Twins?"

"I'm so happy for you guys, " Ebony exclaims as she hugs Sierra and kisses me on the cheek.

"Congratulations, Joe and Sierra. Y'all know I'll be there for you. Mom, I just need some time. I hope you understand, " Diamond says as she gets up and heads for the elevator.

"Take your time, dear. Family and love sets no limits, " Ebony replies as Diamond boards the elevator. "She'll come around. Everything will be all right. I can feel it, " Ebony states as the elevator doors closes. "Well, I think I've taken you from your friends long enough. I'll come by tomorrow and visit you two. Thanks for everything and I love you both so much, " Ebony says, hugging both of us.

I remind her, "You know you don't have to leave, Mom."

"I've done what I wanted to do. Thanks for the thought, though, " Ebony states as she kisses us good-bye.

We watch her board the elevator and Sierra sits on my lap aside the fountain. She puts my hand on her stomach and gives me a luscious kiss. "Thanks for putting up with my family, Joe. You ready for twins, big daddy?" She inquires with her hand around my neck.

"Yes, baby. I'm ready, willing, and able. As long as you're by my side, I can handle anything the world has in store for me."

We get up, kiss, then walk back into the ballroom and join Pretty Kevin, Chase, Vernon, and Gertrude on the dance floor doing the electric slide.

epilogue

VERNON AND GERTRUDE HAVE FINALLY MADE IT TO THEIR master suite on the twelfth floor. The party was a huge success and everyone left very satisfied. Vernon sits on the sofa with his shoes off and his shirt partially unbuttoned enjoying the view of the beautiful twilight Plaza skyline.

"Damn, that must have been some shock for Diamond to see Ebony walk up in there tonight. I sure hope they can work things out. I felt kinda sorry for Ebony, " Vernon talks through the bedroom door, so Gertrude can hear him as she changes into something sexy.

Gertrude explains while opening the door to the bedroom, "I felt sorry for Sierra, she's the one who's been caught in the middle of that family tragedy for three years."

She stands there looking like a phantasm in her see through robe with a crochless teddy clinging to her sensuous body, illuminated by the rose scented candles that flicker behind her in the bedroom. The music of Luther Vandross, 'So Amazing' is beckoning Vernon from the CD player in the room's entertainment center.

Vernon slowly rises as his pinstriped jacket falls to the floor. He walks toward his true love of a quarter of a century, unbuttoning his silk shirt letting it fall to the plush carpet, along with his pants and boxer shorts.

He tenderly embraces his wife and kisses her with all the ecstasy that twenty-five years of devotion and steadfast love can simmer in a man's soul, mind, spirit, and passion. Gertrude leads Vernon to the fabulous brass king size bed. Gertrude throws back the downy covers revealing rose petals that adorn the top of the sheets. Vernon inquires anticipating what his darling has in store for him, "So baby, you been watching those Prince videos again?"

"Yes baby, lay down so I can 'do you' as Prince calls it, " she demands.

Vernon lay on his back as Gertrude retrieves the chocolate tipped strawberries from the small refrigerator. They feed each other the provocative fruit. She fills the two glass flutes full of Dom Perignon Champagne. They toast to each other and drink from the effervescent potion.

"Suck in your stomach, " Gertrude orders.

"What?" Vernon asked wondering what is about to happen.

"Suck in your stomach, silly, " Gertrude asks seductively as Vernon gives in to her demands.

Gertrude pours the sweet nectar from her glass into the bowl shape that has formed in Vernon's stomach and begins to sip up the cold tingling champagne from its human pool.

Vernon asks trembling from excitement, "Damn woman, where'd you learn that?"

"HBO, " Gertrude replies with a devilish grin.

"Hey, let me try that, " Vernon suggests as he copies what Gertrude has done.

After, Gertrude returns Vernon to his spot amongst the rose petals. She disrobes and straddles him. They make passionate love well into the morning, until they both have their fill. The scent of rose petals and sensual delight intertwine like the romantic gestures just performed.

Vernon testifies, "Gertrude, you make me fall in love with you all over again, every time I feel your passion and love for me. Heaven got to feel like this, girl."

"You just as fine and handsome as the first day I saw you at the car wash. Loving you has been the easiest thing in the world to me. I would die for you baby, " Gertrude confesses as they hold each other close and kiss some more.

After they catch their breath from the exotic journey, Gertrude gets up and goes to the bathroom to run some bath water.

Gertrude summons, "Vernon, come in here and take a bath with me. Let's discuss when we'll take the trip to Europe."

"I'll be in as soon as I pull these rose petals out my ass, " Vernon jokes.

He enters the bathroom and slowly climbs into the hot tub with his beautiful wife.

"Lay up against me honey, so I can talk some French to you, " Vernon requests tenderly.

Gertrude replies impressed with her husband's romantic skills, "I never knew you spoke French."

"Woman, I'm full of surprises, " Vernon boasts as he nibbles on Gertrude's ear.

Gertrude seductively moans as she nestles against Vernon's chest in anticipation of the romantic language of love, "Well, speak some French to me then."

"You ready for this woman?"

"Yes, " Gertrude responds placing her hands on top of Vernon's thighs.

Vernon whispers in her ear, "French toast, French fries, French silk pie, French bread, French vanilla ice cream..."
Gertrude bursts out laughing as Vernon joins in with the jovial bliss.

"You're so silly, " Gertrude responds turning to face her husband on their silver anniversary.

"Well how about this, French Kiss?" Vernon says as he takes her in his arms and passionately kisses her.

"Now that's the language I'm talking about, " Gertrude replies as she falls into Vernon's arms happy in life, happy in spirit, happy in health, and happy in love.

Vernon answers as he holds his wife tight and they relax in the hot bubble bath, "I know that's right!"

about the author

Vincent Alexandria - "If Walls Could Talk", "Postal Blues", "Black Rain", & "Poetry from the Bottom of My Heart." (We Must X-L Publishing Co.) He is an author, actor, producer, director, composer, lyricist, vocalist, screen writer, and musician. He is the father of four children. He holds a Masters degree in literature at Baker University and holds a Bachelor's degree in Psychology from Rockhurst College. He's a GED Teacher with the EVENSTART Program in Kansas City, MO. His vision for the Brother 2 Brother Symposium is to enlighten men and women in reading and comprehension to enhance their quality of life. Having nationally published authors show a commitment to their communities and give back to their readers in gratitude of what they have done for them and their careers.